Firecracker

ABBI GLINES

Victoria!
Enjoy! :)

*To every reader who enjoys a slightly twisted, naughty heroine
who isn't afraid to admit it.*

I

There is a charm about the forbidden that makes it unspeakably desirable.
—*Mark Twain*

Chapter ONE

TREV

Horse racing was in my blood. It was the second-most important part of my family's legacy. However, if I was being brutally honest, this was my favorite part of the Kentucky Derby
weekend—the Derby Eve gala. I typically hated fucking galas,
but not this one. I didn't even mind wearing a tux. My best
friend didn't seem to share my sentiments. Saxon Houston
looked annoyed. He was definitely here for the races. Horse
racing *was* his first love.

Smirking, I turned toward him to lay one of my smart-ass
comments that would get a smile out of the guy when my
eyes found someone else instead. All other thoughts left me.
The music being performed onstage by some old famous dude
faded away. It was as if no one else was in the room. Just her.

Fucking hell, she was smokin'.

The lights caught the different shades of blonde in her long,
curly hair. Bare, sun-kissed shoulders and—holy shit—that
body in that formfitting hot-pink dress. She wasn't looking

1

at me. Not directly. Her focus was on the old dude singing. From where I stood, her lips looked full. I wanted to see her eyes. I had a thing about eyes.

"I'll be back—maybe," I said, not taking my gaze off her when I spoke to Saxon.

"Where are you—oh," he replied, and I knew that he'd spotted my target.

He could keep his nice-guy bullshit right where it was. I had seen her first.

Moving through the crowd, I didn't even stop to speak to the Packers quarterback who had grown up in Ocala. Our families were friends. Even if Jon Bon Jovi stepped in front of me—and I was pretty sure he was here—I wasn't stopping.

She took a sip from the drink in her hand and finally let her gaze travel across the room.

Who was she with? Why the fuck was she alone?

Reaching her side, I pulled out all my Hughes charm and decided she was about to fall hard. I'd make sure of it.

"You owe me a drink," I said, leaning down close to her ear.

The tiniest jerk of her shoulders was followed by a slow turn of her body toward me. She lifted her eyes and ... fuck me.

"I doubt it," she replied. Her thick Southern drawl was a smooth, smoky sound.

What color were her eyes? Honey? Could eyes be the color of honey? Because hers looked like warm honey with sunlight shining through. I struggled to get my head back in the game after she'd thrown me off with eyes I hadn't expected.

"Ah, but you do." I flashed her a smile that had been working for me since puberty.

She smirked. "Please continue. I can't wait to hear the rest of this cheesy pickup line."

Okay, fine, it was a pickup line, but, damn, it wasn't cheesy. It was fucking smooth.

"Because when I saw you, I dropped mine."

A grin tugged at those full pink lips, and then she laughed. Score. It'd worked.

"What color are your eyes?" I asked, fascinated.

"Hazel," she replied with another laugh.

I shook my head. "No, I've seen hazel eyes. That is something else. Sunshine and honey."

"Now, what would you have said if they'd been blue? What's your pickup line for that color?"

"That wasn't a line. I'm fucking serious."

"Mmhmm," she replied, taking a sip of her drink.

"You don't believe me?"

She raised her eyebrows. "Does it really matter? I don't even know you."

Ah, but we were gonna fix that.

I held out my hand. "Trev Hughes," I said.

The flicker of recognition in her eyes told me she must be connected to the horse racing world. Not just a guest or someone wanting to experience the Kentucky Derby. She knew the last name Hughes. Her eyes lowered to look at my hand as if she wasn't sure if touching me was something she wanted to do.

What had Dad done to her family? He'd better not have fucked this up for me before it even had a chance.

I started to attempt damage control when she finally lifted her hand and slid it inside mine. Her skin was soft, and her hand was dainty with pink nails to match her dress. I liked how my hand seemed to swallow hers. A weird tightening in my chest that I wasn't familiar with struck me.

"Gypsi Parker," she replied.

I could see in her gaze that she was searching mine for any recognition. But I'd never met anyone named Gypsi in

3

my life, and there was no fucking way I'd have forgotten her. Especially with those eyes.

Reluctantly, I released her hand but stepped closer to her, then bent my head to whisper in her ear. "I know you aren't here alone," I said. "Please tell me there isn't a guy somewhere who has a claim on you."

She laughed again. "That's a tricky question."

No, it wasn't. I needed her to answer me and then point him out so I could make him disappear.

"How so?"

She smirked again and turned to look out over the crowd. "A man did bring me." She paused and glanced back at me. There was a twinkle of mischief in her eyes. "He bought everything I'm wearing." Reaching up, she touched the simple diamond necklace around her neck. "Even the jewelry."

"I'm really hoping he's your father."

She laughed. "No. He is definitely not my father." This amused her. The humor in those honey-and-sunshine eyes was unmistakable.

"Fuck," I muttered.

She tilted her head to the side and reached out to touch my arm. I fought the urge to cover her hand with mine and keep it there. I'd dress her and buy her jewelry better than what she was wearing now, if that was what it would take. I started to say so, but she spoke first.

"You're not what I expected," she replied. "I think we might end up being good friends."

Oh, hell no. She was not friend-zoning me. When she started to move her hand away, I reached up and grasped it.

"I'm thinking something a little more exciting than friends."

Her eyes shifted away from me then, and I saw a change in her expression before she turned to look at me again.

4

"I need to be going."

"I'll go with you," I told her.

She wasn't running off like goddamn Cinderella.

She sighed, and I could see the battle in her eyes before she lifted them to me.

"Okay, fine. You lead the way."

Hell yes! I wrapped my arm around her waist and pulled her close to my side before walking toward an exit. The gala wasn't doing it for me anymore. Time to change locations.

Just as we reached an exit, my cell started ringing. The ringtone was my father's. Fucking hell, this'd better not be family shit he wanted me in on tonight. I considered ignoring it, but I knew I'd regret it later. Glancing down at the girl beside me, I debated on it. She might just be worth my father's wrath.

"You gonna get that?" she asked once we were outside.

With a sigh, I reached into my pocket. "Yeah."

"Get Saxon. Meet Levi and Kye at their hotel suite. There's an issue that needs handled," Dad barked at me.

Motherfucker!

"Saxon?" I asked, making sure I'd heard him right.

"Yes. Kenneth agrees it's time," he replied.

Kenneth was Saxon's dad. He was also part of the family. Saxon hadn't been on any family business before. He never mentioned it, and I had thought he would just handle the horse racing part of our world. Hearing that Dad was bringing him into the other side surprised me. I wasn't sure Saxon had it in him.

"Okay." Irritated, I hung up and turned back to figure out how in the hell I was going to explain this to Gypsi and get her to hand over her phone number.

But I didn't get a chance to figure it out.

She was gone.

Chapter TWO

GYPSI

I loved her. I truly did. There had never been a dull moment in my life. When I was sad, she'd spend money we didn't have on candy, ice cream, chips, and soda for us to eat instead of dinner. If times got hard, she'd turn the small camper we called home into a dance party, complete with hits from the '90s. If there was a new movie in the theater I wanted to see, she'd flirt with the guy or girl at the ticket counter and convince them to let us in for free. Often, she got a bucket of popcorn thrown in too. Fawn Parker was a beautiful, energetic force of nature. She was my best friend, but she was also my mom.

Understanding my mother's decisions was something I'd given up on years ago. When she wanted something, she found a way to make it happen. There was no obstacle that she allowed to set her back. She often left my head spinning while I tried to keep up. This was one of those times.

This time, it wasn't a thing she wanted. It was a lifestyle. The lemon-colored dress she was wearing—which left one shoulder bare while the bow that held the dress up rested on the other shoulder—the ridiculous hat, and the diamond necklace that made me nervous every time I looked at it were stunning with her pale blonde hair she had pulled back in a sleek ponytail. The teardrop earrings matched the diamonds around her neck, and I wondered if it had occurred to her that what she was wearing cost more than what we'd made last year. I doubted it. Her bright smile, which I'd seen reel a man in with its powerful flash, was in place as she stood, watching the racetrack below as if the winner of this race mattered to us. She knew nothing about horse racing, but she lived for the thrill of new things.

"Enjoying yourself?" my mom's newest conquest, Garrett Hughes, asked as he stepped up beside her, placing a hand on her bare lower back.

She turned her man-killer smile on him. "This is incredible," she gushed. "The energy is intoxicating."

The slight lift of his lips and glint of approval in his eyes made me want to groan. This was more serious than she'd let on. When she'd come home with the dresses and accessories for us to wear with designer names, I'd been concerned. Being picked up by a limo, taken to a private airstrip, escorted onto a private jet had all made me question if this was another of those moments my mother's magic had made happen or if it was something more. That the man had fallen for the Fawn Parker enchantment.

I was sure normal girls would be thrilled for their mother. Garrett Hughes was a powerful billionaire. If I believed in fairy tales, I would be right on board. Because if Mom was taken care of, I could finally go start my life. Move out and travel the world. Just me and my camera. Find my own path. I knew college wasn't something I'd get a chance at until later in life. When I'd made enough money to afford it.

However, I wasn't most girls, and my mom was not a normal mom. She was a beautiful face with a wild soul that couldn't be held on to for long. I had to be here when it all fell apart or she needed to run from it all. It was a burden that got heavier with each passing year.

We had only parked our camper in Ocala, Florida, three weeks ago. Enough time for me to get a job at a coffee shop and Mom to get a job as a cocktail waitress at an elite private club. Our plan had been for us to stop long enough to make some money before continuing north. We had spent a year in Miami, and for us, that had been a long stop. Mom was determined that we were going up the East Coast this time. The plan had not been for her to start dating one of the wealthy members from the club where she worked.

I had googled Garrett Hughes. Even if Mom wanted to finally settle down and get married, this would not be the man to do that with. He didn't have a good track record with marriage. The number of beautiful women that he'd been photographed with over the past year alone was impressive. If the day came my mom decided to marry, she needed a man who adored her and the wild, free spirit that she was. The life this man lived was not one my mother knew how to fit into. She was beautiful, but she wasn't elegant and refined, like the other women in attendance. The thing about my mom was, she didn't give one small fuck about that. Fawn didn't know what it was like to feel insecure.

"How would you like to go down to the winner's circle suite for the next race?" Garrett asked my mom. "We can always return here to the mansion if you prefer it."

The fact that this elaborate room with celebrity chefs preparing the food and a concierge waiting on our every need was called the mansion made me want to roll my eyes. Wealthy people made up crap to spend their money on. Until today, I'd had no idea the level of indulgences provided to those who could afford it.

"That sounds wonderful." Mom placed her hand on his arm, then glanced over at me. "What about you? Want to go, Gypsi?"

Her eyes danced with the thrill of adventure. She loved experiencing new things. Me? Not so much. I felt completely out of my element. I also felt as if Garrett wanted some time with Mom today without her nineteen-year-old daughter tagging along. He'd generously provided my outfits and travel for the weekend, along with my mom's. I was happy to let him have her to himself for a while.

"Is it okay if I stay here?" I asked.

"Sure, I think that's fine." She tilted her head back to look up at her date.

Garrett gazed down at my mother's upturned face as if she were the most ravishing creature on earth. He was not her type. She normally went for the bad boys. The unstable, often-dangerous, tattooed sort with motorcycles. He leaned down and brushed a kiss close to her ear as he whispered something that made her sink in closer to him. The heated spark that ignited in Garrett's eyes had me turning my attention back to the track below.

"When does Hughes Farm have another race?" Mom asked. Her enthusiasm wasn't fake. It never was. She was enjoying this.

"Shakespeare races in Churchill Downs soon. We can watch it from the winner's circle suite. You'll enjoy the experience," he replied with clear affection in his tone.

"Oh, that's exciting!"

The obvious joy on her face seemed to please Garrett. His body language and the way he kept my mother close to his side screamed possessive.

Bad idea, Mr. Hughes. Mom isn't the female you try and claim. She belongs to herself. Always has.

"Call me if you change your mind," Mom told me before Garrett led her toward the exit.

I wasn't sure if it was my imagination, but it felt as if people parted like the Red Sea for Garrett as he walked through the room. Many gave him a smile, greeting, nod of their head, but all of them looked at him with an odd reverence. It was unsettling to watch. Something bothered me about that, and I wasn't sure why exactly.

Turning my focus back to the view in front of me, I looked over the crowd. I had never seen so many hats in my life. Many were completely ridiculous. I was thankful the hat—which had been supplied by Garrett Hughes's stylist, who had apparently been the one to choose our outfits—was a simple, floppy cotton-candy-pink hat that would work brilliantly on the beach. The pink dress I was wearing was strapless and cinched at the waist but fluffed out with a twisty chiffon material, stopping just past my mid-thigh. It was much more elaborate than the hat. As were the strappy white heels on my feet. Teardrop pearl earrings and a matching necklace, which was almost a choker, finished off the look. This was the second fancy outfit I'd worn since arriving, and both had been pink. Different shades but pink nonetheless.

Mom had convinced me not to pull my hair back, like hers. My hair was long and curly. My mom coveted it. She also liked for me to display it. The honey-blonde color was darker than hers, but she swore that the different shades of blonde streaks, caused by the sun, created a masterpiece that

I shouldn't keep from the world. To make her happy, I had left it down, allowing it to curl on its own.

"You forgot to leave me a glass slipper last night," a familiar, deep voice said close to my ear.

Closing my eyes for a moment, I sighed, then turned to look at Trev Hughes. I'd hoped to avoid him the rest of this weekend. Last night, he'd given me a moment to escape, and I'd taken it. I shouldn't have, but when I had gotten the chance, I'd bailed. I liked him. He made me laugh. I'd been honest when I told him that I thought we could be good friends. He wasn't at all what I'd expected after being around his father. In the end, I had known that allowing him to flirt with me was wrong. Our parents were dating. He just didn't know.

I turned to study him. Just like last night, I was struck speechless by his shocking gray eyes, outlined in thick black lashes. Ridiculously full lips made me want to touch them and see if they felt as soft as they looked. His black hair was just long enough on top to have a sexy, messy look. Tanned skin—which hinted that he spent more time outdoors than in—a firm jawline, and wide shoulders all created a very nice profile package. He wasn't in a tux today, but he was still devastatingly beautiful.

"Waiting on that excuse, Cinderella."

"Can I just apologize?" I asked.

He shrugged with a serious expression. "I don't know. Might require more than that."

Unable to keep the grin from spreading across my face, I took the bait. "What would that be exactly?"

He cut his gaze from the track to me, and then he winked. "Oh, Gypsi, you shouldn't give me that kind of power."

I laughed.

"I'll go easy on you," he said, leaning down to me, then tapped his cheek with his finger. "One kiss."

11

Putting my lips on him was too tempting. He had no idea what he was asking for. But it was just his cheek. What harm could that do? It wasn't like I was in Florida. We were miles away. This was safe. There was no danger in my past stalking me here. Besides, he was hard to tell no. I turned toward him, and with the heels on my feet, it just took me lifting up a little to reach him. Closing my eyes, I leaned in to make it quick. I gasped, and my eyes flew open when soft, warm lips met mine. When I moved away from him, his gray eyes locked on mine. I wished he hadn't done that.

I watched as he slowly licked his lips, as if savoring the taste. "Damn, that's sweet. Like a fucking lollipop."

This guy. He was too much. I had to keep my head straight. Even if our parents weren't dating, I was trouble, and he had no idea how much.

The sound inside the room rose, and people began moving to crowd in behind where we were standing. The intercom system announced the Churchill Downs race. Trev moved in behind me, as if keeping others from getting too close.

"Do you have a favorite?" he asked.

Smiling, I knew my answer would throw him. "Shakespeare," I replied.

He would think I'd looked him up and I was giving him this answer to flirt. When, in reality, I didn't know the name of any other horse in this race.

His lips curled up slowly at the corners in a way that made my stomach flutter. "Did you do some research last night, Lollipop?"

Lollipop? I wasn't sure I wanted to be called anything but my name. But then again, Lollipop was nothing like princess. I shivered, remembering things I tried to forget. That was behind me. I would move on and be stronger for it. Shoving those memories as far back in my head as I could, I focused on the here and now.

"Why would I do that? I was the one who ran off."

Keep that ego in check, Trev. I'm not going to stroke it. You're wasting time with the wrong girl.

"And I'm still wounded. Another kiss might make it better."

I laughed. If only wounding this man's ego was that easy.

A loud horn went off, and I turned my attention back to the track. The race had begun. I grabbed the rail in front of me as the energy in the room began to build.

"Which one is Shakespeare?" I asked, wishing I had paid more attention to Garrett earlier.

"Did you bet on Shakespeare?"

If he only knew how ridiculous that question was for someone with my lifestyle. He assumed I had money to bet on horse racing.

"No," I replied with a laugh. "I don't bet. But I do want him to win."

"And why is that?" he asked, oozing of swagger that I was sure got him laid easily.

I shrugged, leaning in to see the horses rounding a corner.

"That one." He pointed, caging me in with his body as he leaned over me. "The one in the lead."

"Maybe I should have bet," I teased.

The speaker's voice caught my attention. "And it is going to be Shakespeare to win."

The cheers went up inside the mansion, and I clapped my hands, then turned to hug Trev, caught up in the moment.

"If I kiss you, will I get slapped?" he asked.

I moved back away from him, but he didn't take his hand from my waist.

"Most likely," I replied but smiled to soften the warning.

He sighed with a look of mock defeat. "You going to tell me why you wanted Shakespeare to win?"

"Why? Did you want another horse to win?" I asked.

He smirked and studied me for a moment. "Come on, Lollipop. Let's go down to the winner's circle."

Part of me wasn't ready for him to know who I was. Having him flirt with me felt nice. Mom and I always traveled so much that it wasn't until this past year that I'd had a real relationship with a guy. One that lasted six months. Pushing thoughts of Tyde out of my head before I went to that dark place, I focused on Trev and what had to be done. We could be friends, but even with that, I'd have to be careful. For all our sakes.

Chapter
THREE

TREV

Damn, she even smelled good. I leaned down a little closer and inhaled. I swore it was like a cupcake—or was it vanilla and lavender? Whatever it was, I liked it. I wanted more of it. She could pretend she hadn't gone back to her hotel and googled me last night, but she'd given herself away with the fact that she knew Shakespeare was a Hughes horse. Maybe whoever she was here with had told her.

And who was that exactly? She'd run off before I figured out what man had brought her. He'd better be some fucking old dude. Both times I'd found her, she'd been alone and completely secure with that. Another thing I liked about her. She didn't need people around her. She was fine with being alone. There was something badass about it that turned me on.

My dad was already at the winner's circle with some new blonde I hadn't met. I'd seen her on his arm last night. He'd mentioned a new girlfriend and wanting the family to meet her. Guessed this was going to be our meeting. He'd brought her to Kentucky. She must have come on a different plane. She hadn't been on ours. Had he let her fly commercial? I found that unlikely. It was getting serious if he was introducing her to us, which meant she had probably gotten here on the smaller private jet. I might be getting a new mom soon. It had been a while. I guessed it was about time.

"Trev." Gypsi said my name so softly.

I dropped my gaze to her upturned face. "Yeah, Lollipop?" I asked, suddenly distracted by her biting her bottom lip. I wanted to bite it. Lick it. Suck on it. Like the damn lollipop I knew she tasted like.

"I need to tell you something." She was looking at me almost apologetically. "I should have told you earlier."

I didn't like where this was going. Especially with that look on her face.

"Yeah?"

Please don't let her be fucking married or some shit like that. Let this be one of those stalker things. Like she knew who I was and had set this all up. I'd be okay with it. She could stalk me all she wanted. I'd let her stalk me right into my bed.

She opened those sweet pink lips again.

"Gypsi!" a female voice called.

She winced and whispered, "I'm sorry."

I didn't like those words. Something was about to fucking blow up in my face. I could feel it. Which sucked. I liked her. I wanted this one. Well, I wanted to fuck her. Several times. In many different ways.

"Son," my father's deep voice said, "I see you've met Gypsi."

My eyes stayed locked on Gypsi as she gave me a tight smile. What was going on? She knew my dad. I was almost afraid to take my eyes off her. Last time I had done that, she'd fucking disappeared.

16

"Did you see the race? I wish you'd come down here with us. It was incredible!"

I turned then to see who was talking. Pausing, I stared at my dad, then at the woman on his arm. The woman he was holding close to his side. Possessively. I glanced back at Gypsi, then at the woman, and I saw it then. The resemblance. It was impossible not to notice.

Well, damn. My dad was dating her sister.

That had to be it. They looked too much alike. Gypsi was by far the better-looking one, but they were definitely sisters. What did this mean exactly? Was it weird? I mean, they were sisters. It wasn't like she and I were related. Fuck, I needed a moment to work through this.

"I did," Gypsi replied in a soft voice.

"Fawn, this is my youngest son, Trev," my father said. "Trev, this is Fawn Parker."

I managed a nod, wanting to get the introductions over with so that I could get back to discussing this with Gypsi. Was this why she'd said we were going to be good friends? She'd known who I was, obviously. The *good friends* thing was still bullshit. This didn't mean we couldn't fuck. Sure, when Dad moved on—and he would—it would be fine. I wasn't looking for a relationship. More like a hot fling with sex. Lots of sex. In many different positions. The things I wanted to do to this girl.

"It's nice to meet you, Trev. Where did you find Gypsi?" Fawn asked.

I gave her my Hughes charm and smiled. Didn't need her to know I was mentally fucking her little sister. I needed this woman to like me. Which was a first. I typically didn't give a shit if Dad's women liked me. "Uh, yeah, well, we met last night. But"—I glanced at her, not sure if she wanted them to know she'd kept who she was a secret, feeling the need to protect her—"we didn't realize the connection until today. I saw her up in the mansion."

Dad seemed pleased. "Now that you've met, why don't you show her around? Introduce her to people. This is their first derby. I'm sure she'd like to be around some people her own age."

I nodded. *Thank you, Dad*. I never thought I'd feel like I owed him one. This was a unique experience. It made up for the fact that I'd lost her last night so that I could go handle an issue with security.

"Her hotel suite is on the opposite side of the hall as yours. In case we get separated at the end and she needs a way back, make sure you get her there," he told me.

She had been so close to me last night? What the hell?!

I managed to keep a casual expression on my face. "Yeah, sure. I'll take care of her." *In many, many ways before this night ends, if I'm lucky.*

Fawn's gaze was on Gypsi's. I could see the silent question in her eyes. I looked down at Gypsi just in time to see her give a small nod. The fucking smile that broke across my face was hard to control. Gypsi had just given me the nod. Hell yeah.

"There're the Houstons. I want to introduce you to Melanie. You'll like her," Dad told Fawn and then led her away.

I turned to face Gypsi and raised an eyebrow in question. "You knew all along," I accused her.

She pressed her lips together and looked truly sorry. Maybe I could play off her guilt, and it would help with getting my mouth between her legs later.

"I should have told you. I was about to, but then they showed up."

"When you ran off from me last night, did you know I was across the hall from you?"

She shook her head, eyes wide. "I had no idea, I swear."

18

The fact that we had wasted a night already bugged me. We'd need to make up for it tonight. After I worked my magic. Still pulling the guilt angle, I let my appreciative gaze travel down her body. All the way to the strappy heels on her small feet.

"The man who bought your clothes was my dad."

I liked that. I could live with it. Hughes money had dressed her. Yeah, I fucking liked that a lot. But it did make me wonder why he had bought their clothing. He typically bought the women he dated jewelry, took them to exotic locations. He didn't normally hand over the Black Amex until he got engaged to one. Then, she would fill her closet on his dime. Yet Dad had already dressed this one and her sister. Not that this mattered to me. It was just different.

She nodded.

The smile that stretched across my face was inevitable. Pretending like I was upset with her was pointless. I wanted her naked and in my bed—or any bed, or a sofa, or a fucking floor. Maybe a table. The wall or the shower.

"Since I'm in charge of showing you around and *taking care of you* ..." My added emphasis wasn't missed on her.

She rolled her eyes.

"I thought for sure you'd stop the flirting once you knew," she said.

Was she crazy? It would take a hell of a lot more for me to give up my plan to get her naked.

"Lollipop"—I reached for her waist and pulled her closer to me, and her eyes went wide as she looked up at me—"it would take a lot more than the fact that my dad is dating your sister to stop me from convincing you to let me have those sweet lips."

There was a flicker in her eyes that bothered me. It wasn't what I had been trying for here with this *pull her close and talk smooth* thing I was laying on thick.

She gave me a serious look. Not what I wanted to see. "Fawn isn't my sister, Trev."

I frowned. Okay ... so I was confused. They looked too much alike. As if Gypsi was a younger version of the other woman. I shook my head, not sure if anything else made sense in this situation.

"She's my mom."

I stood there as those words sank in. Mom? How the hell did her mom look like she was thirty years old? How old was Gypsi? Fuck! Had I been hitting on a minor?

I stared at her, waiting for her to laugh and tell me she was joking. She didn't.

I dropped my hands and took a step back, needing to get enough distance that her scent didn't cling to me. Driving me insane. "How old are you?" I asked, feeling like I'd been fucking kicked.

She blushed slightly. "I'll be twenty in a few months," she said softly. "My mom had me when she was seventeen."

Not a minor. She sure as hell didn't look like one. Thank fuck I didn't have that standing in my way. But our parents were dating ... and Dad had dressed them. That was serious. He might be keeping this one.

What did this mean for my future chance of getting between those mouthwatering legs?

Jesus Christ, I needed a drink. No, I needed the whole damn bottle.

I wanted her. Any man who laid eyes on her would want her. But leave it to my dad to make this fucked up. Screwing up my life every chance he got. Because as hot as she was, fucking someone who could be my future stepsister was too twisted of a situation. You couldn't have a fling with someone who might move into your house. When it was over they didn't go away. And the way Dad had been looking at her mom ... FUCK!

Chapter
FOUR

GYPSI

I had to give it to him. Trev sure could switch roles on a dime. It had taken him a moment to process things, and then a smile returned to his face, and he began introducing me to people. Acting like we were the friends I'd said we would be. What I hadn't bargained on was the loss I felt. It stung a little. I should be relieved. He wasn't making this weird. This was all my fault anyway. I should have told him the moment he introduced himself last night. Enjoying his flirting and letting my own imagination think about things that could not happen—it was stupid.

After introducing me to Saxon Houston, his best friend, he excused himself to go speak to someone he had seen in the distance. I watched him walk away as if he couldn't get away from me fast enough. Which, again, my fault.

"He might be gone for a few," Saxon told me.

I turned my attention back to the guy he'd dropped me on and dashed.

"Hughes Farm doesn't have a horse in the next race, but Moses Mile, my family's stables, does. Come on up close with me and watch. I can give you some Horse Racing 101."

That sounded like a great distraction. Sax held out his hand for me to take, and I slipped mine in his as I stood up from the cushioned sofa I'd been left sitting on.

"Want another drink?" he asked me as he reached for the empty mint julep glass in my hand.

I shook my head. "No thank you," I replied.

For a guy who had just been left with a strange girl to entertain, he was being nice about it.

Saxon took the glass and put it on a tray. "Let me know if you change your mind."

"Thank you."

He gave me a smile that caused dimples to appear. I hadn't expected those. His strong jawline and the scar on his left cheek made him appear more rugged. The dimples seemed to wipe that away completely. As did his warm brown eyes. Saxon wasn't Trev level of hot, but he was attractive. At least with him, I wasn't entertaining perverse thoughts.

"Rig is running in this next race. I'll point him out as soon as they're let loose," he told me.

"How many races do you have horses in today?" I asked him.

"We had one earlier, and we have two more after this one, but one of those isn't our horse. It's a horse we board. We don't have a horse in the Kentucky Derby race. We had hoped Lava Run would get a spot, but he didn't. Hughes Farm has Cohiba racing in it though. He'll be hard to beat."

I had no idea what winning a spot meant. I started to ask when I heard female laughter, verging on giggling, drawing closer to us. Glancing back, I tensed only a moment when my gaze found Trev giving a wicked grin to a stunning redhead as he held her close to him with his hand on her butt, then bent to whisper in her ear. She appeared to be completely enamored with him.

Not wanting to be caught watching them, I turned my attention back to the track. This was his way of handling the awkward position. He was going to find a replacement female to flirt with. But I'd already given him the player label. It hadn't been a harsh judgment. The guy was charming, and he used it too well.

"Maybe I do want that drink," I said to Saxon, hoping he didn't realize why.

It was silly really. The fact that it even bothered me. I'd been around Trev Hughes twice for barely any time at all. Knowing the entire time that the fact that our parents were dating would end his flirting. It was also going to save him. When we got back to Florida, I'd need to keep my distance from him and Saxon. Until I knew it was safe to be around a guy again.

Saxon nodded and leaned back, held up a hand, then smiled down at me. "Same thing?"

I paused then, unsure if I needed to have money for this. Trev had gotten me the first one before ditching me. I didn't have any money on me.

I scrunched my nose, feeling more comfortable being honest with Saxon than I did Trev. "Um, depends. How much are they?"

That dimpled grin flashed at me again. "Nothing. The drinks are all on Hughes Farm."

"In that case, yes, please," I replied.

He chuckled, turning to order my mint julep from the server and a whiskey for himself. The giggling started again, and I caught myself rolling my eyes.

"I wasn't going to ask, but I've decided I am. Last night, when Trev spotted you at the gala, did he know who you were then?"

I looked up at Saxon, not realizing he'd been at the gala last night. I shook my head. He did a quick glance back in the direction of Trev and the giggling female.

"And he just found out today," Saxon finished.

I nodded.

He sighed, then gave me that dimpled smile. "That sucks for him." Then, he winked.

Here we go. He was going to flirt. I would have to be sure to keep him at arm's length. Not give him any wrong ideas. He didn't have a reason not to pursue me, like Trev did.

Saxon turned and took our drinks from the server I hadn't realized was behind me. He thanked her, then turned to me, handing me the mint julep.

"So, tell me about yourself. I know you don't live in Ocala. Your face isn't one that a guy forgets."

I felt my cheeks warm. Something about the matter-of-fact way he had said it—without the flirty tone of voice or flashy grin—made me feel as if he truly meant it. "Uh, well, I do currently live in Ocala, but we just moved there three weeks ago."

"Why move to Ocala?"

"It was a stopping point on our way north."

"North? Where were you before? Where are you headed to next?" He asked both questions before taking a drink of his amber-colored whiskey.

"We have been in Miami for the past year. As for where to next, I have no idea. We rarely ever know."

He looked confused. "I'm gonna need the story behind that."

I sighed, thinking of my mother. "Mom likes to move. She never can stay settled long. She doesn't have a plan—never has. We just move."

"Is that why she named you Gypsi?" he asked me.

I nodded, pleased he'd picked up on that. "Her two favorite things in the world should have the same name—at least, she said that was her reasoning when she was seventeen."

He frowned. "She had you at seventeen?"

"Yep," I replied, taking a sip.

"Explains why she looks so young."

I laughed.

"You two look cozy," Trev said, stepping up beside me with the redhead clinging to his arm.

I smiled at the girl, then took another drink, turning my attention to the track again.

"We'll be discussing our wedding plans by derby time," Saxon drawled.

I bit my bottom lip, not wanting to laugh, then looked up at him. He was pleased with my response. His dimples told me so. I had to stop that. Rein it in.

Trev didn't respond.

"Hello, Sax," the redhead greeted him.

"Eliza," he replied. "Felix looked great out there today."

She giggled. "Is that one of our horses?"

Saxon looked down at me and raised his eyebrow slightly, then back at her. "Yeah, he is."

"I don't keep up with that stuff. You know that. I'm just here for all the fun stuff."

Saxon nodded, then leaned down to me. "They'll start from there. Rig is the third one in."

"I think I am asking this correctly ... what are his odds?" I was trying to remember the race talk I'd heard from Garrett the past two days in conversation with others we had met.

"If you're betting, yeah," he replied. "You want some Horse Race Betting 101 now?"

I thought about that, then shrugged. "I'm not much of a gambler," I explained. "After I work for my money, I'm not keen on losing it."

Saxon smirked. "What if it's not your money?"

I tilted my head and studied him for a moment. "Are you offering to give me money to bet?"

He nodded his head slowly while watching me. That was tempting, but it would give him the wrong idea.

"If she wants to bet, I'll place her bet." Trev's voice was hard. Something I'd not heard before.

I turned to look at him, and he was glaring at Saxon. What was that about?

"Hey, I'm just teaching her the ropes. You've got your hands full," Saxon replied.

Trev's jaw flexed, and then his gaze dropped down to mine. "You want to bet?" he asked in a harsh tone that made me flinch.

I shook my head. Even if it wasn't my money, I had a hard time seeing people toss money away. I'd worked too hard for it from the time I was old enough to get a job.

His nostrils flared, and then I watched as he visibly relaxed somewhat.

"Hell, Trev, you growl at her, and she's not gonna want to do anything." Saxon sounded like he was scolding him.

"I didn't growl." Trev's voice still held a sharp bite to it.

"I want a drink," Eliza said. "Can I have the Mint Julip Gold Cup?"

"Isn't that thirty-five hundred dollars?" Saxon asked, sounding annoyed.

Eliza lifted her shoulder. "They have sapphires on them this year. I know they are sold out and there was only fifty made but I also know Trev is a Hughes."

"Let me see what I can do," Trev replied.

Saxon looked at me. "Does that mint julep taste okay in the regular cup?" He was smirking.

I nodded, but didn't look back at Trev or Eliza.

"Sorry about him. Trev isn't normally so tense," Saxon whispered.

I managed to smile as I looked up at him. "No worries."

His gaze dropped to my drink. "If you want a Gold Cup though, he can get you one. Hughes have power here that most don't. Garrett probably bought most of the damn things anyway."

I didn't know much about cocktails or mint juleps, but I thought it was rather nice. I didn't know what a Gold Cup meant, but I did know there was no way I would drink something that cost that much.

"This one is delicious."

He flicked his eyes back over my shoulder, then back to me. "It's a very expensive collector's item that Woodford Reserve sells every year."

My eyes widened. "I prefer this free one."

He chuckled.

The next race was announced, and Saxon leaned into me with excitement dancing in his expression. "Almost time."

I asked him more questions about Rig and Moses Mile. He answered them with enthusiasm, and it was clear he loved horses and racing. I enjoyed listening to the passion in his voice about it all.

Chapter
FIVE

GYPSI

Rig won his race, and Saxon took me with him to the winner's circle. Photographers took pictures, and Saxon put his arm around my waist, then told me to smile. For a moment, I panicked. But this wouldn't be the kind of news that would be seen by everyone. It should be fine. I hated living in fear all the time.

The frenzy was addictive, and when we went back to the suite for the next few races, Trev wasn't around. I found myself enjoying Saxon's company. The next race, Moses Mile had another horse racing, which came in third, and then the last one, they came in second.

When the Kentucky Derby race began, the suite was full, and I noticed Trev standing with Eliza on the other side. Garrett and Mom came to stand with us, and Mom looked from Saxon to me, then gave me a wink. She was getting the wrong idea, but I didn't say anything. She so desperately wanted me to date again. I would soon. When I knew I could do so safely. Garrett spoke with Saxon, congratulating him on the earlier win.

The loud horn blew, and cheering filled the air. Mom squeezed my arm, and I glanced back at her to see the exhilaration on her face. She was loving this. Saxon cheered on Cohiba as if he were one of his horses running. I liked that about him. He was one of the best kind of friends. The good guy always was.

When Cohiba's name was called, the entire suite erupted, and in the frenzy of it all, I turned and hugged Saxon. When I looked back at Mom, she was wrapped in Garrett's arms. He was looking down at her with an affectionate smile. I wanted to be happy for her. She was having a wonderful time. I just didn't know if she realized this man was as serious about her as he was.

He whispered to her, and she nodded before they began to walk off. I knew the direction they were headed was to the winner's circle. She'd been there several times today, but this was the main show. The big one. Mom was going to love this.

Saxon leaned down close to my ear. With all the noise, it was hard to hear him any other way. "Want to hang around here for the celebration party, or do you need to go change or anything before?"

Trev was supposed to get me back to wherever I was expected to go after. I looked around to ask him about that since the party hadn't been mentioned, but he and Eliza were walking behind Mom and Garrett as they headed for the circle.

I looked back at Saxon. "I'm not sure. Garrett told Trev to get me where I needed to go after, but he's got to go do the winner's circle stuff. If you need to leave, I can wait here until they're done."

Saxon glanced back to where I knew the others were headed. "I'm not certain if he remembers that. He's been drinking pretty heavily. I'll check with Levi. He can get directions from Garrett faster than I can. Come this way," he said to me, then placed a hand on my back and led me over to a couple of men standing at the exit of the suite.

Both of them were tall with wide shoulders, their arms crossed over their chests like they were security of some kind.

The one with light-brown hair pulled back in a knotted bun turned to see us, and his gaze locked on me. His eyes traveled down my body before a slow smile curled his lips.

"Levi," Saxon greeted him, and he shifted his focus to him. "This is Fawn Parker's daughter, Gypsi. I need to know where Garrett would like me to escort her from here."

He didn't mention that Trev had been given this job, but I figured it didn't matter. Garrett would see Trev had a date with him now.

Levi nodded, then stepped away.

"Kye," Saxon said to the blond guy with tattoos covering his arms. "This is Gypsi Parker. Gypsi, this is Kye."

The guy smiled at me and nodded his head. "Nice to meet you," he drawled, but he didn't move to shake my hand.

He remained in his bodyguard stance. Was that what he was?

Levi was back almost immediately. "Garrett said to take her back to the hotel so she can get ready for the party. Her mother will stop by to check on her from there."

"Thanks," Saxon replied. Then, he looked down at me. "That sound good to you?" he asked me.

The thought of getting alone time and a hot shower sounded wonderful.

I nodded. "Thank you," I told him, feeling bad that he'd suddenly become my keeper.

31

He bent his elbow and held his arm out to me with a grin. I lifted my gaze to look up at him again.

"Come on. We're friends now. We derby'd together," he teased.

I stepped forward and took his arm. This day had been nothing like I'd expected.

We left the suite and turned to head in the opposite direction as the winner's circle. My eyes, however, landed on Trev as he whispered in Eliza's ear, making her smile. Cameras flashed around them, and for a moment, I envied her, but I knew that I couldn't have done that. The actual Kentucky Derby winner would be all over the media. Photos splashed everywhere. That was a risk I wasn't taking.

Apparently, there was a winner's circle party that we would be attending, but after it was over, Garrett had his own private party that we would move to.

I was limited on time to get changed and refreshed for the winner's circle party. Saxon had said he'd be back for me and escort me there. He had seemed to want to do it, so I didn't argue or tell him he didn't have to. After all, I did feel as if we had forged a friendship today. One I wished I could keep. Maybe I'd feel safe enough to do so soon.

The soft, shiny chiffon of my dress hit just below mid-thigh and clung to my body. The back was a low drop with spaghetti straps that sparkled even more than the black shimmer of the rest of the material. Thankfully, there was no hat tonight. I pulled my curls up with a silver clip that was hidden under my hair to get it off my back and neck.

Mom had stopped by on her way to make sure I was having a good time and ask me about Saxon. She'd met his parents, and she said his mother had seemed thrilled that he was spending time with me. It had been a short visit, but she'd been so vibrant and ready for the evening that I hadn't wanted to keep her.

The doorbell startled me. I'd never known hotel rooms to have doorbells, but then this was more like an apartment. Slipping on my shoes, I headed for the door.

Opening it, I smiled at Saxon, then held up a finger. "Give me one minute," I told him, then bent down to fasten the strap around my ankle.

When I managed it, I stood up and started to apologize for not being ready when my eyes locked on Trev walking out of his door across the wide hallway. The smile that lit up his face was completely different from the angry Trev earlier.

"My friends!" he called out.

Saxon turned then to see Trev heading toward us. "Ready to go celebrate?"

"Hell yeah, I am," Trev replied. "I think I'm supposed to pick up Eliza, but I can't remember where I left her. Besides, I have my dates." He walked up to Saxon and threw his arm around his shoulders. Then, he smacked a loud kiss on Saxon's cheek and threw out his other arm. "Come here, Lollipop."

"Lollipop?" Saxon asked.

Trev grinned. "Yep. Lollipop. Her lips are fucking sweet. Taste like candy."

My gaze swung to Saxon, and he raised his eyebrows.

"It wasn't like that. I was supposed to kiss his cheek, and he turned his head at the last minute," I explained, feeling my face heat up from even having to explain this. I probably hadn't needed to, but it'd made me sound bad. Or maybe Tyde's words were still controlling me.

Trev laughed. "I got moves."

Turning away from them, I closed the door and took a second to regroup before facing them.

Trev held out his arm. "Come on, Lollipop. This is your side."

Not wanting to make this weird, I walked over to him, and he slung his arm around my shoulders. Then, he pressed his lips against my cheek. The scent of whiskey on his breath was intense. Saxon had been right. Trev was drunk.

"Let's go do this thing," he announced and started walking us to the elevator.

I wasn't sure how long we were supposed to walk like this, but it was going to be difficult for us to get into the elevator this way.

"Do I need to text Eliza and find out if you're supposed to pick her up?" Saxon asked.

Trev turned to look down at me. "Is that what I should do?"

Why was he asking me? "Yes, if she is expecting you to pick her up, then that would be a good idea."

He frowned. "Sax always does the right thing. He's good like that."

The elevator opened, and Saxon moved out from under Trev's arm. "Come on in, and I'll text her. Is she staying here?"

"No fucking clue," Trev replied, then laughed as he dropped his arm from around my shoulders, letting it go to my lower back. When his hand touched my skin, he stilled, then peered over my shoulder to look at my back. "Damn, Lollipop. I like this dress."

"Easy there, Romeo," Saxon said to him.

Trev turned his attention to Saxon, but his hand didn't leave my back. "What? I do. It's hot. The damn thing doesn't have a back. She looks hot, doesn't she?"

Saxon glanced up at me, then back at his phone. "Yes, she looks beautiful."

Trev groaned, and his hand fell away from me as he leaned against the elevator wall. "Why do you have to be so damn charming? I can't compete."

Saxon grinned, shaking his head. "We've been best friends most of our lives, Trev. You've never once needed to compete with anyone. Your game is strong."

Trev swung his head back around to look at me. "You think my game is strong, Lollipop?"

I opened my mouth and closed it. How did I answer this? Carefully, I decided. Very carefully. "Yes, you've got excellent pickup lines," I assured him.

He let out a bark of laughter. "Bullshit! You didn't fall for it for a second. My fucking ego was bruised."

"I texted Eliza," Saxon informed him. "She's on the fifth floor. We're stopping to get her."

Trev looked disappointed. "She's getting the wrong idea."

Saxon cleared his throat. "Dude, you should have thought about that before buying her a thirty-five-hundred-dollar cup, groping her, taking her to the winner's circle, and sticking your tongue down her throat in photos that will make it in the news."

Trev covered his face with his hand, groaning again. "Fuck, I did that, didn't I?"

I looked over at Saxon, and he just smiled, shaking his head at me. This must be common Trev behavior. That was a bit of a letdown, but then how long would I really be around Trev? This could be over with our parents by next week. Then again, it could last awhile. Mom seemed to light up under Garrett's attention.

"Just for the record, the mint julep without the gold cup was delicious," I told him.

He looked at me and frowned. "You didn't get a Gold Cup?"

I laughed. "Uh, no. That offends me that you'd ask. Drinks should not cost that much."

Trev banged the back of his head on the wall. "Fucking hell. I didn't even get you a Gold Cup."

"And I assure you, I am happy about that."

"Now, I'm stuck with Eliza," he groaned.

"Look at it this way. Eliza doesn't live in Ocala. After tonight, you won't see her again until Belmont Stakes," Saxon told him.

Trev nodded. "That's good. Yeah." Then, he looked at me. "How'd you like the winner's circle?"

Even with his eyes glassy, he was still insanely handsome. It truly wasn't fair. With his money and looks, what else had I expected? He could do whatever he wanted, act however he wanted, and it was overlooked.

"I liked it. It was exciting," I told him.

He looked pained. Had he wanted me to hate it?

The elevator doors opened.

"Go get your date," Saxon told him.

"I don't know what room," he replied, not moving.

Saxon sighed and walked out of the elevator to look down the hallway while texting, I assumed, Eliza. The elevator doors started to close, and I took a step to stop it, but Trev's hand wrapped around my arm, pulling me back.

"It's closing." I pointed out the obvious.

Trev grinned. "Oops."

I realized that he'd done that on purpose. "Saxon is helping you."

He nodded. "Yeah."

Frustrated with him even if he was drunk, I pulled my arm free of his hold. "I realize that most people just let you get drunk and act however you want, but I'm not cool with it. You need to be a better friend, even when you're drunk."

His smile fell. Good. Someone needed to point out his behavior.

"He deserves it," he said to me.

"No, he doesn't."

Trev nodded, and then his gaze slowly drifted down my dress, legs, all the way to my shoes. "Yeah, he fucking does. You were gonna be my friend. He stole you."

He sounded like a little boy, upset because someone had taken his toy.

"You got busy with Eliza. Remember? You left me with Saxon, and being the good friend he is, he stepped in and babysat me so you didn't have to."

The scowl that touched his brow shouldn't make me want to reach up and smooth it out. "I needed a minute. Eliza was there, and she distracted me. I wasn't trying to get rid of you. We were supposed to watch the race together. You were supposed to go with me to the winner's circle. But you liked Sax better."

The elevator doors opened again, and an elegant older couple stepped inside. I realized we hadn't pressed the lobby button, and the elevator had gone back up.

The man noticed Trev and nodded his head. "Congratulations, Mr. Hughes. Cohiba was a beauty to watch."

He smiled, straightening his stance. "Thank you," he replied.

The man stepped forward and pressed the lobby button, glancing back at us. "Are you two headed to the lobby?" he asked.

"Yes, please," I replied, assuming Saxon and Eliza were down there, looking for us now.

Trev turned to look at me again. "Will you be my friend tonight?"

"I told you last night that I was sure we'd be good friends."

He sighed. "Yeah."

The doors opened again, and Trev waved his hand for the other couple to exit. Then, he placed his hand on my bare back before leading me to follow behind them. His thumb began to make small circles against my skin, and the goose bumps on my arms gave away the fact that it affected me.

"There you are," Eliza's voice called out.

I waited for Trev to drop his hand from my back, but he didn't. His thumb didn't stop its circular caress either.

"What happened to you?" Saxon asked, looking at me with concern.

I cut my eyes back up at Trev, then back at him. He gave me a nod of understanding, then noticed Trev's hand on me, but he didn't mention it.

Eliza's emerald-green dress looked phenomenal with her red hair. It made her green eyes pop. I started to tell her that, but her eyes dropped to Trev's arm behind me, then moved up to glare at me. Why did girls do that? I wasn't touching him. I hadn't asked him to touch me. Why glare at me?

I started to take a step forward to break the contact, but Trev's hand dropped to my hip, and his fingers dug into my skin, holding me still.

"Don't." His tone sounded like a warning.

I lifted my eyes to look at him, and my breath caught when his locked on mine. There was a commanding gleam in his gray depths. I wanted to point out that he had a date. I also didn't want him looking at me like that.

"Trev?" Eliza's tone was clearly annoyed.

He didn't acknowledge her, and it got awkward.

"Trev!" she repeated, louder this time.

There was a darkness that shaded his expression as he turned his head to look at her. "What?"

Uncomfortable was not a strong enough word. It felt as if everyone were watching us, although I knew they weren't. The place was crawling with people, and this small interaction wasn't as big of a deal as it seemed.

"What are you doing?" she asked, shooting a hateful scowl at me before swinging her eyes back to him.

"Touching Gypsi. She feels good and smells like vanilla and lavender," he replied casually.

My face felt warm. I looked to Saxon for help, and he gave me a tight smile, but said nothing. I was alone in this situation.

"Are you serious? Or just drunk?" she snapped.

He smirked. "I'm drunk, but I thought she smelled incredible when I was sober. As for touching her, I assure you, she feels good with or without intoxication. Now, can we go to the fucking party, or are you going to keep asking questions?"

Her flushed face wasn't from embarrassment. She was furious. Tossing her hair over her shoulder, she turned to look at Saxon. "Fine. Saxon?" She stepped over to him. "You can escort me to the party."

"Thank fuck," Trev replied and slid his hand back to my bare skin.

This time, it was lower, and his fingers brushed underneath the fabric that gathered at my waist. Thankfully, I had forgone panties, for fear they'd be seen through the dress, or he'd be touching the edge of them by now.

I stiffened as he began the circling caress with his ring finger, this time entirely too low.

He leaned down. "Relax. It's a friendly touch," he whispered.

My eyes flew up to meet his. "That doesn't feel friendly."

And my thighs were going to get damp if he didn't stop.

39

He winked and continued following behind Saxon and Eliza. When we walked outside, a chauffeur standing beside a black limo stepped forward and opened the door. Saxon walked up, then stepped back, allowing Eliza to climb inside. Then, he looked back at us, and I started to step forward, but Trev's hand was gripping my hip again.

He lifted his chin at Saxon, saying nothing, and Saxon climbed inside. I started to follow him and then realized that bending over to climb in could possibly flash my naked butt. I hadn't realized we would be taking a limo. I'd arrived at the track today in a limo with Garrett and my mom, but Saxon and I had left in a regular Escalade that he had driven.

"Do you need help, Lollipop?" Trev asked me when I didn't move to get inside.

I bit my bottom lip nervously, then looked up at him in hopes that I could trust him. I could trust Saxon with this. It was Trev I was worried about.

I leaned into him and whispered, "I'm worried if I bend over too much, I'll flash everyone. Could you stand behind me and block the view?"

I wasn't going to tell him that I didn't have on panties. That was information he didn't need.

He didn't even try to hide the flare of lust in his eyes. "You can't look either," I told him.

An evil grin touched his lips. "Sure, Gypsi. I'll be sure to block the view."

"And you won't look?"

He winked. "Of course not."

I tried to turn sideways, while keeping one hand on the back of my dress, trying to hold it down and over my bare bottom without falling into the limo. Once I managed to get in, I slid into the seat closest to me and across from Saxon and Eliza.

Saxon was watching me with concern. My awkward entrance into the limo hadn't gone unnoticed. I smiled to reassure him that all was well.

Trev climbed in and sat so close to me that his thigh touched mine. He put his arm behind my back on the seat and leaned close to my ear. "Didn't see a thing," he whispered just as his hand hung over my shoulder, and he began caressing my upper arm with his thumb.

What was with him and the touching? Drunk Trev was someone I needed to stay away from in the future. I wasn't sure how much willpower I would have if he kept this up over time.

"What time is it?" he asked Saxon.

"Almost eight," he replied.

"Ah, perfect timing. We've missed an hour. One hour left before we move it to the better party." Trev's tone sounded pleased. He leaned back as if he owned the world. "Stop the angry scowling, Eliza. It's ruining the mood."

My eyes swung to Saxon, who shook his head with a sigh and turned to look out the window. This night was going to be interesting.

Chapter
SIX

GYPSI

Once we arrived, Trev nodded his head toward the door. "Let them go first, and then I'll go out before you." He was offering me a way to get out without worrying over my dress riding up.

Trev waited for me to exit, holding his hand out for me to take. The moment I stepped out, I realized cameras were going off.

Trev kept his hand locked tight on my hip as we walked toward the entrance. Several photographers called out his name, and he pulled me close to his side as he smiled. This could be trouble. I didn't have time to escape him, and if I did, it could cause a scene I didn't need. I managed to smile, but the entire situation felt as if I'd been tossed into an alternate universe. When we finally stepped inside, past the media craze, I took a deep breath. That was probably as safe as the pictures I'd had taken with Saxon today. I doubted it was something that would make national news. I hoped not. For both our sakes.

Saxon was alone, waiting on us. I looked around, but didn't see Eliza anywhere. His gaze met mine.

"Lost your date?" Trev asked him.

"No. I lost yours."

Trev laughed. "I owe you one."

Saxon shook his head, looking amused. Trev's behavior didn't surprise him or bother him, but then they'd been friends forever. He was used to it. I was the one struggling with the strange swing in his mood.

"Let's get a drink," Trev suggested, keeping his hand on me as we walked into the crowd of people.

"Are you going to keep your hand on me all night?" I asked him. "Eliza left. It worked." And I was mentally exhausted, trying to fight off sexual thoughts about him.

Trev frowned, looking down at me. "My touching you didn't have shit to do with Eliza. I'm just making sure you don't leave me to go make friends with another guy. You're my friend tonight. Sax got you already. It's my turn."

I laughed. "I can be both your friends."

Trev scowled. "I don't like sharing." He pointed across the room. "There're our *parents*. Want to go say hello?"

"Um, only if you want to," I replied.

I wasn't sure how his father felt about him being intoxicated. He was twenty-one years old, but still, I didn't know their dynamic.

He chuckled. "Yeah, then no. I'd rather not."

"Trev!" a guy called out in greeting as he walked up to us. "I missed you at the track today. Spent a fucking lot of time in the winner's circle, as usual."

"It's the Hughes way," Trev replied, clasping the guy's outstretched hand with the one he didn't have almost down the back of my dress.

43

The guy laughed. "No shit," he replied, and then his eyes shifted to me. "I thought I saw Eliza in the winner's circle photos with you earlier. Looks like you traded up."

"Gypsi, this is Xavier. His family owns Lighthouse Stables in Knoxville, Tennessee. They've had a former derby winner. Xavier, this is Gypsi, my new friend."

The guy laughed, then gave me a close inspection. "Since when did you start friend-zoning beautiful women?"

Trev chuckled, but said nothing.

"It's nice to meet you, Xavier," I replied, hoping to change the subject.

Saxon appeared at my other side, holding a mint julep out for me. "Wasn't sure what else you liked. If you're tired of this already, I can go get something else. Just tell me what."

I took the drink. "Thank you, Saxon. This is perfect."

"Seriously, dude. She's my friend tonight. Stop making me look bad."

Saxon rolled his eyes.

"You sure you don't want one of the Gold Cups? They're not selling them but I know where I can get one."

I shook my head. "I would be furious."

"So, she is a friend?" Xavier asked, looking from Saxon to Trev, then locking in on me. "How exactly does one get in line for this friendship?"

Trev's hand moved to my waist, gripping me tightly. "You don't."

I shifted some, trying to get him to ease up on his hold. It stung. His heated glare dropped to me.

"You're hurting me," I said softly.

His expression softened, as did his grip. "Sorry, Lollipop," he replied, looking truly bothered by the fact that he'd caused me pain.

44

"Excuse us, Xavier," Trev said as he moved us toward the bar. "I've got to go get a drink since Sax didn't bring me one."

Xavier laughed and began talking to Saxon as we walked away from them.

"I didn't mean to hurt you," he said, leaning closer to my ear so I could hear him.

"It's fine," I assured him.

"No, it's not. I can kiss it and make it better," he offered.

A laugh bubbled out of me, and I shook my head. "That won't be necessary."

"You sure? I don't mind. That's what friends are for."

I looked up at him. "No, Trev, it isn't."

The disappointed look on his face bothered me. He was drunk and acting out of character. When he had been sober, he hadn't wanted anything to do with me. As much as I liked him being close to me and I enjoyed his attention, it was a disaster waiting to happen.

"Don't be mean," he replied.

I reached up and placed a hand on his chest. "If you were sober, we wouldn't be standing here together. Sober Trev understood how impossible this situation was. I'm not saying that our parents will end up married. Knowing my mom, we could be in Virginia next week. It's how she is. But if by some miracle your dad manages to change her mind and she stays, they get married, what then?"

He said nothing as he stared down at me. I continued when it was clear he wasn't going to respond.

"If we are friends, then it'll be easy. If we are friends, no one gets hurt."

Trev's hand fell away then, and he took a step back. It was as if my words had sobered him. The playful glint in his eyes was gone, and I missed it. That wasn't a fair reaction, but I missed it just the same.

"You're right," he finally said.

Then, he glanced over my shoulder before turning to walk into the crowd. I didn't watch where he was going. Girls would be throwing themselves at him any minute now, and I wasn't in the frame of mind to watch it.

"You okay?" Saxon asked from behind me.

With a sigh, I turned around to look at him. Saxon would make a good friend. What I felt when I was with him was what I needed to feel when I was with Trev.

"Not really," I replied honestly.

"It was the right thing to do. He needed that reminder. Most girls wouldn't have done that." Saxon's approval was clear in his voice and his expression.

"Yeah, well, part of it was self-preservation. I'm not ready for anything more than friendship, and neither is my trust. Even if it's just sex he's after."

Saxon held out his arm for me. "Want to leave and go talk about it? Or find a movie to watch? Or sit outside and watch the sunset over Churchill Downs?"

He was giving me an escape. It was tempting.

"What about the party after this one?"

"We can go there later if you want to. Probably should show our faces, but I can be a rebel when needed. If you'd rather go see a movie, I'm in."

I glanced over to where Mom and Garrett were. People surrounded them. Mom looked like she had been born to do this. Garrett kept staring down at her with an expression that told me he was getting attached to her. The future was about to get complicated. If she married him, I'd be leaving. She'd be safe. It was what I hoped happened, if she wanted that.

"Maybe we should stay around a bit first. Trev would be hurt if we left," I replied. He'd asked me to be his friend tonight. Running off would be unfair to him.

46

"Uh, he looks like he might have gotten distracted," Saxon replied, looking over my shoulder.

I turned my head to see Trev talking to a blonde and a brunette. The blonde was touching his arm, and the smile on his face said he was enjoying the attention. They were beautiful, so I could understand why.

"Yeah, he does. I guess stepping outside would be nice," I agreed.

Saxon smiled and flashed his dimples. Things were just easier with him.

Chapter
SEVEN

GYPSI

"Having fun?" Mom asked me, pulling me over to a corner, away from the others. She glanced back at Saxon, who was talking to Garrett. "He's cute," she added with a grin.

I shrugged. "Yeah. But it's a friends thing. I'm not ready to even think about dating yet."

Her concerned frown was immediate. "Gypsi, you can't go the rest of your life scared of guys and dating. Don't give Tyde that kind of power."

"I'm not. It's just that I had missed the red flags with him and I realized too late. I'm not giving him power. I am playing it safe."

She sighed and tucked one of my wayward curls behind my ear. "Sweetie, he was mentally unstable. It was my fault you even met Tyde. I was the one who made the poor choices, and I will never forgive myself for putting you in danger."

I held up a hand. "Stop. We've gone over this a million times. None of it was your fault. I was eighteen years old and perfectly aware of the choices I was making. Now, forget this. I don't want to talk about it anymore. Go back to your billionaire boyfriend and have a fantastic night."

She glanced in Garrett's direction and blushed. That was a first. Fawn Parker did not blush. She really liked this one. I just hoped she wasn't setting herself up to get hurt.

"He makes me feel like a princess," she whispered. "I've never been treated the way he treats me, and I'm not talking about the money. It's how he acts … as if I'm … special. I mean something to him. He wants to protect me." She smiled and rolled her eyes. "I sound silly."

Not wincing when she had said *princess* was difficult, but I managed not to react.

I reached over and grabbed her hand. "No, Mom, you don't. You sound like you've finally found a guy who is worthy of you. Maybe," I added.

She laughed and leaned in to kiss my cheek. "I love you, Gypsi Lu. I want you to be able to enjoy life, boys, dating, sex."

Only my mom would add sex to that. She never acted like sex was something bad. Maybe that was why I reacted to it the way I did.

"I will. Just probably not with Saxon. Especially since he's Trev's best friend and … well, there's that chance that Trev might end up being my stepbrother."

Her musical laugh made me smile. "Don't get carried away. We are just getting to know each other. That man could have any woman he wanted. I don't think he'd give a woman like me his last name. But for now, I'm gonna live it up and have the best time. Make memories—"

"Of the best times so you can daydream during the bad." I finished her favorite motto.

She'd been telling me that all my life. It was the way she lived.

Mom winked at me, then squeezed my hand. "I'd better get back to my hot date, and you try and enjoy the cutie you're with."

I smiled, but said nothing.

She shifted her gaze, then leaned in close. "That Trev gets around, doesn't he? There was a redhead with him in the winner's circle, who he was kissing and groping. Now, he's got a blonde pressed up beside him, and I think that other girl is trying to get his attention too."

I glanced in their direction, and it did look like things were escalating. "Yeah, he is a player. Saxon and he couldn't be more different."

And yet it was Trev who made me feel something. I had terrible taste in guys.

She looked back at me. "Yeah, but then it's the bad boys who can be irresistible."

"Maybe to some, but not me. At least not anymore," I lied. I'd thought that. I really had, but then Trev proved me wrong.

We walked back over to Garrett and Saxon. After I assured Garrett I was having a good time and that Saxon was being an excellent escort, we headed for the exit. I was ready to get away from the temptation of watching Trev flirt. Poor Eliza. She was having to watch that too.

The private party that Garrett was holding for special guests was in a ballroom at the hotel. Trev had left in the limo with his two female friends, so we ended up riding with the two guys I'd met earlier today in the winner's circle suite, who I'd thought were bodyguards. I still wasn't convinced they weren't, but the way Saxon talked to them, they seemed like friends of his.

Levi drove the SUV and dropped us off at the entrance. When we walked inside, there was celebrating still happening everywhere.

"What did you think of your first derby?" Saxon asked me as we made our way to the ballroom.

"You mean, my only derby?" I replied. I seriously doubted I'd get invited to one of these again unless my mom did marry Garrett.

"Why your only?"

I shrugged. "Unless my mom and Garrett are still seeing each other next year, I can't imagine we'd get invited to another one of these."

Saxon looked down at me. "And here I thought, we were friends."

"We are," I replied.

"Then, even if your mom and Garrett aren't together, as my friend, if you want to come back, you have a standing invitation."

I couldn't help but smile. Although I didn't see that happening since Saxon's and Trev's families were so close, but it was nice to think I'd get to keep him as a friend long-term.

"You're a good guy, Saxon."

He smirked. "Is that what I am?"

The guy at the door recognized Saxon, and we were granted instant access. It was stunning inside, and a live band was playing on a stage. A few couples were on the dance floor, and others were standing in groups, drinking. Appetizers were on fancy silver trays, being walked throughout the crowd by servers. Saxon took two cream-puff-looking things from a tray and handed one to me.

"These are awesome. You're not allergic to seafood, are you?"

I shook my head and took the puff. "Thanks."

We made our way to the bar while I casually looked around the room for Trev. I was just curious, nothing more. However, there was no sign of him. My thoughts immediately went to what he might be doing in that limo with two females. Aggravated with my imagination and the fact that it made me envious of them, I turned my attention to Saxon.

"Want a drink, or would you rather dance?" he asked me.

The idea of dancing with people watching made me feel self-conscious. "A drink for now."

He grinned as if he knew what I was thinking. "Want to try something new? Or do you have a favorite cocktail?"

I laughed and shook my head. "I'm nineteen. I typically don't get served alcohol like I have been this weekend."

"How about I surprise you?"

I nodded. "I'm up for it."

While he was ordering our drinks, I turned to see Mom and Garrett arrive. He had her close to his side, leaning down and whispering in her ear while she smiled at whatever he was saying. I started to turn back to Saxon when Trev came walking in after them with the blonde by his side. She was holding on to him as he talked to a guy on his other side, then laughed loudly at something.

"Try this," Saxon said to me, and I was thankful he'd distracted me.

I took the glass from him. It had a pretty red color to it. Taking a sip, I smiled. It wasn't too sweet, but it had a nice flavor.

"Perfect."

"It's a cosmopolitan. I won't lie. I don't know much about cocktails. My mom likes those. I figured it was a good bet."

The band started an upbeat song. I looked out over the crowd on the dance floor while younger people made their way to the floor. Trev was grinning as he pulled the blonde with him to the center. I wasn't the only one watching him. He was hard not to look at. With the wicked grin on his face, he tugged the blonde against him and began to move his body in a way that was insanely sexy. This I didn't need to watch. Right when I began to turn my attention back to Saxon, Trev's gaze locked with mine. He winked, then bent down to whisper to the girl he was with.

"He's gonna regret that tomorrow. Gretchen isn't an easy one to shake. She's been after him since we were kids," Saxon said beside me.

Realizing I'd been caught staring at Trev, I put my back to the dance floor and gave Saxon my full attention. "He seems to make a habit of that. I feel bad for Eliza."

Saxon shook his head. "Don't. She knows the score with him. The thing about Eliza is, she doesn't go stalkerish. Gretchen does. He's had too much to drink. That's the only explanation for it."

"You don't seem to, uh, hook up with the females here. It seems you all kind of know each other. Is that why? No one new?"

The corner of his mouth kicked up a touch. "Yeah. You could say that. I've dated a few of them. Hooked up with some over the years."

But he didn't go back once he was done. Or when he was drunk, like Trev. Not a player.

"You're more of a relationship guy," I said.

He nodded. "Yeah, but I just got out of a long relationship about six months ago. Not looking to jump back into anything."

"I understand that, although my last one wasn't a long one, but it was the longest I'd ever had. I guess it could be considered my first relationship really. It was a mistake."

Saxon sighed. "Mine was a mistake. One that was off and on for years."

I finished my drink, and Saxon took the glass and set it on a tray that came by.

"Is he treating you right?" Trev asked as he and Gretchen joined us, looking flushed from their dirty dancing.

"He's set the bar high for all my future derby dates," I replied, giving Saxon a teasing grin, not wanting to look at Trev and his blonde too long.

"Ah, love match in the making," Trev drawled. "Want a drink?" he asked Gretchen, then pressed a kiss to her lips.

"Champagne," she replied, gazing up at him adoringly.

"You two have fun," he said as he and Gretchen headed for the bar.

"He needs to drink some water," Saxon said, frowning. "But he's in a mood. Telling him that will piss him off."

"He seemed to be in a good mood to me," I said.

Saxon chuckled. "Trust me, he's not."

Deciding that talking about Trev and asking questions would only make me think about him more, I changed the subject to college. I asked Saxon about his major, future plans, past, ex-girlfriend, and hobbies. I learned that the more I found out about him, the more I liked him.

When I covered my yawn, he set down his glass and held out his arm to me. "Ready to be delivered to your suite?"

Smiling, I nodded and left without looking back for Trev once. I was proud of that. Tomorrow, I would go home and back to work. I doubted I'd see Trev much after that—unless Mom and Garrett got serious.

Saxon waited until I unlocked the door and was inside before he left me. I didn't know if he was going back to the party or not. I hadn't asked. He had given me all his attention tonight, and I felt bad about monopolizing his time. But I was grateful for his company.

Slipping off my heels, I started walking toward the kitchenette area to get a water when my eyes locked on something sitting on the dining table. I froze. My shoes fell from my hand and hit the floor with a clang. It echoed through the suite. The room blurred as the cold sweat of fear crawled over me. That wasn't possible. There had to be another explanation.

Slowly, I made myself walk to the table to be sure my mind wasn't playing tricks on me. I couldn't swallow. It was as if a hand had wrapped around my throat. There, on the wooden table, was something so small and inexpensive. I didn't touch it. I stared down at the plastic gold ring and fake, large blue stone. It was a duplicate. The original I had thrown into the lake.

Turning around quickly, I scanned the area. How had this gotten in here? My door was locked. I was in Kentucky. It was far from Miami, Florida, and the man who would have done this.

"Tyde?" I called his name as nausea rolled through me.

Nothing.

Walking slowly through the suite, I began to open closet doors and look under furniture, in the shower, on the balcony. Each time thinking that would be the spot where he was hiding. And if it was, what would I do?

There was no one here with me. Just the ring. I picked it up and walked to the trash can, throwing it away while shaking. There was no explanation that made sense other than Tyde had put it in here. But how had he gotten in here?

The answer to how he had known where to find me was clear. He was stalking me. Even here. Watching me. We hadn't left him behind. He hadn't let me go, like Mom had thought he would. Deep down, I'd feared this.

I went to get my phone to text Mom, but stopped when I reached it.

This would ruin her night. The rest of her trip. She didn't deserve that. No one was in the room with me. But someone had gotten in while I was gone. My gaze lifted to the door, and I ran to it, throwing the bolt that would keep out someone even if they had the key. Standing there, staring at it, I decided to check the suite one more time.

Chapter
EIGHT

TREV

I boarded the plane, barely glancing at Sax, who was already in a seat, drinking coffee. He looked refreshed, awake, and not even a little hungover. Asshole. Dropping into the seat facing him, I groaned and laid my head back closing my eyes.

"Fun night?" Levi asked.

I opened one eye and saw him grinning at me as he took a seat closer to the restroom.

I grunted, which only caused him to laugh.

"You were killing it on the dance floor. I think you had every woman at the party wet. Especially the married ones."

Sax chuckled. The only thing keeping me from putting my fist in his face was my pounding head. He was my best friend, but right now, I fucking hated him.

"You danced some more last night?" Sax asked.

"He closed down the party," Levi replied.

"I want to know if you fucked both those chicks you were with," Kye said.

I hadn't realized he was on the plane already. Closing my eyes, I grunted again.

Both of the girls had been asleep in my bed, naked, when I snuck out this morning. I'd stepped over six used condoms. What the fuck had I been thinking?

"What about you, Sax? You took off with the hottest piece of ass there. Did you tap that?" Kye asked.

My eyes snapped open then, and I glared at him. He was already looking at me, smiling as he sipped his fucking coffee. I was going to kill him.

"No, Kye, I didn't," he said, glancing over his shoulder. "I walked her to her suite. Told her good night. Then went back to my room, got a shower, and went to bed. Alone."

I dropped my head back again, relieved. If he'd fucked Gypsi, I wasn't sure I could have recovered from that. Hell, she'd messed me up yesterday. Trying not to look at her and go to her had taken a lot of fucking whiskey and distractions. This morning, I felt like shit, but at least I'd managed to stay away from her last night.

"That's a fucking shame," Kye said, taking a bottle of water from the bar and sinking down on one of the single leather chairs near a window. "Someone should have gotten a piece of that. We don't know how long Garrett will keep her mom around. While she's available—"

"Shut up!" I growled, not wanting to think about any of them fucking her.

A phone started ringing, and I winced. "Fuck, make that stop."

"It's Garrett." Sax sounded as confused as I was. "Sir?"

I lifted my head to look at him. Why was Dad calling Sax? Levi and Kye were here. I was here.

"Yes, sir. I'll go straight there. Yes, sir."

Sax was frowning when he hung up and dropped his phone beside him. I sat there, waiting on an explanation. He just stared at me like he didn't know what I fucking wanted.

"You gonna tell us what that was about?" Levi asked.

"Gypsi had to leave early this morning and couldn't wait to fly back with us or Garrett and her mom. She got some cheap-ass flight and took an Uber to the airport at four this morning. Her mom said she left her a text, saying she needed to get back because of work. Fawn didn't get it until this morning and it was too late. Garrett said Fawn was worried about her, and when we get back, he wants me to go to the coffee shop she works at, stay there until it's time for her to leave, and drive her back home. Apparently, she walks to the coffee shop from their trailer."

They lived in a trailer? Did I know anyone who had ever lived in a trailer? Where had my dad found Fawn?

More importantly, "Why the fuck is he asking you to do it?" I asked, in a worse mood than I had been in before.

I was his fucking son. Why not me?

Sax sighed. "We're friends."

"I'm her fucking friend too. It's all we can be as long as my dad is hooking up with her mom."

"No, Trev, you're not. You spent yesterday with three different females. I spent it with Gypsi."

Scowling at him, I leaned forward, resting my elbows on my knees. "I met her first."

Sax rolled his eyes at me. "So, tell me, what's her favorite movie? Color? Dessert? Favorite time of day? When is her birthday? How long has she lived in Ocala? Where did she live before there?" He raised his eyebrows. "Don't know? Well, I do. I talked to her. Got to know her. Garrett knows that."

How the fuck did he know all that? What did he do, grill her with questions all damn day? No wonder she ran her ass

59

back to Ocala before the sun came up. She was worried he'd ask her twenty questions on the flight back.

"Did you kiss her?" I asked through clenched teeth.

He looked annoyed. "No, I didn't. Like I said, we are friends. I can read women, and I'm not the one she's attracted to."

"What's that supposed to mean? Who the fuck is she attracted to?" My hands fisted as I glared at him. Who had he let her talk to?

Sax laughed and shook his head. "Please tell me you're not that blind."

"She's got the hots for little Hughes?" Kye blurted out. "Now, that's fucking hilarious."

I scowled at Kye until his words sank in, and then I snapped my gaze back to Sax. "Me?"

Sax stood up. "Good Lord, I need more coffee for this shit."

"She said that?" I asked, unable to keep the smile off my face.

"She didn't have to say it. She struggled not to watch you all over Gretchen and her friend last night. Before that, she watched you with Eliza. I felt bad for her, but it was best she figured out you were a whore now."

I fell back in my chair. Fuck. She'd been watching me with them. I didn't do it to get to her. I didn't think she gave a shit. I had been doing it to keep me from touching her like a crazed man.

"You keep that *good guy friend* shit up, and she'll spread those pretty legs for you, Sax," Levi said while grinning at me.

"Keep it up, Levi, and I'm gonna get up from here. I'm not a fucking kid anymore. I can take your ass, old man," I warned him. "And that stupid fucking beard."

"Warn me first. I want to get my popcorn ready," Kye drawled.

60

"Hey, don't diss my beard. The bitches love the feel of this between their legs. Should have grown one years ago," Levi replied, more amused than anything.

"Whatever. You're both assholes." I scowled, then turned to Sax. "I'll go to her work and stay with her today."

Sax shook his head. "No, you won't. And if you do, I'm still going. Garrett gave me orders, and I'll do what I was told."

"Fuck," I growled. "I swear to God, you'd better not fuck her." I closed my eyes again. My head was pounding.

"What, today? If you think there is even a chance Gypsi would do that, then you really don't know anything about her. She's not a Gretchen or Eliza."

I didn't open my eyes to look at Sax. I was too fucking pissed that he knew things I didn't. That he could be her friend when I struggled with keeping her in a friend zone. But, fuck, she had obviously been struggling too. She wasn't immune to me like she had led me to believe.

What the fuck did I do with that though? Nothing had changed. Our parents were still dating. That made it complicated. And if she didn't fuck for fun, then she required a relationship. I wasn't in the market for that. Never would be. Goddammit, why did she have to make this hard?

"You saying she's a relationship kinda girl?" I asked sourly.

"Yep. That's exactly what I'm saying," Sax replied.

He sure knew how to throw ice water on my dirty daydreams. Fuck.

"I want to know where she's lived, how long she's been in Ocala, her favorite movie, dessert, all that shit. Tell me."

"What are you gonna do with it? Even if your parents weren't dating, you don't want what she wants. You would only hurt her. Hell, I think you hurt her without meaning to last night."

I clenched my teeth and opened my eyes to glare at my best friend. Why the fuck would he tell me that? I hadn't needed to know I'd hurt her. That fucking made me feel bad. It made my chest ache, and I didn't like it.

"Tell me about Gypsi," I ordered angrily.

Sax sighed. "Fine. They lived in Miami for a year and moved to Ocala three weeks ago. Ocala was a stopping point on their way north. She loves anything peanut butter and chocolate. She loves watching the sunset. Favorite movie is *The Godfather*—and, yes, I almost spit my damn whiskey all over her when she told me that one."

I sat up, grinning. "She seriously said that?"

He nodded. "Hard to keep from laughing, too, but I managed to keep a straight face. She loves pink. Her birthday is August 31."

Sax had taken the time to get to know those things and remembered them. He'd paid attention to her. He hadn't mingled and found a hookup. Things he normally did at events like that. He was a fucking good guy. He was a relationship guy. There was no danger of his dad dating her mom. He was fucking perfect for her. The kind of guy she deserved.

I ran a hand over my face in frustration. That was why he was the hero and I was the villain. Because I wasn't going to let him fucking have her.

Chapter
NINE

GYPSI

It had cost me fourteen dollars for an Uber to the airport, eighty-three dollars for the flight, and sixty-two dollars for the Uber ride from the airport in Gainesville to the coffee shop. One hundred fifty-nine dollars I shouldn't have spent. But I'd had to get out of that suite. That hotel. And out of Kentucky. I'd stayed awake all night, staring at the door. Trying to figure out how Tyde had gotten in there. If he had. Wanting another explanation, but unable to come up with one.

I finished the cappuccino my current customer wanted and took her ham and cheese melt from the microwave, then handed them to her. It had been busy since I'd arrived. Leaving Kentucky early put me here for the last half of the morning shift, and since they were so busy, my boss had told me to clock in. I figured the money would help with what I'd spent to get back here.

The bell on the door rang, and I lifted my eyes to see Saxon walk in. The smile that curled my lips wasn't forced. Seeing him was nice. Deep down, I normally tensed up every time someone new walked in. Terrified it would be Tyde. Even if Saxon was just here to get a coffee and go, it made me feel less alone for the moment.

"Hello," I greeted him. "I didn't expect to see you again so soon."

He shrugged. "You left me no choice, running off before the rest of the world woke up."

"Did we talk about where I worked?" I asked him, realizing this wasn't a coincidence. He wasn't here for coffee.

A guilty grin made his dimples pop. "I might have asked your mom."

That was so sweet. He'd asked about me. Asked my mom. And he was here. Why did this not give me flutters? What was wrong with me? I should get that giddy, excited feeling. Right?

"Well then, choose your poison. It's on me," I told him.

The bell chimed again. I looked over his shoulder, and my eyes collided with gray ones. The butterflies erupted in my stomach. A smile spread across my face before I could stop it. Why? Because I was stupid. A very stupid girl. But Trev Hughes's sexy smirk, formfitting T-shirt, and khaki shorts, which showed off his muscular, tanned lower legs—it was lethal.

"Hey, Lollipop," he drawled, and my heart did a weird tightening thing.

"Trev." I said his name, unable to keep the pleased sound from my voice.

He noticed. I could see it in the way he was looking at me. He knew he was sex on a stick, and he enjoyed the effect it had on females.

"You ran off on me. Not even a goodbye." The teasing twinkle in his eyes made my nipples pebble because I was a glutton for punishment.

"Work," I stated the obvious.

"If I'd known you needed to get back earlier, Lollipop, I'd have made that happen. You should have told me."

"During or after your orgy on the dance floor last night?" Saxon asked.

Trev ignored him, keeping his eyes fixed on me. "You left last night without a goodnight too. My feelings are hurt."

I rolled my eyes. We both knew his feelings were not hurt. "I am sure you survived just fine last night."

He placed a hand over his heart. "You wound me. I looked for you, and Sax had taken you away."

"You had your hands full. Literally," I shot back at him, then worried that I'd sounded bitter about that.

"Lollipop, there were only two. My hands were definitely not full."

"Ooookay, rein that shit in," Saxon said, glaring at his friend, then turned back to me. "I'll have two espresso shots and a slice of the carrot cake. For here." He paused, then slapped Trev's stomach with the back of his hand. "Order some food and let her work."

Trev shot Saxon a very brief, annoyed look before turning his megawatt smile on me again. "Just a black coffee, whatever sandwich you suggest, a brownie, and that chocolate peanut butter cake."

"A slice?" I asked, wanting to laugh that he'd started this order with "just," then ordered way more than Saxon.

He smirked. "The whole cake."

"You want that entire cake?" I asked, looking at the cake that Geoff, the baker, had just brought up here thirty minutes ago.

He nodded.

"Um, I have to go ask how much the whole cake is," I told him.

"Will this cover it?" he asked, holding out two one-hundred-dollar bills.

I frowned at the cash, then lifted my eyes back to meet his. "That's way too much. It might be a hundred for all of Saxon's food, yours, and the cake."

"Excellent," he said, dropping the two bills on the counter. "The cake is to go."

I picked up the money and handed him back a bill. He shook his head and winked before walking over to the table closest to me and sitting down.

"Trev, this is too much," I tried again.

"He's not going to take it back. Might as well give up," Saxon said.

"This is crazy," I muttered, then took the other bill and placed it in the tip jar.

I split the tips with the morning shift. Donja and Jerry would be thrilled.

I took the cake and put it in a box, then bagged it before someone came in and asked for a slice. Then, I went about making two sandwiches instead of one since he'd given me too much money and filling the rest of their order. Saxon had gone to sit across from Trev, and I tried not to look at them until I had their orders ready. I placed everything on a tray and turned to take it to them but Trev was standing at the counter.

"I'll take it," he told me.

I handed it to him, and he nodded at the cake. "That's yours."

"Mine?" I asked.

"You like anything peanut butter and chocolate. Right?"

I nodded.

"The cake is for you."

A shocked laugh bubbled out of me. "I can't eat that whole cake." But it was sweet.

Trev Hughes was trying to be sweet. He was also more than likely trying to get in my pants. Not that I was against that idea. I just knew better. We didn't need to go down that road.

"Then, come to the house tonight. We can share it."

"Your house?" I asked, my heart rate speeding up. This was a terrible suggestion.

"Certainly not Sax's. I have the better pool," he replied. "Sax can come too. We will make it a small party. But the cake is yours regardless."

I looked past him to Saxon, who was watching us from the table. Why did it feel like if I agreed, he would be disappointed in me? He was Trev's best friend. Besides, he would be there. It wouldn't be just me and Trev. There would be other people. Girls. There would be other girls. Trev would have one or more hanging on him.

My stomach knotted up. "Uh, um ... I don't think I can tonight. I need to do laundry this evening, and I have work tomorrow morning." It was lame, but I couldn't go to his house and watch him with some bikini-wearing girls rubbing all over him.

"You turning me down for laundry, Lollipop?"

"No. I'm explaining why I can't tonight."

He wasn't accustomed to being told no. It was obvious. He finally turned around with the tray and walked over to the table. The doorbell chimed, and I had never been more relieved to have a customer.

Over the next hour, I barely got a break. Trev had left after finishing his sandwich. I'd been busy, but he saluted me as he backed out of the door. Seeing him leave had made me sad. Which was another reason I had done the right thing by telling him no. The cake had been left with Saxon, and every time I glanced over at it, my chest squeezed.

Trev had come here to make amends in his own way. It wasn't his fault he was so dang gorgeous. The one-hundred-dollar bill in the tip jar only made me feel worse. He was trying to be friends, and I hadn't been very accommodating. I had let my fear of seeing him with other girls again stand in the way.

When three o'clock came around, I went to lock the door, then turned to Saxon. "It's closing time. As much as I like seeing you, you can't sleep here," I teased.

He chuckled. "Damn. That was my plan."

When he didn't stand up to go, I walked back over to the register to begin balancing the drawer before cleaning up.

"He was being nice, and I was a jerk," I said, frustrated.

"You were not even close to being a jerk," Saxon replied. "You were being smart."

I pulled out the money from the tip jar and sighed. "But why? He wants to be friends. Our parents are dating. I should stop pushing him away."

Saxon stood up. "Do you really think he just wants to be friends?"

I held Saxon's gaze a moment, then sighed. "No. Yes. I don't know. Trev is a player. I don't think he can do anything but flirt." I pointed to the cake. "He bought me a cake. A peanut butter and chocolate cake. I've always wanted to try it, but every time we have it, the thing sells out before my shift is over. And he bought me the entire cake. I shouldn't have turned down his invitation."

My cell phone dinged, and I pulled it out of my back pocket. It was from my mom.

I'M GOING TO DINNER WITH GARRETT TONIGHT. AND HE'S ASKED ME TO STAY OVER AT HIS HOUSE. ARE YOU OKAY? HOW DO YOU FEEL ABOUT THAT? I'M NOT SURE I SHOULD LEAVE YOU AT THE TRAILER

ALONE UNTIL WE KNOW _ IT'S SAFE. WHAT IF YOU STAY OVER AT GARRETT'S TOO? WOULD YOU DO THAT?

I read over the text three times. It was as if fate was trying to right my wrong.

Lifting my gaze, I looked at Saxon. "My mom wants to stay at Garrett's tonight but wants me to stay too. So she won't worry about me being alone."

Saxon chuckled. "You want to go, Gypsi? Then, go. I'll take you home. Get your things. Then, we will head over to Trev's."

I would be going to his house after all. The buzz of excitement over seeing him again today was not a good sign.

Chapter
TEN

GYPSI

Standing in the living area of the camper—also known as my bedroom—I clutched my bikini while staring in horror at the small plastic ring on my pillow. Gold and blue. Another replica. I backed away until my back hit the kitchen sink, gulping for air.

He'd been in my home. He'd been around my things. My mom's things.

This was happening. I hadn't imagined it. I'd thought leaving would fix it. He'd let me go. How wrong I had been. And now … now, my mom was happy. I couldn't ask her to leave it all. Not because I'd trusted the wrong guy. This was my problem. Not hers. I needed to figure out how to protect her.

Forcing my legs to move, I walked back to the ring, picked it up, and shoved it into my bag. It wasn't safe for Saxon here, and he was sitting out there in the car, waiting on me. I had to get him away from this place. Grabbing the last few things I needed, I hurried out of the trailer, locking it behind me.

Although I wasn't sure what good that did. Nothing seemed to be able to stop Tyde.

Hide. I had to find a place to hide. Get a new job somewhere safe. Maybe Mom would start staying at Garrett's more. I could move the camper. Find a more hidden place to park it. Explaining that to my mom though would be difficult. I couldn't let her suspect anything. If she did, we'd be gone within hours.

Saxon was out of the car and holding open my door when I reached the vehicle. I gave him a smile that hid the terror currently gripping me.

"Sorry it took so long," I apologized.

He frowned. "You were barely in there."

It had felt like I'd been in there for years.

I climbed into the car and buckled up, then studied the trailer for signs of Tyde being there. I heard Saxon get in and close the door. He didn't need to come back here. I was putting so many people in danger. I would leave tonight if it wasn't for my mom. She'd panic. Freak out and find me. I had to do this so that she stayed calm.

"You good?" he asked me.

No. I was so far from good. "Yeah, just tired."

"That's understandable. You've had a long day."

I simply nodded. Thankfully, he didn't ask more questions on the drive to Trev's house. Other than asking me about my music preference, we sat in silence. It gave me time to think, although I didn't have an answer to my problem by the time we drove under the big arch leading into Hughes Farm.

"Wow," I whispered when we pulled up to the mansion that the Hughes called home.

"It's impressive," Saxon agreed.

"They live here?" I asked, already knowing the answer but still amazed.

He chuckled. "Yep."

I wished I could have seen my mom's reaction the first time she saw this place. She would have been thrilled. This was a new, exciting experience. Her favorite things in the world. There was no way I could take this from her.

Opening the door, I stepped out, still taking in the sprawling property.

"Looks like Trev invited some people. I know those cars," Sax said, carrying my cake that Trev had bought me in his hands.

I glanced over to see two expensive sports cars and three luxury SUVs parked to the far left of us.

"I'm giving you a heads-up now. There are at least three girls here who would lick his fucking feet if he told them to. One for sure will be topless. Trev's pool parties normally end up a little wild."

Topless? Great. I was going to get to see Trev making out or groping boobs. Not what I was in the mood for today of all days. I simply nodded. If that was the case, then I knew which bikini I was wearing. I'd brought two. That information made my decision for me.

"Thanks for preparing me," I replied.

We walked up the stairs to the house, and Saxon rang the doorbell. A short, round, older lady opened the door and beamed up at Saxon, then turned to me, still smiling.

"Come in," she said, stepping back. "It's always good to see you, Saxon. How are your parents?"

"They're doing good, Ms. Jimmie," he replied. "Uh, is Garrett home yet? This is Gypsi Parker—"

"You're Ms. Parker's daughter. Of course! You are as beautiful as your mother. Come, come. I have your room all prepared for you. Mr. Hughes and your mother have gone out to dinner, but they'll be returning soon. Trev is out at the pool

72

with friends if you want to get changed and join them. I was just about to take out some refreshments to them. What is this you brought, Saxon?"

"Chocolate peanut butter cake. It's Gypsi's, but she's going to share."

She reached out and took it from him. "I'll go put it in the kitchen cooler until she wants it," Ms. Jimmie said to him.

I was glad Mom wasn't here. It would give me time to relax. She knew me too well, and fooling her was more difficult than it was with others.

"Thank you," I replied.

I glanced at Saxon. "Do you want me to wait on you, or you wanna just meet me outside?" he asked.

"I can show her around. Give her the lay of the land so she doesn't get lost," Ms. Jimmie said to him.

He nodded but kept his eyes on me, waiting on a response. As much as walking out to a group of people I didn't know alone sounded uncomfortable, I was willing to face that if I didn't feel rushed. A few minutes to think and gather myself would be nice.

"Go on out. I'll be there shortly," I told him.

"Okay." He flashed Ms. Jimmie his dimples, then headed off to the left.

"I'll show you around first, then take you to your room," Ms. Jimmie told me.

I followed her around as she walked me through the first floor of the Hugheses' mansion. You could park three of our campers into the kitchen alone. It got my mind off things, as I was awed by each new room. There was even a movie theater. I almost laughed when she took me in there. I didn't know people had these in their homes.

Once we made it to the second floor, she walked me down a wide hallway with several doors. The last one on the right was open, and she waved a hand for me to enter. It was white and gold. A crystal chandelier hung from the ceiling. The king-size bed sat on a platform in the middle of the room with plush white bedding.

"Through there is your en suite," she replied.

I had no idea what that was, but I glanced in there to see a bathroom that made my jaw drop. I wondered if I could skip going out to the pool and just get in the copper bathtub that could fit five people.

"The closet is here," she told me, opening the door to what I thought was a wardrobe but it just looked like one.

Inside was a walk-in closet larger than our entire trailer, complete with floor-to-ceiling mirrors, a white sofa, and a television. Who watched TV in their closet?

"If you need anything," Ms. Jimmie said, "that button right there will call me. I can bring you whatever you need."

There was a button in the closet. I would not be asking this sweet lady to bring me anything, but I thanked her anyway. If my room was this outrageous, what was the master bedroom that Mom was staying in like?

Ms. Jimmie left me with the reminder to call her if needed. "Even if it's just a glass of ice water."

She'd shown me the kitchen. If I needed water, I could go get it myself.

Once she was gone, I walked over to the chaise lounge and sat down. This was overwhelming, but thankfully, it was also distracting. I glanced at the windows covering the far left wall and wondered if I could see the pool from here. Afraid of what I'd see if I could, I didn't get up. A knock on the door, however, startled me.

"Uh, come in," I replied, standing up.

The door opened, and Trev stepped inside. He was wearing swim trunks. That was it. A girl needed a warning before being faced with a barefoot, bare-chested Trev. His dark hair was damp and messy, only making him even more attractive. I tried very hard not to stare at his washboard abs, but it was difficult. Dropping my gaze, I realized the man even had sexy feet.

"You like the room?" he asked.

My eyes snapped back up to meet his. There was a smirk on his face that said he knew I'd been checking him out. I guessed I hadn't been very subtle after all.

"Oh, um, yeah," I replied, turning to look at my surroundings. "It's ... wow. The entire house is wow."

"I'm glad you like it. You are coming outside, aren't you?"

I turned back to him and wished he would put on a shirt or something.

"Yes, I was. I mean ..." I paused, not sure I could handle it if he was going to be all over some girl. Not today. I just didn't have it in me today to watch it. "I don't have to. If you have company and—"

"I came to get you, Lollipop. I've been watching the damn door since Dad texted that you were going to be staying the night."

Ugh, the Lollipop thing. Why did him calling me that make me tingle in areas I had no business tingling?

"Okay, well, I need to get changed."

The corner of his mouth turned up. "I can wait."

"Just for the record, I'm keeping my top on outside," I informed him.

He laughed. "Sax has been talking, I see."

I nodded. "He was giving me a warning. He also mentioned that three of the girls here would lick your feet if you told them to. Please don't have them do that. Not sure I want to watch it. Licking feet is gross."

75

He tilted his head slightly to the left, and his gaze drifted down my body, then back up. "I've got some pretty feet," he said with a smirk. Then added. "Lollipop, if you're out there, I'm not going to be aware of anyone else."

This time, I laughed. "We both know that's not true."

Trev walked over to me, stopping just inches from his bare chest brushing against me. I held my breath after the smell of coconut on his warm skin hit me. If I had to look at him, it wasn't fair that he smelled like something I wanted to taste.

"I don't lie about shit like that," he said, looking down at me.

I did my best not to look as completely turned on as I was. "You had no problem looking at other females in Kentucky," I reminded him.

The dark smile that touched his lips made me shiver. Damn, this man was dangerous. I could forget why doing the things I wanted to do with him was a bad idea.

"Lollipop, if you thought I was looking at other females, then you are very mistaken. I struggled to remember their names. My eyes stayed on you. Followed you. I was doing my best not to go get you and haul your ass away from everyone so I could have you alone. You weren't even wearing fucking panties. Do you know how that shit messed with me?"

My eyes widened. I hadn't told him I wasn't wearing panties. Did he see when I got inside the limo? I had thought I kept my dress pulled down.

He smirked, then leaned close to my ear. "No one saw but me."

His voice made me shiver. I needed to get away from him. If I didn't, I was going to grab him and run my tongue over his nipples. He had no idea how close I was to doing it.

Trev ran a fingertip down my bare arm. "You have goose bumps, Lollipop," he said softly.

76

I swallowed hard. "Yes, and that's not a good thing," I said, trying to make myself move away from him. My feet, however, felt cemented to the floor.

"Why? Because of our parents? Because it could make things awkward?"

I nodded, unable to use my words while he continued caressing my skin. His finger trailed over my collarbone and up my neck.

"I'm struggling with that," he said. "I'm not so sure it's a big deal. If they break up, that doesn't affect us. Not really. It's not a relationship I'm looking for. I don't do those."

I didn't do them either. Not anymore. I tried it, and I was still paying for it.

"What if they get married?" I asked, wanting him to make this okay. Give me a reason why licking his bare chest wouldn't be a bad idea.

"Then, we'll be really close stepsiblings. I could be your stepbrother with benefits. We can call it steps with benefits." He grinned as he said it.

A laugh bubbled out of me.

Trev's fingers wrapped around my upper arm, and he jerked me against him, then brushed a kiss near my ear. "That sounds nice, doesn't it? No strings. Just me making you feel good."

I was breathing hard. He was too close, his skin was hot, and I wanted to melt against him.

"Come on, Lollipop. Tell me yes or, fuck, even maybe. Just give me some hope that I'll eventually get to bury my face in your sweet little pussy."

I had to grab his bicep to keep my knees from buckling under me. He was really good with the dirty talk, and he had no idea how much I liked it. This wouldn't end well. What if he turned out like Tyde?

77

I had thought Tyde was charming in the beginning. He was so gentle with me until he realized he'd unleashed a nympho. At least, that was how I felt. Once I got a taste of sex, I was insatiable. That had turned Tyde into a possessive psycho, who became abusive and twisted.

Thinking about him cooled me off.

I stepped back from Trev, still trembling some from his effect on me and my needs. "You think you want me, but you don't know me. Maybe we should get to know each other as friends first."

His heated gaze stayed locked on mine. "If that's what you want, I'll do whatever you ask. Just give me some whisper of hope that we can add the benefits part to our relationship eventually."

That was something I wasn't sure I could promise, but I wanted to. Sexual thoughts of Trev were going to haunt me. If I didn't have my massive pile of fears about where that would all lead, this would be an easy answer.

"You don't know that you want to do that. Not really. I can be demanding." As soon as the words came out of my mouth, I regretted them.

His gaze darkened. "Lollipop, if you're talking about fucking, then I'm going to need more details than just demanding. Because all you did was just make my dick harder than it already had been."

I covered my face with both hands. God, he needed to stop talking about his dick. I needed air. This was bad.

His fingers wrapped around my wrists, and he tugged my hands down. I gasped as those gray eyes blazed down at me. The things this man made me want were very dirty.

"Right now, I want to bend you over that bed, rip these shorts off, and fuck you. Hard."

I closed my eyes and inhaled. That didn't help. He smelled too damn good.

"Now, I've been brutally honest. Your turn." His voice took on a deep, raspy sound.

I opened my eyes slowly and looked back up at him. "I recently went through a bad relationship. I'm still dealing with it." That was the truth. I was dealing with it. I was being stalked by the psycho. But I wasn't telling him that. "Yes, the thought of you bending me over and fucking me hard turns me on. You turn me on." I waved a hand at him. "All this would turn anyone on. Even males. You're beautiful and sexy, and why do you smell so good?" I groaned. "Anyway, I just don't think I am emotionally ready for a sex fling. Or friends with benefits. Or whatever this would be. Do I want it? Yes. But I think we should get to know each other. Become friends first before we add benefits. I need to be able to trust you." Although I wasn't sure I could ever trust a man again.

He narrowed his eyes. "Did the fucker hurt you?" he asked, looking like he was going to do something about it if he had hurt me. The level of hurt I had endured wasn't something I would ever share with Trev. The things Tyde had accused me of and the things he'd called me still made me feel as if I were somehow warped. If he had been right.

"No," I lied. "Sex just made things different. He was different." He was insane, and I had loved it at first. Until I didn't.

"I'm gonna be the best damn friend you've ever had," he said, reaching out to wrap one of my curls around his finger. "You're gonna be saying, 'Saxon who?' when I'm done."

I laughed.

He raised his eyebrows. "You think I'm joking? Sax might be the good guy who says and does all the right things, but, Lollipop, when the bad boy makes you his priority, it's gonna make your pussy wet." He let my hair slip from his finger, then winked at me. "I'll wait for you to get changed." He nodded his head toward the closet. "Then, we'll go get some of that cake I bought you."

I was pretty sure I had started to pant. Needing to get away from him, I hurried past him, grabbing my bag, and went into the large mirrored room, closing the door behind me. My bag fell to the floor, and I closed my eyes for a moment to catch my breath. Trev Hughes was going to be hard to resist. Even with Tyde stalking me and the threat of what he would do if he got me alone, I still reacted to Trev. One would think my crazy body would be scared to let another man touch me.

Trev was making himself a target. If Tyde ever saw us together, he'd snap. If men had even looked at me, he'd lose it. But it was me who paid the price. I had been the one he hit, slapped, kicked because, in his eyes, it was my fault for making the man look at me.

I liked Trev, but even if I didn't, I wouldn't want to unleash Tyde's crazy on him. Or anyone. When I'd left, he had warned me he'd kill me and any man who touched me. If Mom's ex-boyfriend hadn't been there, helping us get away from Tyde, I'd never have gotten free.

Chapter
ELEVEN

TREV

While Gypsi was changing, I should have gone to the bathroom and pumped one out to get some fucking relief. The girl already turned me on, but damn if she hadn't insinuated with those crazy-sexy eyes of hers that she might be a little naughty. Now, I was going to be hard all damn night. And that see-through cover-up thing she had on over her bikini was not helping. I wanted to rip it off her so I could see that ass she was practically baring and get my hands on it. The tiny glimpse I'd gotten last night had been a tease.

She wanted to be friends first. Fair enough. She was right; we didn't know each other that well. I knew the few things Sax had told me and that I wanted to fuck her like a dog in heat. But that was it. I hadn't spent much time with her. That was about to change. We were going to be fucking BFFs.

Sorry, Sax.

I pulled the cake from the cooler and walked back out of the pantry with it. Gypsi was perched on one of the barstools, watching me.

Friends, Trev. You've got to be friends. Stop fucking her in your head. Eyes off her crossed legs.

"How big of a slice do you want?" I asked her as I set it down in front of her.

"Are we not taking it outside?"

I shook my head. "Fuck no. I bought this for you. Those bastards will eat it all. You'll just get one piece."

She laughed. "I told you, I can't eat this whole thing."

I grabbed two forks from the drawer and held them up. "I didn't say you were. We are sharing. Some cake tonight, then tomorrow, then the next day."

"Who says I will be here tomorrow and the next day?"

I wiggled my eyebrows, making her smile. "My dad. He's hot for your mom. She's not going anywhere."

There was a flicker of worry in her eyes, but she smiled anyway. What about that worried her? Was it because we could end up as stepsiblings? I'd already cleared that up. I had made it okay in my head and I thought I'd smoothed it over for her too. Steps with benefits sounding real damn good to me.

I put a plate and fork in front of her before taking the lid off the cake. Picking up the knife, I sliced two large pieces that made her laugh and placed them on our plates.

"I'm gonna need milk for this. What about you?" I asked.

"Water would be nice."

Turning from her, I went to the fridge and pulled out a bottle of water, then got the milk. I could feel her watching me as I poured my glass and put the carton away. She liked looking at me, and I liked her doing it. I would prefer she put her hands all over me, but eyes were good for now. I'd never had to work at it to fuck a girl. This would be fun. I could think of it as a game. A challenge was different and I had grown bored with my sex life I realized. Gypsi was giving me some excitement and she didn't even know it.

I pulled out the stool beside her and sat down. "So, if our parents get married, would you move in here? Or are you headed off to college in the fall?"

She smiled as she used the fork to cut a small portion of the cake on her plate. "I would travel. Take the camper and just go. College isn't something I can afford right now, but one day."

Frowning, I stared at her. "What camper?"

"The one we live in," she replied, then put some cake in her mouth.

I thought she lived in a trailer. Not a camper. I started to ask her why she lived in a camper, but she closed her mouth and moaned. Words left me as my cock twitched in my damn shorts. Fuck, that was hot. She even made eating cake sexy.

Her eyes fluttered open, and she grinned. "This is the best cake I've ever had. Thank you. And you're right. I don't want to share anymore. We can eat it all."

I chuckled, then turned my attention to my cake just to stop eye-fucking her. Clearing my throat, I moved the topic back to her living conditions. "Why are you living in a camper?"

"We've always lived in it. We don't normally stay in one place long."

What the fuck?

"So, you're an actual gypsy?"

She grinned. "Yep."

Did my dad know this? He was dating a woman who lived in a camper and moved all the time? How had that worked when Gypsi was growing up? Did she ever make friends and get settled somewhere long enough to get attached? This bothered the fuck out of me, and it shouldn't have. Not my problem. I wasn't looking to fix her life. I was looking to fuck her.

"Do you like living that way? Is that why you would leave if they got married?"

She shrugged. "I want to have roots one day. It's just … if Mom gets married, she doesn't have to move me into her new home. I'm not a child. I'm almost twenty. We live together now because it's just us. But if she has a husband, then I need to be an adult and live my own life. And traveling is all I know. Maybe I'll find a place I love and get a good job, save up, and go to college, make a life for myself there. I just don't know yet."

Why was this hot? She had no fear. She was a free spirit. The idea of living in a home like this when all she'd ever known was a camper didn't seem to appeal to her at all. She didn't give a fuck about our money.

"Lollipop."

"Yes?"

"How long do we have to be friends before I get to fuck you?"

She laughed, and her twinkling eyes met mine. "Why do we have to put a time frame on it?"

"Because you might up and leave. I've got to crank up the friendship game hard before I miss out on getting my hands, mouth, and dick on and inside that hot little body."

She took another bite of cake and chewed it. My eyes locked on her lips. She had great lips. They'd look real nice, wrapped around my cock.

When she finally swallowed, my eyes dropped to her neck, watching her throat.

"I won't leave before that happens. I promise," she said, and my eyes snapped back up to meet hers.

"You promise?" I asked.

She grinned, then dropped her eyes back to her cake. "Yes."

"So, this friends thing ... can I kiss you?"

She pulled her full bottom lip between her teeth, and I wanted to groan. It popped free, and then she cut her eyes at me. "I don't think that's a good idea."

"Because you think I'll want more?"

She shook her head. "No, because I think I will."

I ran a hand through my hair. "Fuck, Lollipop. You're killing me."

A soft laugh escaped her, and she went back to eating her cake. I had female friends ... well, a female friend. My sister-in-law, Maddy. Sure, I'd been attracted to her and wanted to fuck her when we first met. But that was before she became my brother's girl. The difference with her was, she didn't make me feel like this. I didn't fight the urge to push her against a wall and fuck her like a crazed man. It had been easy to be Maddy's friend.

I tried to think of things I had done with Maddy as friends before my brother laid claim to her. I needed to do those things with Gypsi. I should probably stop calling her Lollipop too. Every time I did, I thought about places I wanted to lick her.

Damn, this was going to be tough.

Gypsi finished her cake just as Ms. Jimmie walked into the kitchen.

"There you are. I was wondering where you'd run off to when I took the snacks outside. I was coming back to get the cake to take out there."

I shook my head. "No. The cake stays in here. It's just for Gypsi. That's who I bought it for."

Ms. Jimmie gave me a look that I knew too well. "You bought her that cake?"

85

I nodded.

"It had better be because you were being nice and she wanted it. Not because you want to get into her bed," she said, then looked at Gypsi. "I love this boy, but you need to be careful with him. Don't fall for that charm. He loves women. All of them."

"Hey, that's not true, Ms. Jimmie. I only love you. I just like all the other women," I told her, then winked.

She shook her finger at me. "You see what I mean?"

Gypsi laughed, and the musical sound of it made me feel all warm and shit. Damn, I needed to fuck her out of my system. She stood up and took her plate, then mine, then walked with them to the sink.

"I'll take those. You two go outside," Ms. Jimmie told her.

"Thank you," Gypsi said, then headed in my direction.

I took the moment to enjoy the view.

I didn't want to share her. The idea to have friends over had suddenly lost its appeal. "What's your favorite movie?" I asked her, although I already knew.

"*The Godfather*," she replied.

Damn, that was still funny.

"That's a classic. Why don't we go to the theater and watch it?"

She frowned at me. "What about the pool and your friends?"

I shrugged. "Sax can be the host. I'm not in the mood to swim anymore. It's been a long day, and I'd rather not be around people."

She glanced down at her cover-up. "Can I go change into clothes?"

I wished she would just take off that cover-up and sit in my lap while I sucked on her tits, but since that wasn't going to happen, I nodded.

"Yeah. I'll go get changed too. Meet you in the theater in fifteen." I told her.

She headed for the stairs, and I pulled out my phone and sent Sax a text.

NOT IN THE MOOD FOR THE POOL. YOU CAN CARRY THE PARTY AND SEND THEM HOME WHEN YOU WANT.

He replied

WHAT THE FUCK ARE YOU DOING?

Grinning I typed out my response and sent it.

GOING TO WATCH *THE GODFATHER* WITH GYPSI. ALONE.

He didn't need to get any ideas about joining us. There was no response to that, so I headed to my room to get changed.

Chapter
TWELVE

GYPSI

The theater was big enough to fit fifty people. When I walked in, I could smell the popcorn. Turning, I found Trev standing in front of a theater-style popcorn machine, scooping some into a bucket.

He grinned. "We've got soda, water, wine, beer, whiskey—oh, and I think there is some apple juice and cran."

"Apple juice sounds good," I replied.

He lifted his chin toward the room. "Pick a seat. I'll bring it to you."

I looked out over the tiered rows of black leather chairs that looked like they reclined. I walked down to the middle, then went to the center of the row. The seats were so big and plush that I pulled my bare feet up and crossed my legs.

Trev walked up and put my apple juice in the cupholder on my seat, then looked down at my legs. "Yeah, that's not gonna be distracting at all," he said, sinking down in the chair beside me with the popcorn.

"What?" I asked.

"Your bare thighs wide open," he said pointedly.

I was wearing a pair of shorts and an oversize sweatshirt in case it was cold in here. I didn't think it was at all revealing or flattering. "Do you want me to sit another way?"

He smirked. "I'm joking. The lights are about to go out. It's fine. Sit how you're comfortable." He held out the bucket of popcorn to me. "Want some?" he asked.

I reached into the bucket and got a handful, then shifted in my seat to put my knees together and bend my legs up beside me. Trev looked at my legs and grinned, then turned back to the screen.

"Ready?" he asked.

I nodded, and he held up his hand, then put it back down. The lights went out, and then the screen lit up.

"How did you do that?" I asked, amazed.

"I didn't. Ralph did," he replied. "He's up in the box where the projector is."

"Who is Ralph?" I asked.

"Ms. Jimmie's nephew. He does, uh … odd jobs around the house," he replied.

I sank back onto the leather and watched the screen. Reaching over to get popcorn occasionally.

"When did you see this movie the first time?" he asked me.

I grinned. "It was playing at a dollar movie theater. Mom and I went to see it. I was thirteen."

"And at thirteen, you decided this was your favorite movie?"

I nodded. "I used to pretend I was part of the Corleones. I made up an entire story about it in my head."

He chuckled and shook his head, then tossed a handful of popcorn into his mouth. How was eating popcorn sexy? I sighed and turned back to the movie, trying to focus on it and not the way Trev looked while eating popcorn.

89

"How long has he been in Sicily? It's been months, and he's still got the damn bruise on his face," Trev said.

"Yeah, they messed up there. And when they realized it, they wouldn't go back and refilm it because they'd already gone over budget. They fixed it by saying the punch broke his cheekbone and caused a permanent black eye."

Trev turned to me. "Really?"

I nodded. "Yep. I watched a documentary on the making of it. Did you know they offered Michael's role to Jack Nicholson, but he turned it down?"

Trev laughed. "Fuck, I wonder how long he regretted that."

"I imagine he still regrets it," I replied, then tossed popcorn in my mouth.

"Oh! You're watching *The Godfather*!" my mom's voice called out.

I turned to see her walking in, followed by Garrett.

She was grinning at me. "And there is popcorn? How much fun!"

She walked down to our row and came to sit on the other side of me. Garrett went over to the popcorn.

"What do you think of the house?" she asked me.

"It's massive," I replied.

She rolled her eyes and laughed at me. Then, she leaned over to look at Trev. "Don't let her fool you. She's impressed."

He just smiled at her.

Garrett handed Mom a bucket of popcorn, and she reached up to grab the front of his shirt and pulled him down until she could kiss him.

"Thank you," she said against his lips, then released him.

He cupped her face with his hand and brushed his thumb over her cheek as if she were something precious, then moved to take the seat beside her. He had also brought her a glass of rosé in a wineglass, putting it in her cupholder.

"This has been Gypsi's favorite movie since she was a kid. I took her to see it at the theater, and she became obsessed with it," Mom told Garrett.

Trev leaned back in his seat, and I saw him look at his dad with a smirk on his face. Mom was terrible about being quiet during movies. I wondered if Garrett knew that flaw about her yet.

"Oh, and don't ever do that to me again," she said. "You scared me this morning."

I had known she'd get worried. "I'm sorry."

She patted my leg, then took a handful of her popcorn, then turned to say something to Garrett. I tried not to stare, but I checked to see if he was annoyed by her talking instead of watching yet. The grin on his face said he wasn't.

I looked at Trev. "I hope you're not really into this movie," I whispered. "Because she can't shut up and watch one. She'll talk the entire time."

His gaze dropped to my mouth, then back up to meet my eyes. "I've seen it enough times. It's fine. Besides"—he glanced around me to look at them—"my dad looks so damn happy that I'm not sure I recognize him."

"Yeah, Mom has that effect on men," I told him, then turned my attention back to the screen.

"What's that guy's name who's in charge?" Mom asked me. "The don?"

She nodded, then turned back to Garrett. "She used to pretend the don was her dad." Mom laughed.

Thanks, Mom. I wasn't going to share that bit of information. At least it was dark in here and my blush wouldn't show.

"You like Don Vito?" Garrett asked me.

I nodded. "He's the best part of the movie."

Trev cleared his throat, and Garrett grinned, sitting back in his chair.

I turned to Trev. "You don't agree?"

He shrugged. "I'm a fan of Michael. It focuses on him turning into a badass. That's the point."

"He is ruthless," I pointed out.

Trev grinned. "Like I said, badass."

I gave him an amused grin and reached for more popcorn.

"Did you go swimming? I saw Saxon and some others leaving when we arrived," Mom asked.

I shook my head.

"We could go tonight," she said, smiling, then turned to Garrett. She whispered in his ear and then did that thing where she curled up close to talk more.

When she stood up, she gave me a smile and a little wave, then followed him out of the door.

Yep, she was going to either get hurt or get married. Mom was in love.

Chapter
THIRTEEN

TREV

The damn horse was a mistake. Frustrated, I took off my Stetson and ran a hand through my sweaty hair before putting it back on my head. Getting this horse to calm the fuck down was impossible. He was two years old and should be more controllable. I didn't give a shit who his sire was. This wasn't a winner.

Glaring at the practice jockey, Eddie, I waited for him to get to me.

"He's a waste of goddamn time," I said with disgust.

Eddie glanced back at him. "He's got potential, but he's picky. Maybe we need to try another rider."

Eddie knew more about this shit than me. Hell, two years ago, I hadn't had anything to do with this side of the family business. Dad had forced me into it last year, and now, here I was, invested.

"Still throws me for a loop when I see you in a hat, talking about horses," Sax said from behind me.

I turned to look at him.

"Yeah, throws me too," I replied.

"Still having issues with Trigger?" he asked.

"Yeah. Think we could borrow Tim?" I asked him. Tim was the practice jockey they kept at Moses Mile full-time. "We've tried Eddie, Hill, and Darcy. I'm out of jockeys to try."

Sax nodded. "Yeah. I'll send him over."

I turned to walk back toward the stables, and Sax fell in step beside me.

"Haven't heard from you all week. Wanted to make sure you were alive."

I smirked. "Between working with this damn horse and being the best damn friend Gypsi's ever had, there hasn't been much time for anything else."

"Gypsi still here?" he asked me.

He was trying to sound like he didn't care. But he did. I didn't like that he cared.

"No. She and her mom went back to that fucking camper they live in three days ago. Dad has been a damn monster since Fawn left. He hates the camper. But Fawn doesn't want Gypsi there alone and told Dad that she isn't after his house and money. She just wants him. And she thinks them staying here is unfair to him." I laughed, thinking about how messed up that woman was making him.

"You think he's going to marry her?"

As much as I wished he weren't—simply because I was afraid it would make shit with Gypsi harder—I nodded. "I can't remember ever seeing him this gone over a woman. Neither has Blaise."

"Wow," he replied.

If he was thinking that Gypsi being my stepsister meant he was going to get a chance at her, that wasn't the case. At least not until I got over this thing I had for her. Then, it would be fine. If Sax wanted to do the relationship thing with her, I didn't care. Or at least I wanted to think I wouldn't care. If it was any other girl I wouldn't care. So I shouldn't care if it was Gypsi.

Except my hands were fisting like I cared. Whatever. I just needed to fuck her. That was all this was. No girl had made me wait before. Made me work for it. Typically, I smiled at them, and they dropped to their knees and sucked my dick.

"What're your plans this evening?" he asked me.

"Why, you want a reason to get Chanel over here, topless, and fuck her again?" Yeah. I knew they'd fucked in the pool house. She'd made sure to tell everyone.

He frowned. "That was a onetime thing."

"You tell her that? She's planning the engagement party. Saxon Houston fucks you, then you're relationship material," I teased him.

He rolled his eyes. "Shut up."

I stopped at the office door to see if Maddy was still here, but she was gone. The lights were off. My brother had probably summoned her home. The man was pussy-whipped.

"Who all knows about Chanel?" he asked me.

I glanced over at him. "You worried about Declan finding out? I'm gonna assume she knows."

"I don't care about Declan or what she knows. I went ahead and fucked Chanel, knowing she'd tell Declan, in hopes that it kept her from texting me."

I stared at him. Who was he worried about finding out?

My eyes narrowed as I looked at him. "You asking if Gypsi knows?" I asked, more pissed than I should be.

He shrugged. "You're the one who said you just want to fuck her out of your system. Why are you getting so damn angry about my wanting something more than that ... possibly? If she could get over you, that is."

95

Fuck this. I stalked toward the exit, not looking back at him.

Sax had been my best friend most of my life. We'd never fought over a woman. Not even when Maddy moved in with him and we had both thought she was hot. Before Blaise, of course. But right now, he was pushing me.

"If you like her for more than a fuck, then tell me," Sax said, following me. "I'll let it go. But she's … she's different. There is something about her—"

I turned and glared at him. "You can have her once I'm done. But stand the fuck back until that happens."

His jaw flexed, and I knew he was angry. I didn't care.

"She's not the kind of girl you just fuck. She deserves more."

I knew that. I was fucking aware. He didn't need to remind me. I hated hearing it.

"Stay out of this. Unless she tells me she doesn't want it, then I am getting what I want. She wants me. Until she gets my dick, she's not gonna be ready to move into a relationship with anyone."

Sax took three long strides until he was almost in my face. "You're a fucking asshole," he said through clenched teeth.

"Yeah, I am, but she still wants my cock," I snarled.

He muttered a curse and stalked off back to his truck. Good. He needed to leave. Gypsi would be here soon, and I didn't want him in the way.

I'd bought every chocolate and peanut butter snack I could find. We were going to my room to play Grand Theft Auto for the evening while our parents entertained some of Dad's friends who he was having over for dinner.

If I was lucky, I'd get between her pretty legs. At this point, if it was just my damn hand, I'd be happy.

"Trev! Saxon!" Kye called both our names. Turning, I saw Kye walking from the house and in our direction. "We've got a job. Suit up."

"Why the fuck is Sax going?" I snarled.

Kye shrugged. "I'm not the fucking boss."

Sax was walking back toward us. His scowl still directed at me.

"What's the job?" I asked Kye.

"Some stupid son of a bitch tried to undermine your dad."

I sighed. "Fuck. So, we're killing."

"We are taking. Delivering underground. Huck, Gage, and Levi will be there to handle the rest."

At least I'd be back to spend time with Gypsi without blood on my hands.

Chapter
FOURTEEN

GYPSI

I couldn't go back to work. I'd have to find another job.

Glancing over at Mom as she smiled, looking down at her phone, I wanted to tell her. Every night we spent in the camper, I was putting her in danger.

Today, I'd gone to the restroom at work, and when I returned, there was a plastic gold ring with the fake blue stone lying on the counter. He'd been in the coffee shop. He had come in when I was away from the counter. He had been watching me.

I shivered.

I'd convinced her to stay at Garrett's tonight. It had taken me promising to stay, too, but at least we would be safe. Garrett had sent a driver to get us in a Bentley. The Louis Vuitton duffel bag she'd packed her things in surprised me. She had blushed and said Garrett had acted hurt when she said she couldn't accept it. Mom didn't like hurting him. Now, she had a designer piece of luggage. What next?

Garrett had told her that he loved her this week.

I hadn't been expecting that news. When I asked her if she loved him, she had smiled and said yes. Almost giddy about it. He wanted her at his house all the time, and I knew she wanted to be there. It was me standing in the way. I couldn't keep staying there. He wasn't my boyfriend. I was an adult. It was time I took the camper and moved on. Mom would be safe and happy. Convincing her to let me go was another thing.

She looked up from her phone, smiling like a woman in love.

"Garrett?" I asked, already knowing the answer.

She nodded. "Thanks for staying tonight. I miss him."

She had seen him yesterday, but I didn't point that out.

The car pulled through the entrance to Hughes Farm, and she leaned forward, like she was ready to jump out of the car and run to the man. I looked out of the window at the stables we passed. They were as impressive as the house. A few horses were out in the fenced-in areas. I was curious about the horses. I'd never been around them, but they were beautiful. I'd like to get a chance to see them up close and maybe ride one before I left Ocala.

When the car stopped, Mom was beaming. She had the door open before the driver could get out and open it for her. I watched her, knowing I had to figure out a way to let her have this life without being a part of it. My situation would put them all in danger.

The driver closed Mom's door and started to my side. I let him open my door simply because it gave me time to prepare for facing Trev. He had been a complete gentleman all week. Every time I was with him, he took the friend thing to a new level. We had laughed, learned a lot about each other. Tonight, we were playing some stupid video game that he loved. He was twenty-one and still played video games. He could be cute, sexy, charming, and sometimes a little dark. Or maybe that last one was my imagination. Tyde had made me paranoid. Trusting a man would be hard for me to ever do again.

I expected Ms. Jimmie to open the door, but it was Garrett who stepped out. His gaze locked on Mom, and a smile spread slowly across his face. He'd been watching for her. He took off the brown cowboy hat on his head and ran a hand through his hair as she reached him.

When he lowered his head to kiss her, I looked away. Watching my mom make out wasn't on my list of things I wanted to see. Not sure if I should go inside or not, I stood there, looking out over the property.

"Lol—Gypsi." Trev called my name, and I shifted my gaze to see him walking up from a building out to the far right of the stables.

I smiled at him almost calling me Lollipop in front of my mom and his dad. A black cowboy hat was on his head and he was wearing jeans with black combat boots. The black T-shirt he was wearing was stretched tight across his, chest. Trev Hughes was droolworthy.

"Things handled?" Garrett asked.

Trev gave his father a nod, then turned his attention back to me as he approached the steps. "You hungry? I was thinking pizza. I can get some ordered before I get a shower."

I glanced back at my mom. She was whispering to Garrett with her hand on his chest as he held her against him. They were in their own little world.

I turned back to him. "Sounds good," I agreed.

He looked behind me and rolled his eyes, then grinned. "Come on," he told me, then reached for the bag in my hands with my overnight things. I let him take it and then followed him into the house.

Neither Mom nor Garrett seemed to notice. I wondered what that felt like. To be so wrapped up in another person that the rest of the world faded away when you were with them.

"He's been fucking irritable all damn day. Maybe she will chill him out," Trev said, glancing back at me.

Looked like he was pretty happy to me.

"Hang on," he said to me when we reached the stairs.

I watched as he walked over to the arched doorway.

"Ms. Jimmie!" he called out and waited.

"Yes?" I heard her reply.

"Can you order up some pizza?" Then, he looked at me. "What kind do you like?"

I shrugged. "I like all of it."

He frowned as if he didn't believe me. "So, if I order anchovies and pineapple, you're good with that?"

"You like that?" I asked, horrified.

He chuckled. "Fuck no. I was just making a point." Then, he turned his head back in the direction of the kitchen. "Order a meat lovers, buffalo chicken, and a cheese," he called out.

"Will do!"

When he turned and started back toward me, he reached up and took his hat off. The messy, sweaty mop of dark hair made me want to run my fingers through it. I tucked my hands in the pockets of my shorts to keep from reaching out.

"Are you inviting more friends?" I asked, trying not to sound disappointed.

He shook his head. "Did you want me to?"

"You ordered three pizzas."

He grinned. "I'm hungry." His booted foot hit the first step. "Come on, Lollipop."

I allowed myself to enjoy the view of his butt as he climbed the stairs. The way it flexed when he walked. I had to get control of my thoughts. Thankfully, we reached the second floor, and he turned to head in the direction of the white-and-gold room I used the last time I'd stayed the night here.

When we reached it, he opened the door, stepped back, then handed me my bag. "Come on to my room when you're ready. A shower won't take me long."

I took the bag and went inside. The room smelled like lavender. It hadn't the last time I stayed in here. I walked through and set my bag down inside the closet before heading to the bathroom. There was what I assumed was an oil diffuser on the counter. It hadn't been here last time. I walked over to it and could smell the lavender coming from the vapor. I loved the smell of lavender. Who had put this here? It couldn't have been for my sake unless Mom had said lavender was my favorite scent and Ms. Jimmie had set this up in here.

However it'd gotten here, I loved it.

Chapter
FIFTEEN

TREV

I heard her come in the front room of my suite. Walking out with only a towel wrapped around my waist, like I needed to grab something before dressing, was probably not cool, but I did it anyway—and on purpose.

I fucking loved it when I caught Gypsi checking me out, and it happened a lot.

I made sure to flex my arms to make them look even better as I ran another towel over my head and stepped into the first section of my two rooms. The area where the sofa, flat screen, pool table, darts, and minibar were located. Dropping my hands, I let my gaze go to Gypsi.

A grin curled my lips because she was looking—and not at my face.

"Sorry. I didn't hear you come in," I lied.

Her gaze snapped up to my face, and she blushed. "Oh. Do I, uh, need to—should I have, uh, knocked?"

She was flustered. I fucking loved it.

"No, you never have to knock. I'll go get some clothes on." I paused and smirked at her, unable not to point out she'd been looking at my body. "Unless you'd rather I just wear the towel."

Her eyes widened, and then she pressed her lips together, as if she were holding back a laugh. "Go get dressed," she said finally. "Yes, I was looking. You've got a nice body."

"Nice?" I asked, looking down at my bare chest. "Maybe I should take the towel off if this only gets a *nice*."

She held up her hand to stop me. "No! That won't be necessary! You've got an incredible body. You know that. Stop fishing for compliments. Your ego is big enough."

That was better. "My ego still likes to hear you say it, Lollipop." I pointed to the table in front of the sofa. "I bought some snacks. If you want something before the pizza gets here."

I didn't wait for her to see every one of those snacks was a combination of peanut butter and chocolate before walking into the bedroom portion of my suite. I thought about closing the door, but why? If she wanted to look in here and see me getting dressed, then I'd be happy to let her watch. Or just get naked with me and lie on my bed and let me finally get my hands on her.

"You bought all my favorites," she called out.

Grinning, I pulled a pair of gray sweats from my closet and put them on. "Yeah, I did."

"That's really sweet, Trev."

Taking the T-shirt I was going to put on with me, I walked to the open door to look at her. Letting her get one more look of my chest before covering it up. I was trying to break her down, and my body seemed to be what did it for her. I would use it to my advantage.

"I'm not just sweet, Lollipop. I'm fucking precious," I told her.

She turned to look at me, and like always, her gaze traveled down my body.

"You want me to keep the shirt off?" I asked.

She jerked her eyes off me and looked back over at the snacks. "No. Stop teasing me."

Walking over to her, I knew I needed to stop. I'd been good all damn week, but I was only so strong. "That wasn't teasing, Lollipop. It was a question. If you want the shirt off, I will happily keep it off."

I watched as she pulled her bottom lip between her teeth. Fuck, the girl was sexy. She was also cute, funny, easy to talk to, and a damn good daughter. Things I'd learned about her by being friends. Sax no longer knew more about her than I did. I'd made sure of it. Even down to the fancy-ass diffuser I had bought and put in her bathroom with lavender.

"Shirt on," she replied, glancing up at me quickly, then reaching down to pick up a Reese's Cup before sitting down on the sofa.

I pulled the T-shirt on, then grabbed a piece of the peanut butter and chocolate fudge I'd special-ordered at the chocolate shop in town. "This shit is delicious. You have to try one."

"I'd better eat some pizza first," she said. "If I let myself, I'll get full on all this."

"We've got all night," I told her, then reached for the game remotes. "How was work?"

I liked hearing about her job. The people she worked with and the drama in their lives. She got so fucking animated, telling me about it. At times, I wanted to grab her face and kiss the hell out of her for being so damn cute.

"It was my last day," she said, not looking at me.

I studied her profile. Something was off. I hadn't known she was quitting. Was she planning on leaving? I wasn't ready for her to leave.

"Did something happen? I didn't know you were quitting."

She wasn't leaving me. Not yet. I had a lot of shit I wanted to do with her first.

"No. I, uh, just thought I needed to find a job that pays more. Maybe a waitress or something. Mom isn't working as much at night because she's with your dad a lot. They've said the L-word, and I don't know what that means for him, but my mom doesn't tell men she loves them. So, I'm thinking I'll be on my own soon. I need to start saving more money."

It meant Dad was going to marry her. That was what it meant. I'd seen it coming. But knowing he'd told her he loved her meant this was not going to end the way I wanted it to. Why couldn't he have drawn this out? Let me have more time with Gypsi before things got complicated.

"Where would you waitress?" I asked. "Would you really make that much more, doing that?"

She shrugged. "I figure tips would make more than working for ten dollars an hour at the coffee shop. The tips there aren't much."

"You know, if they get married, my dad will expect you to move in here. Your mom would be happy, and that would make my dad happy. You leaving is going to upset her. You two are tight." *And I want to keep you around awhile. Preferably on my cock.*

She gave me a sad smile. "Yeah, I'm worried about her being upset too. But I will be twenty soon, and I can't just move in here. I'm not a child she has to take care of. I'm an adult. There is no reason for me to live with my mom."

"I'm twenty-one, and I live with my dad still," I pointed out.

She laughed. "Yes, but you work here too. This is a family business. It would be stupid for you to leave just to come back here every day for work. Plus, this place is massive."

"Exactly. It's massive, and you already have a bedroom here."

"I just can't, Trev. It feels wrong."

Fuck, she was stubborn. That was going to be an issue when she became family. Dad wasn't going to allow her to take the fucking camper and travel alone in it. "You traveling alone in a camper feels wrong. Have you looked in a mirror? Are you aware how fucking gorgeous you are? It's not safe for you to travel like you're planning on doing."

As the words I'd said sank in, the tightness in my chest was uncomfortable. I didn't like the idea of her being in danger. I wasn't going to be okay with it, I realized. Her leaving would be an issue. I knew my dad and he wasn't going to want her to leave but I also didn't know how much power her mom would have over his decision. Would her mom let her go if that was what she really wanted?

"Mom and I have traveled like this most of our lives. Sure, we've had some times that got a little scary. But we've learned the ways to keep safe. I will be smart about it."

Her words caused a clawing unease inside of me. They'd been scared? What the fuck had happened? Did Dad know this? Why the hell was he allowing them to stay in that camper? I needed to think about something else. This conversation was pissing me off. Everything she was saying was making me furious.

"If your mom marries my dad, then you're under the family's protection, just like she is. Fuck, if Dad is in love, then you're already under the family's protection. Moving in here is the best way to keep you safe." My words came out with the same fucking urgency that was building inside of me.

She laughed softly. I wasn't fucking joking, so why was she laughing?

"The way you say *the family* reminds me of the Corleones."
The smile on her face eased me some.

Telling her that it reminded her of it because that was what
it fucking was I couldn't do. Dad would have to offer that
information or tell me that I could trust her with it. But if he
was in love with Fawn, then had he told her? No, I doubted it.

"The Hughes name is powerful," was all I said.

Her expression was a cross of hopeful and unsure. "Some
things you can't be protected from. You have to handle that
battle yourself."

What the hell did that mean? If she needed protection, I
sure as fuck could do it.

"No, Lollipop, you don't. You need protection and I can
promise you, it'll happen."

A knock on the door stopped her from saying whatever it
was she was about to say, and then the door swung open as
Fawn walked in, carrying the pizzas.

"Delivery," she said, smiling brightly. "Ms. Jimmie was
going to bring it up, but I wanted to."

I jumped up and went to take the pizza boxes from her.

"Thank you, Trev," she said to me, then turned to look at
Gypsi. "I wanted to talk to you and see how you felt about
something."

Gypsi started to stand up, and her mom shook her head.
"It's not a private thing. I, uh …"

She reminded me of Gypsi when she smiled like that.

"Would you mind if Garrett and I left for a couple of days?
He wants to take me to Paris. Paris, Gypsi. I just … I hate to
leave you, but … it's Paris."

Gypsi's smile was genuine as she listened to her mother. "I
would be mad if you didn't go," she said, then stood up. "Go
have fun. Take pictures and text them to me."

I watched as she went to hug her mom.

"You'll be fine? Right?" Fawn asked her.

Gypsi laughed. "Mom, I'm grown. I'll get a ride back to the camper in the morning since we don't have the car here. It'll give me time to look for a better-paying job with the car all to myself."

Fawn was frowning, her eyes wide. "You aren't going to stay here?"

"This isn't my home. I can't just stay here."

"Yes, you can," I interrupted.

She was not going back to the motherfucking camper alone.

Fawn looked at me, smiling again. "See, Trev doesn't mind. Garrett wants you to be here so I won't worry. I can't enjoy Paris if you're alone at the camper."

Gypsi sighed heavily. "Mom—" she started, but Fawn cut her off.

"Please, honey. This is a once-in-a-lifetime thing for me, and I get to be with Garrett. Let me enjoy it. Don't go back to the camper. And why are you looking for a better-paying job? Do you need money? You know where the savings jar is. Get what you need."

Gypsi shook her head. "That is our savings. Not just mine."

Fawn grabbed Gypsi's shoulders. "You would tell me if ..." She paused, her gaze flickering to me for a moment, then back to her daughter. "If I needed to know something?"

Gypsi stiffened slightly. I didn't like it. "Yes, of course. I just need to start putting back money for the future. That's all."

Fawn closed her eyes briefly and took a deep breath. "Listen to me. I need you to stay here. Where you are safe. Don't go looking for a new job until I get back. We will talk when I return and figure out the future together. Just stop being stubborn. Stay here in that beautiful bedroom and enjoy yourself."

109

Gypsi stayed silent for a few seconds, and I realized I was holding my breath, waiting on her answer. Not butting into this conversation and telling her that she was staying her ass in this house was hard.

"Fine. Okay. Go enjoy Paris. I will stay here like some spoiled heiress and mooch off Garrett's hospitality," she said grudgingly.

Her mom laughed. "You are so far from a spoiled heiress, and you're not mooching. Garrett wants you here." She waved a hand at me. "Trev wants you here too."

"Yep," I chimed in.

Gypsi just nodded.

Fawn beamed brightly, then kissed her cheek, hugging her tightly. "Okay. I was going to go back to the camper to pack, but Garrett is refusing to let me. He wants to buy me clothes when we get there." She paused and bit her lip, looking unsure. "I feel bad, letting him," she said softly to Gypsi.

"Stop worrying, Mom. If the man wants to dress you in Parisian clothing, let him," Gypsi told her.

Fawn's smile wavered some, unsure, but she finally nodded. "I love you."

"I love you too," Gypsi replied.

Fawn hugged her one more time before she waved at me, then left the room, closing the door behind her.

Gypsi's shoulders lifted and fell with another heavy sigh, and then she walked back over to the sofa and sank down beside me. I leaned forward and got a piece of the meat lovers pizza and handed it to her.

She looked at it, then back at me. "You are no help. You know that?"

I smirked. "Sorry, Lollipop. But I want you here."

She took the pizza from my hand and took an aggressive, angry bite that made me laugh.

They were going to be gone. I'd have her here all to myself. It was game time.

"I'm not expected to go topless, am I?" Gypsi asked me as we reached the door leading out onto the veranda.

I'd invited over friends since the parents were gone. I figured it was an excuse to get Gypsi in a bikini and outside at the pool with me.

"No. You keep your top on. I'll hurt someone if they look, and they'll fucking look. They're gonna be looking anyway. They'd look, no matter what you were wearing."

She laughed softly, and the need to cover her mouth with my own was beating in my head like a drum. Since I'd opened my eyes this morning and remembered that I had Gypsi alone in the house, my dick had been hard. Ms. Jimmie didn't count. She never got in the way of anything going on in the house. But after working in this house and seeing the things that had gone on here, she'd learned long ago to stay quiet and out of the way.

I opened the door for Gypsi, then followed her outside. The sun was in my eyes, but I could see Chanel was now also topless and currently draped on Sax's arm. Not surprising. Declan might be her friend, but she was definitely more a *guys before friends* kinda girl.

Her eyes locked on us as we walked toward a set of lounge chairs. Sax was looking this way too. I knew he was annoyed about me having Gypsi alone in this house. He was still set on the fact that I couldn't fuck her without a relationship. She had agreed to the *friends with benefits* thing when she was ready. I didn't need his permission. She wasn't his.

"You've been gone forever, Trev," Chanel called out.

I'd left them all to go get Gypsi, who had been taking too long, and I was afraid she had decided not to come.

I started to say something when Gypsi pulled the cover-up off her body, and my mouth went dry. Jesus Christ, it was better than I'd imagined. Perky, full tits, covered up by a triangle of white with hot-pink piping around the edges. Then, the matching bottoms covered very little. Her asscheeks were completely on display.

I stepped over to her and picked up the flimsy thing she'd been covered up with and handed it to her. "Please put this back on."

She frowned. "Why?"

"Because I'm not going to be able to do anything but think about fucking you."

A slow grin spread across her lips. "That sounds like a you problem."

"Fuck," I groaned, and she laughed.

"There are topless girls out here. You were going to think about fucking someone. Might as well be me."

I shook my head. "I've already fucked them. I don't have to imagine it."

A small shadow crossed her face, and I wondered if I'd said the wrong thing. I didn't normally think about what I said to girls. I never had to before. Damn, I needed a how-to course from Sax.

Chapter
SIXTEEN

GYPSI

Mom had already texted me this morning from the plane. I was happy for her. She'd always talked about Paris and wanting to see it one day. Garrett was making that dream come true. The fact that I was having to stay here in order for her to enjoy it was the only issue I had. Trev, in his swim trunks and bare chest, was making me light-headed. I was struggling not to look at him constantly.

When Mom returned, I'd have to face her and convince her to let me move. Tyde couldn't find me here. I didn't think he could. But if he'd followed me, then maybe he could. I wasn't sure. The property had a lot of security. I'd noticed that. It gave me a sense of peace. I had slept better last night than I had all week.

Trev introduced me to everyone. Chanel, the topless red-head who wanted to fuck Saxon. Jeremey was a toned and tanned surfer boy, who was home from Mississippi State for the summer. Bea was the other topless female out here. She was blonde, and her boobs could not be real. They looked fake. She was also determined to get Trev's attention. I had become her enemy without doing anything. Daphne was a brunette and the only other female here who was wearing a top. She also looked like she and Jeremey were a thing. Aston was a blond guy with tight curls and blue eyes. He was talking to Saxon and drinking a beer. He went to college in Gainesville and had changed his major six times already.

Trev had made all the introductions, whispering the extra information in my ear. I'd struggled not to laugh.

"Let's get in the pool. It's hot as fuck out here," he said.

I agreed and followed him to the water's edge. The pool's entry reminded me of a beach without the sand. I went in slowly, getting used to the cold temperature of the water. The water was halfway up my calves when Trev scooped me up in his arms and ran the rest of the way down the sloped entrance until my body was submerged in the water.

"TREV!" I screamed as the freezing water shocked me.

He grinned, letting my legs go so that I was standing in front of him.

"You're mean," I complained.

"It's easier this way, Lollipop. You get used to the temperature faster," he assured me as his hands stayed on my waist.

Moving away from him would be smart, but it felt good. He had nice, big hands, and feeling them on my skin was getting to me. But he had been getting to me since he'd tried that ridiculous pickup line in Kentucky. We were friends now. I could say that and mean it. But he hadn't mentioned the benefits thing again.

"I've heard that argument before, but I still prefer to go in slow," I told him.

He smirked. "Aston was looking at your ass. I didn't like it."

114

This. This was my issue. This kind of behavior made me hot as hell. It was why I'd made the mistake with Tyde. Why I liked this in a guy I didn't know. Maybe I had daddy issues since I'd never known mine.

"Stop frowning at me, Lollipop. You're my friend, and I was protecting your ass from those who would ogle it."

I laughed, and he started to grin.

He was a flirt. That was different from Tyde. They weren't alike. Tyde hadn't flirted like Trev did. But Trev wasn't dangerous. Tyde lived in a dark world I didn't know that much about. He'd tried to keep it from me. I had to stop comparing Trev to him. Trev wasn't a psycho. He was a rich, spoiled kid with epic abs and a panty-dropping smile.

"Then, I guess you're my hero," I told him.

He leaned down close to my ear. "I'm the villain, Lollipop."

I shivered, and he pressed a kiss right beside my ear, then pulled me closer to him until I could feel his erection against my stomach. I stiffened, and he chuckled, his warm breath tickling my skin.

"It's a friendly boner, I swear," he whispered.

I didn't laugh. I was too busy trying to breathe. My body no longer felt cold.

"Lollipop," he said, looking down where our chests touched.

"Hmm?"

He didn't say anything for a moment, then muttered a curse as his hands flexed on my waist. This would be the time I should move away from him. Give us some space and cool off. I didn't though. I placed my palm against his chest, and his pec flexed under my touch.

"Um," I managed, then forgot what I was going to say. Lust was throbbing between my legs, and I was going to need some alone time if he kept this up.

"Completely friendly." His voice dropped to that deep, raspy sound.

"I'm not so sure," I whispered.

He chuckled low in his chest. "Okay, fine. I'm standing here, thinking about sliding those bottoms over and pushing inside of you. But in a friendly way."

My fingers curled, and my nails bit into his flesh. I needed to move him away. Like, now.

"Dude, you gonna fuck her in the water?" Aston called out, and Trev's entire body tensed.

I stepped back so that our bodies weren't touching and looked up at him. His jaw was clenched, and his gaze was a mixture of anger and need. He kept a hand on my side, then turned to glare back at Aston.

"Do you want to fucking leave?" The threat in his voice was clear.

The other guy's eyes widened, as if he was surprised by Trev's response. Then, he shook his head. "Sorry, man. I was just kidding."

"Don't," Trev bit out.

When he looked back at me, he relaxed some. I watched him as his eyes dropped to my chest. My nipples were so hard that they ached. I knew he could see that through the top I was wearing.

"Still cold?" he asked, lifting his gaze to meet mine.

"No," I replied softly.

His eyes flared, and he sucked in a deep breath. "You're gonna fucking kill me, Lollipop."

I took another step back, and he let his hand fall away from my side. My skin felt like it was on fire from where his touch had been. But most of my body was currently zinging with heat.

116

A splash to our left startled me, and I turned just as Chanel giggled, sitting on the edge of the pool. Saxon's head broke the surface of the water, and he swam over to her. It was odd to see Saxon like this. He ran his hands up her legs, and she opened them so that he could continue on. She bit down on her bottom lip as he slipped a finger in the crotch of her bottoms. I turned away quickly then.

Trev's gaze was still locked on me. "Does that bother you?" he asked me.

I frowned. "What?"

He lifted his chin in Saxon's direction.

"No. I just didn't want to watch. I'm not a voyeur."

He stepped closer to me, and I inhaled deeply.

"You don't care that he's sliding his finger inside her cunt?"

I let out a small laugh, shocked by his words. "No. I don't care whose, uh … cunt he slides a finger inside of."

Trev looked pleased with my answer. He had been worried I had some kind of attachment to Saxon.

"He's a friend," I told him.

Trev raised his eyebrows. "I'm a friend."

"Yes, and I have seen you grope all over several girls in our short friendship," I replied. "I'm surprised you're not all over one now." That sounded way too bitter.

"Sounds like it bothered you when I was groping these other girls," he drawled as his hand slid around my waist until it was at my back.

"It did. I was jealous," I admitted.

"You're not jealous of Chanel?" he asked me.

"No. I don't want to fuck Saxon."

Trev pushed my back until I was pressed against him again. "But you want to fuck me?"

"Yes."

"Why are we waiting again?"

117

I laughed. "Because we want to be friends first. I need to trust you and know that when we fuck and you're over it that we won't be awkward around each other."

Trev rubbed my bottom lip with the pad of his thumb. "We're friends now, and, Lollipop, you say that as if I'm gonna be over it after fucking you one time. Let's be clear. I want to lay you back and eat your pussy until you come on my face. I want to see your big, plump lips wrapped around my cock. I want to fuck your hot little pussy as you're bent over my bed, in the shower, in this goddamn pool, against the wall, on my pool table, on that lounge chair, and I'm sure I'll come up with a few more places. No, I don't want a relationship. But one fuck isn't all I'm asking for here. I'm gonna need a lot more than one to get you out of my head. That's the whole *friends with benefits* thing."

I stood there, staring at him. Rubbing my thighs together, in need of some relief. I'd come close to orgasming from his words alone. That was a first for me. My breaths were coming in short and fast. Reasons why we couldn't just do one of the many things he'd just mentioned seemed to be lost on me right now. I'd never been this turned on in my life.

"Tell me what's going on in that head of yours," he said.

I swallowed. "That if you had kept talking, I would have gotten off, and that's shocking. I didn't know someone could get off like that. Without being touched."

The dark look he gave me only made the ache he'd caused between my legs to throb harder.

"Are you serious?" he asked.

I nodded.

He grabbed my waist with both hands and spun me around. "Under the waterfall. Now," he growled.

He was bossing me around. It was one of my kinks. I walked until I had to swim, then swam out to the waterfall.

I ducked underwater to get under it until I was on the other side of it. I found a ledge underwater that I could stand on and keep my head above water. Trev's arms caged me in, and I turned to look at him. His wet hair was slicked back, and his gray eyes were glowing as he stared at me.

I tensed as he leaned in and brushed a kiss on my cheek, then my jaw before running the tip of his nose along my neck, inhaling deeply.

"I want to slip my hand inside those bottoms and play with your pussy while watching you get off," he said against my ear, then buried his head into the crook of my neck. "Let your sweet cunt squeeze my fingers, like I want it to do to my dick."

His warm breath on my skin made me tremble. A small moan came from my throat.

"I want to feel you as you come on my fingers. Hear you cry out my name." He pressed a kiss to the corner of my mouth. "I've jerked off, thinking about how you'll taste. How sweet your cum will be on my tongue. What your juices running down my face will be like."

Reaching out, I grabbed his arms and squeezed. I was so close, and it was almost painful. I wanted to stick my hand in my bottoms and get there already before I passed out from the agony.

"You like hearing about me licking your pussy, Lollipop? All you have to do is say the word, baby. I'll get on my knees so damn fast that it'll make your head spin." His hot tongue ran up my neck. "I want to feel your hands in my hair, pulling it and pressing my face harder as you ride my tongue."

My head dropped forward onto his chest, and I let out a cry, hoping the sound of the waterfall muffled it. I jerked and started to slip my hand inside my bottoms when Trev grabbed my wrist and pulled it out.

"That's mine," he growled.

119

He shoved his hand inside and pressed one of his fingers against my clit. I bit down on his chest to keep from screaming. He began to slide his fingers along the folds until he got to my entrance and pushed a finger inside of me. My hips rocked forward. I needed him to go deeper.

"Ah, fuck, this is a tight pussy. You're gonna squeeze my dick so good."

I realized I was still biting him and released his skin. His free hand came up and held the back of my head, keeping me pressed there against him.

"Bite me," he ordered in a husky whisper.

My teeth sank back into his skin, and a deep sound came from his chest. I moved my hips as he slid a second finger inside me and pumped them. I was close again already. Feeling the frenzy of lust clawing at me, I stopped biting him and licked his nipple, like I'd fantasized about.

"Fuuuck, Lollipop."

The sound of his pleasure triggered me. I forgot about where we were. The rest of the world faded.

"I need you to fuck me," I panted, looking up at him. "Please," I begged.

I shouldn't have let him start this. I wanted it too much. He had no idea how quickly he was going to get me out of his system.

"Jesus Christ, baby. You're going to decide that right now? We have an audience, and I don't have a condom." He sounded like he was in pain.

I reached inside his swim trunks and wrapped my fingers around his erection. "Oh God, it's big," I moaned.

It was bigger than Tyde's had been. Much bigger.

Trev's head dropped to my shoulder. "Talk about it being big while you've got your hand wrapped around it, and I will fucking blow," he said.

120

"But it is big. I want to see what this feels like inside me. Please … just a little. Let me feel," I begged.

He lifted his head to look at me. "Lollipop," he breathed. "Stop talking."

I held his gaze while I jerked against his hand. "I love your fingers in my pussy, but I really want to feel your big dick."

The flare in his eyes brought me so close to the edge.

"You're a dirty talker," he said in a shocked whisper. "My Lollipop is a naughty little brat."

"Please, just a little," I begged.

"You want me to fuck you where they can see us?" he asked.

"The waterfall is blocking them," I said as I began pumping his thickness.

"Not good enough," he groaned, then pulled his hand from my bottoms and took my hand out of his pants.

He grabbed my waist and picked me up, walking me over to where he could set me out of the pool. I stood up as he pulled himself up and out. He didn't look back at anyone as he took my hand and pulled me toward the door, stopping to grab our towels.

"Here," he said, shoving mine at me, and then he wrapped his around himself and pushed me toward the house.

"Where y'all going?" Aston called out, then laughed.

Trev didn't look back or reply. Once we were inside, his hand wrapped around my arm, and he pulled me through the house, up a flight of stairs I hadn't seen yet, and then we made two turns before stopping at his bedroom door.

He pushed it open and yanked me inside with him before slamming the door closed and locking it. I was against the wall, and his mouth was on mine instantly. His tongue ran along my bottom lip, and I opened for him. It wasn't a sweet kiss. It was savage. Out of control. Hungry and wicked. I ran my nails down his arms as he took the bikini top I was wearing and tugged it down, then covered my bare breasts with his hands.

I reached for his bottoms, pushing them down, then grabbed his swollen shaft in my hand and pumped it. He made a deep, guttural sound in his chest.

"Let me suck it," I said, breaking the kiss.

He shook his head. "Not this time. I'll fucking explode. Condom," he said, taking my arm and walking farther into the room.

Trev opened a drawer in the end table beside the sofa and took out a silver package, then ripped it open with his teeth.

"Get the bottoms off," he ordered me.

I hurried while watching him roll the condom down his erection. He dropped the swim trunks and stepped out of them, then grabbed me and pushed me up against the wall.

"Can't wait," he hissed, then pulled my right leg up onto his hip before shoving into me with one hard thrust.

My head fell back against the wall as I cried out. Trev pulled back slowly, then pushed back inside of me harder, sinking all the way in this time.

"FUCK, that pussy is tight. Can barely get it all in," he panted.

"Harder," I pleaded. "It's so big. I want to be fucked with it hard."

"That fucking dirty mouth is gonna make me blow too fast," he warned me, slowing his pace.

"Trev," I moaned, "I've never been stretched like this. It feels so good. I need it hard. Get it all the way in. Deep."

"Fuck," he swore. "Your pussy's so wet; I can hear it."

Then, his hand squeezed on my leg he was holding, and his other hand gripped my hip so tightly that it almost hurt. He rammed into me then until he hit a spot deep inside

122

that I hadn't known was there. It sent my body into a frenzy. Wanting more, I clawed at his back, begging him.

"Is that it, Lollipop? That's where you want my cock?"

"YES!" I cried, never having felt this kind of delirium.

Trev pumped harder. Our bodies slapping against each other and the wet sounds of my pussy sliding over his cock were the hottest things I'd ever heard. When my body spun out into its release, I clung to him as his name fell from my lips over and over.

I felt him tense under me, then jerk before he shouted, "FUUUCK!"

I kept my arms wrapped around him as he thrust out his release inside me. I lay against him, panting. He'd made me come harder than I ever had. There wasn't a word for how incredible that had felt.

When he finally stilled inside me, he leaned us both against the wall as he gasped for breath. I let out a disappointed whimper as he pulled out of me and gently put my leg back on the ground.

"Holy shit, Lollipop," he said, resting his forehead against mine. "I expected it to be good, but, damn, that was off the fucking charts."

I smiled as he stood up straight.

"I need to go get rid of the condom. I'll be right back."

"Let me take it off?" I asked, blushing when his eyes widened in surprise.

"Uh, okay."

Even semi-hard, he was still thick. I took it in my hand, pulling the end down before rolling the base back up. When it was off, I ran a finger over his wet tip and played with the cum still clinging to him.

He hissed. I sank down to my knees in front of him and licked it off, then lifted my eyes to look up at him. The astonished heat in his eyes urged me on. I wasn't freaking him out yet. That was good. Sticking my tongue out, I licked at the tip again, then ran my tongue around the head.

"Lollipop, you're a naughty, twisted girl." His voice was hoarse.

I wrapped my lips around the head only and sucked gently before letting it go and standing back up.

His eyes followed me, looking at me like he wanted to fuck me again. That was the point. I was ready for another round.

"How soon can you do it again?" I asked him.

"You start talking with that filthy mouth, and I'll be ready for round two," he replied.

His phone dinged just as he took a step toward me, and he scowled over at it like he might smash it against the wall.

"Check it. I'll wait right here."

His gaze traveled down my body, and he let out several curse words before walking over to his phone and picking it up.

"Dammit!"

"What?"

He shook his head and pressed a number, then put the phone to his ear.

"Can this wait?" he bit out.

"As a matter of fact, yes." His eyes cut to me briefly.

He listened to whoever it was, then cursed again. "I'll be there in fifteen." He ended the call and stalked back over to me. His gaze traveled down my body. "Fuck, I hate my life."

"You have to go somewhere?" I asked, ready to beg him to stay.

He nodded. "Yeah. It's work-related. Can't wait," he said.

"When will you be back?" I asked, sounding desperate.

His eyes locked with mine, and then he lowered his mouth, pressing a kiss to my lips. "Real fucking soon. As fast as I can."

He stood back up and walked over to pick up one of his shirts that was lying over the back of the sofa. "Wear this. Stay in my room. There are drinks and your snacks from last night over in the minibar. I'll send the others home."

I took the shirt from him, then reached up and untied the bikini top, letting it fall to the ground while he watched me. He was breathing heavy while looking at me standing there, naked. I wasn't playing fair.

"Jesus Christ, Lollipop. Please put my shirt on," he urged.

I took my time slipping it over my head and letting it slide down my body, knowing I had his complete attention.

His gaze lifted from my body to meet my eyes. "Keep it on. I like it on you."

Then, he turned and headed for his closet. I followed him into the bedroom part of his rooms and went to his massive bed. While he got dressed, I crawled onto his bed and buried my face in the pillow, smelling him. I was probably going to have to get myself off in here once he was gone.

"Damn," he swore, and I looked over at him pulling on his jeans while looking at me. "Please be right there when I get back."

I nodded and watched him finish getting dressed. His gaze kept shifting back to me. The hungry gleam in his eyes only made me ache more. Rubbing my thighs together, I shifted, pulling the covers down from underneath me, then tugged them up over me. Trev's scent was strong now. I held the covers to my nose and inhaled.

"Are you smelling my sheets?" he asked me.

"Mmhmm," I replied.

He ran a hand through his hair and stalked over to me. I looked up at him as he stared down at me.

"You need to rest because when I get back, I'm fucking you all night."

"Promise?" I asked.

A wicked grin curled his lips, and he ran the back of his finger over my cheek. "Yes, I promise."

II

There's a dark side to everything.
—Prince

Chapter
SEVENTEEN

TREV

"That was longer than fifteen minutes," Gage barked at me when I walked into the house he shared with Levi and Huck.

It had once been my brother's, but he'd moved Maddy into a house on Hughes land. Huck's fiancée also lived here, and Gage's girlfriend was now living here too. It was a high security setup, but the security here was more obvious than that at the farm. Dad's security was more intense, but it was hidden better. He didn't like his home to feel like a place for our operations.

I closed the office door behind me and looked around the room. Levi and Kye were here.

"Where's Huck?" I asked Gage.

"In Paris."

I nodded. Should have thought about that. Dad had taken Huck as security.

"You said on the phone that I interrupted you fucking," Gage said, leaning back as he studied me.

He'd actually asked me, "What am I interrupting, a hot fuck?" and I'd said, "As a matter of fact, yes."

"Sax is on his way but had to run home from your house to get changed. I asked him where you were, and he said, 'Upstairs with Gypsi.' That's Fawn's daughter, right?"

"Yeah," I replied, annoyed that Sax had told Gage shit.

Gage chuckled. "You remind me of Blaise when he was younger. He won't admit it, but he let Gina suck his cock back in the day. Having a hot piece of ass as a stepsister has its perks."

I didn't like him talking like Gypsi as if she were a fucktoy. "It's not the same."

Gage raised his eyebrows. "Don't tell me you got feelings."

I scowled at him, not caring that Gage was the craziest son of a bitch I'd ever met. "We're friends. I respect her."

"But you also fuck her," he added.

My hands fisted at my sides.

Levi laughed. "Leave him alone. You've got him worked up enough. We have shit to do."

Gage continued to smirk as he glanced over at Levi. "Fine. You're right. Sax will be here soon, but he's not ready to do more than watch and learn."

"Someone's been trying to get on the ranch at night. It's happened twice now. Both times, Six was on duty. When the guy saw him, he took off."

"On foot?" Kye asked.

Gage shook his head. "He's on a Harley. Nice one. Six didn't see any cuts on his leathers. We don't think it's an MC. But we also haven't been able to get close enough to take him. The only common denominator between the two nights is, Fawn and Gypsi were there." Gage locked his gaze on me. "Do you know any connection those two have to MCs or gangs?"

I shook my head. "No."

Gage nodded. "Garrett doesn't want us asking either of them. He said it would upset Fawn, and he won't allow that. But if someone is trying to get to them, he wants them caught, questioned, and killed only after he speaks to him. The one thing that makes it unlikely that he's after the women is that they were at their trailer all week and were fine. That could be because Garrett had Bart placed as their security. His being outside would have kept anyone away."

"He's done this twice?" I asked. "Six couldn't have been more prepared the second time?"

Gage shrugged. "First time, he thought it was a fluke. Some biker had gotten lost. It wasn't until this next time that we got concerned. If they show up again, he's been ordered to take the shot. But not a kill shot."

The door opened behind me, and Sax walked in. Our eyes locked for a moment, and then he dropped his. He knew I was pissed. Good. Gypsi wasn't his concern.

"I'll give Sax the update. Levi, you take Kye to set up extra security at the house. Trev, now that you know what's going on, go back to the house. Fuck the girl but keep her safe. Watch her though and listen. Garrett trusts Fawn and has done a complete background check on them. The only questionable thing that has come up is some time that they were in Miami. It's almost as if they were off the map for a while. Nothing. No jobs, no trace of the camper, nothing at all."

More than once, I had thought something was off with Gypsi's reactions to certain things. And she'd said a few things that didn't sit well with me. I turned and walked out of the office, ready to get back to Gypsi. I didn't like her being there alone. I'd know if she tried to leave. Six would stop her, but the need to protect her was now battling with the need to fuck her for top position.

She was asleep. Curled up in my bed with her blonde curls spread out over my pillow. I watched her as I undressed. I didn't want to wake her, but I was not going to be able to stay away from her. I'd gotten one hot, quick fuck. I was ready for more than that.

I pulled the covers back and climbed in behind her. I ran my hand over her bare bottom and up her side, slipping it under my shirt she was still wearing until I had one of her tits in my hand.

She stretched and made a sexy little sound before turning her head to look at me. A sleepy smile touched her lips. "You're back."

I pushed the shirt up and over her breasts before leaning down to suck on her right nipple. She moaned and arched into me. Her hands threaded through my hair as I made my way down her stomach, kissing the smooth, soft skin as I went. I pushed her thighs open and stared down at her slick folds.

"You're already wet," I said, looking back up at her.

She bit her bottom lip. "I might have gotten myself off earlier."

"You masturbated in my bed?" I asked, my cock throbbing. The image of her legs open while her pretty fingers pleasured herself under my sheets was going into the gold section of my spank bank.

She nodded. "The pillow and covers smell like you. It got me all worked up."

The talking had to stop, or I was going to blow too fast again. Growling, I lowered my head, taking her legs and putting them over my shoulders. Lifting my eyes up to watch her face, I took my first lick of her pussy, and, fuck, it was sweet. Her mouth fell open as she watched me. I began to make hard, long strokes with my tongue before flicking her clit, then pulling it into my mouth to suck on it.

She threw her head back and moaned loudly.

"Yes! Lick it harder," she panted. "That feels amazing."

I ran the tip of my nose over it, loving the smell of her arousal. I began to fuck her tight little hole with my tongue, and she bucked against my face.

"Oh, oh, oh, Trev."

Licking back up to her clit, I replaced my tongue inside her with my middle finger.

"OH! GOD!"

Her hands grabbed my hands, and she held me against her swollen, throbbing nub. I licked it continuously as I finger-fucked her. She was about to come. I could taste her release. Like a man possessed, I began licking hard, needing it on my tongue.

"Trev! I'm gonna come! Yes, please! Just like that, please!" she begged. As if I could stop.

Her hips came off the bed as her body shuddered while she screamed my name.

I continued licking as she slowly came back down from her climax.

"Fuck me," she said, pulling at my hair to get me up. "Now. I need you to fuck me."

"Condom," I said, starting to get up.

"I need you in me now," she cried.

"What about the condom, baby?" I asked, looking down at her open legs lifting to me. Fuck.

"I'm on birth control, and ... I've been tested since I had sex last." She stared up at me.

I'd never fucked without a condom. I was religious about it. I looked back down as she moved her hand to slide over her dripping wet cunt. Fascinated, I watched her start to play with herself.

"Go get the condom if you want to," she breathed. "I'll wait."

No, I realized. I didn't want to. I wanted to feel that. All of it. I'd lost my damn mind, apparently. I covered her body with mine and leaned down to kiss her lips, unsure if she would let me really kiss her after I had my mouth covered in her juices. She opened to me immediately, and her tongue plunged into my mouth like she couldn't get enough of me.

Grabbing her thigh, I moved it over and slid inside her. The wet heat that pulled me in was more than I had prepared for.

I tore my mouth from hers. "FUCK!" I shouted. "Jesus Christ." I stared down at her, sinking all the way in.

This was a nirvana I hadn't known existed.

She pulled her knees up to my hips and let out a long moan. "Oh God, you're inside me bare."

Yeah, and if she started that talking shit. I was done. This was already more pleasure than I'd ever had.

"I need to feel you come inside me. I want you to fill me up so that I can feel it leak out of me when I play with my pussy."

"Lollipop! You have to stop talking. I can't handle it," I said through clenched teeth.

She lifted her hips, pressing me deeper. "Give it to me, Trev. Fuck me with that big cock."

Something snapped in me. A fucking roar tore from my chest as I began pounding into her. The harder I got, the more she cried out in pleasure. My hand covered her breast as I looked down at her head thrown back. She grabbed my hand and moved it to her neck. What the fuck?

Opening her eyes, she held my hand there and stared up at me. I tightened my hand around her throat, and her eyes fluttered.

"YES!"

Fuck, that was hot.

"You want me to choke you, Lollipop?" I asked, feeling like I'd lost any control I had.

"Yes! Choke me while you're filling my cunt with your cum," was her strangled response.

"I need you to come, baby," I groaned.

I was too close. I'd never fucked like this. The girls I'd had weren't into kinky shit. They did what I told them to do, but my imagination hadn't been this damn good.

Her eyes were locked on me as her mouth fell open and her eyes rolled back in her head. Her body convulsed under me as her first wave of release washed over her. She was fucking gorgeous.

"TREV!" She cried my name, her cunt squeezing my dick with each tremor.

My hand tightened on her throat as I pumped into her two more times before I exploded inside her. I ran my hand from her neck down to her stomach as my cock continued to jerk inside her.

"Oh, that feels amazing," she said, rocking her hips against my cock. "I can feel it. All of it."

"That fucking mouth of yours is going to be the end of me. Keep it up, and I'll stay buried in this pussy."

Her eyes flashed with excitement. "Promise?"

I laughed, dropping my head to her chest. "You are a very bad girl, Lollipop. I had no idea."

"Are you okay with it?" she asked softly.

I lifted my head and stared at her. "Am I okay with it?" I repeated.

She nodded her head.

"Yes, baby. I might be obsessed with it."

She smiled so damn sweetly that it was hard to believe that pretty mouth could say such naughty shit.

"One problem," I told her.

I saw worry flicker in her eyes. I hadn't meant to do that. Why had she gone there so quickly—thinking something bad was going to happen?

I reached up and cupped the side of her face. "This *fuck it out of our systems* setup we have?" I said. "It's going to take much longer than I realized."

"Oh," she replied.

"Yeah. Oh. You've talked dirty with that sweet mouth, begged for me to come inside you so you could *play with it*, had me choke you while I fucked you. Yeah … I'm gonna need this longer than anticipated."

A small laugh bubbled out of her, and the way she was looking at me didn't scare me off. It should, but damn if my dick wasn't getting hard again. I moved inside her and watched as her mouth made a cute little O.

"I'm gonna need some more of that," I told her.

She opened her legs wider and smiled up at me. "You had a list of places you wanted to fuck me. Should we move to another location?"

I shook my head. "No. Right now, seeing you in my bed is all I need."

She pulled her bottom lip between her teeth, and I continued my slow thrusts, watching her. The mixture of our releases made her so slick that I easily slid in deep. It was fucking heaven. She reached up and ran her hand over the bite mark she'd made on me in the pool.

"I like to bite," she whispered.

"You can bite me whenever you fucking want to," I told her.

138

"I want to bite your stomach and …" She stopped.

"And what?"

"I want to straddle your abs and get off on rubbing against them while you jerk off."

I closed my eyes and sucked in a breath through my teeth.

"I know … I should have warned you. I … I have these kinks. And once I start, I want it a lot. I crave it."

I hung my head as my cock jerked inside of her. Where the fuck had she come from? Was this shit really happening?

"Lollipop," I said, lifting my head back up to look at her, "you're telling me you like to do kinky shit and that you like to fuck a lot as if you need to apologize for it." I shook my head in amazement. "I don't know who made you think something was wrong with that because I'm trying to decide if this shit is real or if I'm having the world's best wet dream."

She laughed and ran her hands up my arms. "It's real. And, Trev, will you let me straddle you so I can bite your chest when I come this time?"

I grabbed her hips, rolling off her and pulling her on top of me. "You fuck me all you want. Bite the hell out of me," I told her, running my hands up her thighs. "I'll happily wear your teeth marks all over my body."

She beamed at me, then leaned down to kiss me.

We might fuck each other to death before this was over.

Chapter
EIGHTEEN

GYPSI

While we showered, I counted three bite marks on Trev's chest along with one on his abs and then one slightly lower. After he bent me over while washing my back and fucked me. Trying not to be needy, I didn't go down on him once we got out of the shower. But I kept looking at his still-semi-hard cock. He had dried off, but stayed naked while brushing his teeth and putting on deodorant.

I tried to do the same, but he was distracting. Keeping me in here with him probably wasn't the best idea. He'd gone and gotten my things from the room I'd been staying in and brought them all in here. Even my toiletries.

"Lollipop." He said my name, and I lifted my gaze from his cock to his face.

I blushed as he studied me. "I … I was just … I want to suck it."

His eyes heated immediately, and he turned to face me. "Then, suck it."

Dropping the towel I had wrapped around me to the floor in front of him, I went down on my knees and took it in my hand. Slowly, it began to stiffen completely as I stroked it. Leaning in, I licked at the tip, then up the sides, watching him swell with the attention.

Lifting my eyes up to look at Trev, I opened my mouth and slid it all the way back until it touched my throat and I gagged. I did it again harder, making my eyes water.

Trev pulled my hair back with his hand and held it in his fist. "You want me to force you, don't you?"

I nodded.

"Fuck," he whispered, then shoved me forward hard, groaning as I made choking sounds when it filled my throat. "Too much?" he asked me.

I shook my head, and his eyes blazed. He pulled my head back and shoved it forward again. I grabbed the fronts of his thighs to keep from falling forward and moaned as he began to fuck my face.

"Jesus Christ, Gypsi," he growled. "You like this? Taking my dick like a whore?"

I cried out, then sucked harder.

"You like being called names," he hissed.

I nodded my head, and he let out a hard laugh.

"Fucking hell."

"Okay then. Suck my cock like a dirty little slut."

I slipped a hand between my legs and began to rub my clit. I was throbbing.

"That's it. Rub that hot little pussy while you take my dick," he groaned and pumped his hips as he controlled my head.

I began to come, and I cried out with my mouth full of him. Our eyes locked before I felt the pulsing of his hard shaft in my hand. His mouth fell open, and a desperate groan tore from his chest as he began to coat my throat. I swallowed all over it, running my tongue over the head when he finished.

He let go of my hair, and I continued to lick him. He jerked as I ran my tongue over the head. Smiling, I let him go and stood up.

I met his gaze as he stood there, breathing hard.

"Lollipop," he said in a hoarse whisper.

"Yes?"

"That's the best blow job any man has ever had on the fucking planet."

I laughed as he pulled me against his chest.

"If you're trying to ruin me for all other women, you're doing a very good job. I give you an A-plus."

Smiling, I pressed a kiss to one of the bite marks on his chest. That wasn't what I was doing. I was just making it harder for myself to leave. And I would. He would tire of me eventually.

Mom had texted me pictures. Once Trev and I made it out of the bedroom, I checked my phone to see what all she had sent me. She was having the time of her life. Smiling, I read each caption she'd sent with the photos. Most of them were just of her. I figured Garrett was taking them for her. But in two of them, he was with her. The way he stood with her made me feel like she was safe from anything. There was a protective stance that was hard to describe. It made it clear to anyone who looked her way that she was untouchable.

Trev had gone down to the kitchen, and I stopped to reply to her many texts. She'd asked if I was having a good time and if Saxon had been over to visit. I laughed at that.

Wrong guy, Mom.

I wasn't going to tell her about Trev though. That wouldn't go over well. It wasn't like this was headed to anything serious.

Once I was done, I continued down the stairs and headed for the kitchen. I had worked up an appetite. Trev wanted to go swimming, just us, but we both needed food first.

"Not your business," I heard Trev say to someone, and I stopped.

"It's family business. That makes it mine," a deep voice replied.

"No, it doesn't. You're not the boss yet. Dad is still the fucking boss. You're my brother. Back off." Trev's tone sounded annoyed.

"Do not push me, Trev."

I backed up, not sure I should be listening to this.

"What do you want to know, Blaise? You want details? What the fuck is it you need me to tell you?" Trev raised his voice.

"Garrett is going to propose to Fawn Parker. He's bought the goddamn ring. He knows there is shit we don't know about her, but he doesn't care. He's fucking infatuated. That's why I care. If you are fucking her daughter, you're gonna need me to protect you from Garrett."

I covered my mouth so the gasp that escaped me was muffled. Mom would say yes. This wasn't a what-if anymore.

"Like you didn't fuck Gina," Trev shot back at him.

"I was in high school, and she just sucked my cock," he replied. "This is different."

"You don't know what's going on. How do you know it's different?"

"You were late to a meeting, which you hadn't wanted to go to when called because you told Gage you were fucking. Sax had informed Gage you'd gone inside with Gypsi. You can't let pussy get in the way of the job."

"HA! Like you didn't? Do I need to remind you just how *in the way* you let Maddy get?"

A loud slam made me jump.

"Fuck, Blaise. Calm your ass down!" Trev yelled.

"Don't bring Madeline into this." His voice made me shiver.

I didn't know Blaise Hughes, but I didn't think I liked him.

"Whatever. You know I love Maddy. I am just pointing out that you're drilling me over something you did."

"No. I was in love with Madeline long before she walked into this world here. It is not the same. You are fucking Gypsi. You don't love her."

Trev was quiet. "Okay, fine. I'm sorry I was late to the meeting. Won't happen again."

"No, it won't. Because next time, it might not be a meeting about some dipshit on a motorcycle trying to get onto the property. It could be more serious."

I stopped breathing. What was he talking about? Was he talking about someone on a motorcycle trying to get on this property? Here? Oh God.

"If he shows again, Six will wound him, and we'll take him underground for questioning. You need to be ready for that call."

"I will be. Now, let me fucking eat. Gypsi will be down any minute," Trev grumbled.

Wound him? Underground? Questioning? He was being serious. Trev hadn't laughed like Blaise was joking. He'd not even been surprised by his words. Who was Six?

I backed up and leaned against a wall.

The motorcycle could be Tyde. He had found me here, but couldn't get on the property. They were looking for him. Waiting.

Maybe they weren't in danger. But did that mean I should stay? Tyde would go away if I did. Mom would freak out if I left. She'd come rushing home from Paris. I heard footsteps, and I straightened, then made my way to the kitchen. My mind was reeling with one question after another. If this was Tyde, they thought they could wound him. But he wasn't a regular criminal. They wouldn't be prepared for his level of dangerous ... or would they? They had an underground for questioning. That sounded pretty dark. Wouldn't they just call the police?

"Ms. Jimmie is at my house today, helping Madeline with Cree," Blaise said as I stepped into the kitchen.

Both sets of eyes turned to look at me. I forced a smile and turned my gaze to Trev.

"Hey, Lollipop. Come sit down. I'll get you some pan-cakes that Ms. Jimmie left us," he said to me, then glanced at Blaise, who was studying me. "Oh, and this is Blaise, my brother. He's currently pissed at me. That's why he's scowling. He scowls a fucking lot. And as you know, Blaise, this is Gypsi Parker."

"Nice to meet you," I said to him, wishing he'd leave. He made me nervous.

He nodded his head once. "Looks like my father and brother have the same taste in women," he drawled. "You're a replica of your mom."

I laughed nervously. "Um, yeah, I guess."

"Stop fucking scowling at her," Trev told him. "Come sit, Lollipop."

Blaise raised an eyebrow. "Lollipop? Do I even want to know?"

Trev smirked. "Probably not."

Blaise shook his head, as if disgusted. These two could not be any more different. Granted, Blaise was ridiculously

145

good-looking, but then so was Garrett. Hughes men were nice to look at.

"I'll be at the stables most of the day. You coming down soon?" Blaise asked him, then looked at the swim trunks he was wearing with his T-shirt. "Or are you swimming?"

Trev grinned. "Swimming."

Blaise muttered and turned to stalk out of the kitchen. When he was gone, I felt like I could relax a little. That man was frightening. I walked over to sit on the stool beside Trev.

He pushed a plate of pancakes with fresh berries over to me, then held up a can of whipped cream. "Want some?"

"Yes, please."

He covered the berries with the whipped cream, then squirted some in his mouth before setting it down.

"Yes, he's an asshole one hundred percent of the time," Trev said to me.

"Um, no comment," I replied.

Trev chuckled. "Wait until you meet Maddy. You're gonna wonder how the fuck that match happened."

Probably because his brother was hot, but I didn't say that.

Trev shoved a bite into his mouth, and I stopped watching him to focus on my food. I was starving. However, my head was going back to the motorcycle and Tyde. If he had tried to get in here to get to me and they stopped him, he'd be pissed. He would come back, prepared with a plan. They might have some underground and security, but they didn't know that world. Heck, I didn't know that world. I knew there were drugs involved, and I thought porn too. I hadn't known about any of it until I got serious with Tyde.

He had said it wasn't a gang, but it felt like it was. What little I saw or heard. Tyde had kept me separate.

The battle on if I should leave or not was waging a war in my head. I didn't want to worry Mom, and I wasn't ready to give up Trev yet. Especially after having sex with him. I wanted more of that.

Tyde hadn't been that good in bed. He was controlling, and I liked that. His dick size, however, didn't compare to Trev's. In the beginning, when I started asking for more things during sex, Tyde liked it. But then he started getting angry.

The slapping my face when I said anything during sex was the start of it.

The slapping my face whenever I said anything anytime that he didn't like was next. Then, when men looked at me, I'd pay for that in private. The face slapping soon turned into arm twisting. Slamming my head against the wall. Shoving me into things, then kicking me when I was down.

The kicking was the last straw. I'd left him then.

"You're real quiet, Lollipop," Trev said, sliding his hand over my thigh.

"Sorry, I was hungry," I replied, trying to smile.

He brushed some hair off my shoulder, then kissed it. "You sure that's it?"

I nodded.

"You finished?" he asked.

"Yes."

He turned my stool so I was facing him and slipped his fingers into my hair, then pulled me to him. Our mouths touched softly at first as he licked at my bottom lip. I ran my hands up his chest, then locked them around his neck. He tasted like berries and cream.

"Mmm," he said, pulling back, then pressing one more kiss on my lips. "You taste good."

"We both do. The berries and whipped topping might have something to do with that."

He looked amused. "No, you always taste fucking sweet. Like a lollipop."

I ran my fingers up his neck and into his hair. His eyes closed.

"Can we fuck again?" I asked him.

He laughed, opening his eyes. "You want more?"

I nodded. "It's your fault for being sexy."

The pleased gleam in his eyes made me feel warm in my chest. I wasn't sure that was a good thing. The warm feeling. It seemed like dangerous territory.

"Let's go to the pool. I want to fuck you in there," he said, standing up. "But I want you naked." He took my hands and pulled me up, then ran his palms down my arms.

"Or we could fuck right here on the bar," I suggested, feeling impatient.

"You want it that bad?" he asked.

"Yes," I replied honestly.

He held my face in his hands again, rubbing his thumb over my bottom lip. "I think my Lollipop might be a nympho."

I laughed, and the tender look in his eyes when he smiled at me made that warm feeling come back. I had to make that stop. This was just sex. Really good sex. *Friends with benefits* sex.

"I think we're gonna have to move from friends with benefits to steps with benefits," he said softly.

I couldn't let him know I'd overheard.

Choosing my words carefully, I replied, "I doubt it. Even if they do get engaged, they'll have to plan the wedding. We would have it out of our systems by then."

His brows drew together in a frown. "Will we?"

I wasn't sure if I needed to answer that. It felt more like he was asking himself and not me. I stared up at him.

"Bottoms off," he ordered, letting me go.

I hurried to slide them down my legs while he watched. When I kicked them out of the way and looked back up at him, he had his dick in his hand stroking it. I wanted to touch it, too, but I didn't. I just watched him.

"The way you look at my cock is really fucking good for my ego," he drawled.

I lifted my gaze to his. "It's a great cock."

"What do you want, Lollipop?" he asked me. "Use your dirty mouth to tell me."

I licked my lips, and he chuckled.

"As tempting as that is, I want inside of that pussy this time. You can suck it later."

"Sit on that chair," I told him, pointing over to the plush white high-back chair over by the entrance to the sunroom.

I walked over and pushed his shorts down to his ankles. He sat down, his cock standing straight up. I pulled my cover-up off, then untied my bikini top, dropping it to the floor. I went to straddle him, and his hands went to my waist as I sank down on him.

"AH!" I winced as he stretched me. I was tender from all the sex, but it was the good kind of pain. It made me feel more.

"Does it hurt?" Trev asked, brushing hair from my face.

"Yes, but I like it."

"Tell me how it hurts."

"I'm sore from being stretched by your dick."

A pleased rumble vibrated in his chest.

I lifted myself up and sank back down, then picked up the rhythm as I coated his length with my arousal, getting him slick. Once I was done, I began to bounce up and down. Each time I dropped down onto his cock, it hit that spot deep inside that felt so incredible.

"Fuuuck, Lollipop," he groaned. His hands went to my breasts, letting them jostle around in his palms with my movement.

His heated gaze was on my tits in his hands.

"Pinch my nipples," I told him.

He glanced up at me for a moment, then began to gently rub them between his thumb and forefinger.

"Hard, Trev. Pinch them!"

His clamp on them became intense, and I moaned.

"YES!"

"I fucking love your tits," he growled. "Pretty pink nipples."

I cried out as I slammed down on his cock hard. "Bite them!"

He looked up at me, then grabbed my waist, pulling me to him. His teeth teased one before putting enough pressure to make it feel amazing.

"AH! It hurts. I want more."

His teeth bit down harder, and the exquisite peak rushed through me. Throwing my head back, I shouted Trev's name. His arms wrapped around me, holding me to him as he thrust into me, burying himself deep, filling me so good that it hurt. My tight walls felt the pulses from his thick shaft as each spurt shot inside me. His body locked up, then jerked as he held on to me.

"*Fuck.*"

I listened to him gasp for air. His head dropped to my shoulder, and he inhaled deeply. I savored the connection. Having him stay inside me. When we were locked together like this, I felt something that my body craved. In that moment, I wasn't scared. The worries I carried were gone.

I didn't want to move. If I could keep him like this forever, I would. That was my sickness though. Not his.

"Do you need more?" he asked, pressing a kiss to my neck.

I always needed more, but I was also afraid he'd end this too soon if I didn't give him a break. "Do you?" I asked.

He leaned back, and his beautiful gray eyes looked up at me. "We can't break your pussy, right? Because you keep wanting it harder and you're so tight."

A laugh caught in my throat, and he grinned.

"Why don't you try to break it?"

He groaned and pulled my face to his for a kiss. "Don't tempt me."

Chapter
NINETEEN

TREV

Ten times. I shook my head, grinning as I walked down toward the stables. Since I had opened my eyes this morning, I'd fucked Gypsi ten times. That wasn't counting the two porn-worthy, Hall of Fame blow jobs she had given me. My dick had never been used so much in such a short time. The last thing I wanted to do was leave her and go down to the fucking cellars.

Whoever this bastard was, we needed to get it handled. Gypsi had been getting in a bubble bath when I left. If I had stayed, we'd have fucked again. I could not sate that woman. She was so damn hungry for my cock that it was crazy. And the times she'd had me choke her, I had come even harder. I had seen fucking stars. Which meant I was some kind of twisted. I was a Hughes, so that made sense.

When I got back, the only way she was getting off was with my tongue. She had to be sore, and I needed to take care of her. Besides, I wanted to taste her again. I liked having her sweetness on my tongue.

"Jesus, Trev, get that look off your face," Levi said as I walked down the concrete stairs to the underground of our property.

"What look?"

"The *I've just had the best fuck of my life* look," he replied.

I smirked. "Fuck is singular," I replied. "That's not the look I have."

He frowned a moment, then rolled his eyes when he realized what I was saying. "Come on, lover boy," he snapped, turning down one of the tunnels that led back to the different rooms.

I heard Gage's voice before we got there. He was shouting.

"This guy showed up during the daylight?" I asked, surprised he'd had the balls.

"Yep. Dumb fucker."

"Six get him?"

"No, Blaise did."

"He got past Six?"

"Yeah, don't mention it though. Six is in deep shit with Blaise. Mattia is at main security now."

We stepped into the room, and the guy—whose wrists were locked together, hanging from the ceiling—looked to be about my age. Several tattoos. Not what I'd been expecting.

"You can talk, or I'll put a bullet in your other knee," Blaise drawled as he casually leaned against the wall, watching the man. He shifted his eyes to me. "Look who could stop fucking long enough to show up."

"Shut up," I snarled.

Blaise turned to look at the guy again, but the guy was glaring at me and solely at me.

"Looks like our friend here doesn't like you, little brother," Blaise said, pushing off from the wall and walking over to study him closer.

He tilted his head and got close to the guy, who finally tore his angry glare from me to look at Blaise.

"What did Trev do to you?" he taunted him. "He never makes anyone mad. That's my job. I'm the fucking bully."

The guy's eyes swung back to me, and Blaise slapped the shit out of him. "I said, look at me, motherfucker."

Levi glanced over at me with a questioning look. I shrugged. I'd never seen the guy in my life.

Blaise turned to look back at me too. His eyes narrowed as the wheels in his head were turning. He'd have this figured out long before Dad got back. He wouldn't let it rest until he did.

"Only thing Trev's ever done to piss someone off is fuck their bitch," Gage said with his cigarette in his mouth while he sat on a stool across the room, dangling his Glock between his legs.

"He fuck your bitch?" Levi asked the guy.

The guy's teeth were clenched so tightly that he was going to break one.

"Couldn't have been recent," Blaise said, circling the guy as he hung there. "Trev's too busy fucking the hell out of Gypsi Parker. Can't keep his goddamn dick out of her."

The guy growled and jerked at the chains holding him. His glare, full of hate, was leveled on me.

Blaise froze, and I knew he was looking at me. I held the guy's gaze as a sick knot formed in my stomach. A tightness in my chest made it hard to breathe.

"I think he might know who Trev's new fuck buddy is," Gage drawled.

I turned to Gage. "Don't fucking call her that," I warned.

He shrugged, then nodded his head to the guy hanging. I looked back at him, and the guy was seething. This was about Gypsi.

"Did you get his bike?" I asked.

"Yep," Levi replied. "Florida license plate."

"Get his wallet? Identification?" I asked.

"Timothy Arnold Hall, twenty-two years old, one hundred seventy pounds, 45 Normand Street, Doral, Florida. Bike is registered to Henry Ray Hall, same address. Background check is being run," Levi informed me.

My hands fisted at my sides as I walked closer to him. "Who the fuck are you?" I demanded.

This guy had no claim on Gypsi. Doral was near Miami. Had she met him when she lived there?

"She'll leave you," he snarled at me. "She'll get you addicted to her pussy, and then she'll walk the fuck away!"

My fist slammed into his face before I realized what I was even doing. Blood poured from his nose as he grunted. Needing to see more blood, I did it again and again. A hand wrapped around my arm, pulling me back.

"Easy there, little brother. Let's not kill him yet. We need answers."

He shook his head as blood covered the bottom part of his face and ran down his neck.

"You came on my property. Where my family is. That's fucking ballsy or just stupid. Do you know who I am?" Blaise asked him.

"I don't fucking care," he said, then spit blood from his mouth.

"Is that a yes or no?" Gage called out. "I'm just trying to figure out if you're ballsy or a dumbass."

The guy's eyes swung back to me. "I don't know, and I don't care."

"Dumbass," Gage muttered.

Blaise shook his head and chuckled. "You never go on someone's property without doing your research."

"Gypsi came here. I followed her."

Blaise scowled at him. "Yeah, I gathered that."

"I want to know about the fucking toy rings he's got a bag full of," Levi said.

My blood ran cold as I turned to look at Levi. "What toy rings?" I asked him.

"These," Gage said, then tossed me a bag.

Jerking it open, I looked down at the rings in the bag. They were all the same. Replicas of the one I'd found in Gypsi's things when I went to move them from her room to mine. I saw it and picked it up, thinking it was real. The stone was huge, and I had a moment of jealousy. Thinking someone had given it to her. I'd smiled when I realized it was plastic and dropped it back into her bag.

I lifted my eyes to find the guy glaring at me with a smirk on his blood-covered face.

"She's got one, doesn't she? She kept it."

I dropped the bag to the ground and started toward him, rage pounding in my chest.

Blaise stood in front of me, stopping me. "Not yet."

"Who the fuck are you to Gypsi?" I yelled.

His blood-coated lips curled into a smile. "The man who took her virginity. The man she loves. I'm not someone she fucked because she needed it. Yeah, I know how she is. She can't get enough. She's got all kinds of fucked up kinks. She's a damn sex addict, the freak. She would take it from whoever would give it to her, but I kept her in check. I reminded her who she belonged to. I fucked her first. I own that pussy."

Someone moved behind me and grabbed my arms while Blaise planted his hand against my chest.

156

I fought against them as an angry roar ripped from my chest. "SHUT UP!"

"Easy," Blaise said.

"You can have my Glock when we're done," Gage said near my ear. He was the one holding me back.

Blaise turned his head to look at the guy. "It seems you've walked into a situation you won't be walking out of. In your pointless quest to chase a woman who had left you, you managed to follow her onto our property. No one walks onto our property without permission and lives."

He spit more blood. "I have family. They'll call the cops. Men you don't want to fuck with will come looking for me."

Blaise's evil chuckle filled the room. "That's the beauty of doing your research." He held out his hands. "Look around. Does this look like anything other than what we are using it for right now? Do you think you're the first person we've brought down here and questioned? As for men I don't want to fuck with, those men don't want to fuck with me."

The guy glared at him, saying nothing.

"We have the cops in our back pocket, along with the senator and the governor—in several different states. Even those cops back in Miami. Yeah, them too."

"What, are you the fucking Mafia?" he asked, spitting more blood.

"Ding, ding, ding," Levi replied.

Blaise just kept his trademark evil smile on his face. "I don't give a fuck who looks for you. They won't ever know."

"You're lying," he said, sounding less confident.

Gage's laugh was twisted.

"Let her see me. She loves me. She doesn't want me dead," he said.

I pulled against Gage's hold on me. Why the fuck it made me so furious to hear him claim Gypsi loved him I didn't want

157

to delve into, but it did. Jealousy, fury, and possessiveness were crashing together inside me, spiraling out of control. I didn't like knowing he'd touched her. Been inside her. That he'd taken her virginity. I wanted to fucking tear his limbs from his body.

Blaise looked back at me. "Gage, you take first shift. Levi, you take the next. Kye can come when he's done with the shit he's handling now. Trev, you go talk to Gypsi. Find out who this son of a bitch is to her, and I want to know about Miami. All of it."

He turned to Gage. "Walk him out first. I don't trust him loose in here. He'll break the idiot's neck. Put a wire on him."

Gage nudged me toward the exit as he held on to my arms. "You won't get shit out of her, walking in with your bruised fist covered in blood."

"I'll wash it."

"Don't scare her either. You gotta remain calm. You fucked her. You knew someone else had been their first. Take a deep breath. You're making this personal. You can't do that."

I glared back at him. "You burned down a fucking frat house once over a girl."

He grinned. "That wasn't a girl. That was my woman. There's a difference."

"Huck killed the people who hurt Trinity," I told him.

"And you'll get to kill that fucker down there. But first, we need answers. You can get them from her faster than that fucking background check. Sounds like he might be involved in a gang. If that's the case, the background check could be messed with. Just like Fawn's and Gypsi's were."

"How were Fawn and Gypsi's messed with?" I asked feeling a tightness in my chest. I needed Gypsi to be exactly who I thought she was. Why wasn't Dad concerned about this? Why hadn't I known?

"Not much," Gage replied. "Levi is a fucking pro at digging shit up on people. Most wouldn't have caught it. But there was a short time where their location isn't accurate. They weren't living in the camper but their address is unknown."

I wanted answers, but I was also fucking terrified of what she might tell me. He had seemed real damn sure she wouldn't want him dead. If she loved him, then I would question everything I thought I knew about her.

Chapter
TWENTY

GYPSI

When my eyes opened, I sat up, surprised I'd fallen asleep. I hadn't meant to, but after my bath, the bed had looked so comfortable. Rubbing my face with both hands, I started to get up when my eyes focused, and I saw Trev sitting in a chair across the room, looking at me. The serious expression on his face was unexpected. He didn't look like the same guy who had left me a couple of hours ago. Something was wrong.

"Is my mom okay?" I asked, feeling a panic rise up in my chest.

"Yes," he replied in a flat tone I had never heard him use.

"Then, what's wrong?" Because something clearly was.

"That's a loaded question," he replied. "Let's start with this."

He tossed something onto the bed, and I looked down. I stared down at the plastic ring that haunted me. Why did he have that? Oh God, did Tyde get in this house?

"Where did you get this?" I asked as my heart hammered against my chest.

"Why? Does it mean something?"

My eyes burned with tears as fear clawed at me. I shouldn't have stayed here. The moment he had left the ring in Kentucky, I should have fled. Mom would have been safe, and I'd have called her later. She could have gotten over me leaving after a while.

"I have to go," I said, moving to get off the bed.

Trev was up and across the room before my feet touched the ground. His hand gripped my shoulder, pushing me back down.

"You're not going anywhere, Gypsi. Not until you talk."

I swallowed hard. He was hurting my shoulder, but I deserved it. I'd brought danger here.

"I'm sorry. I shouldn't have stayed. I should have left. Did he get into the house?" I asked.

Trev looked down at me like I was crazy. "In this house? Fuck no. Not even the FBI could get into this house unless invited."

He was naive if he thought that was true. He didn't know Tyde or people like him.

"But you had a ring. Where did he leave it?"

"Who?" Trev asked me.

There was no use in not telling him now. He needed to know. Tyde had been on this property. In this house. The house he thought was so secure. He deserved a name and information.

"Tyde Hall," I said. "He's dangerous. If he left that ring anywhere on this property or in this house, then your security isn't strong enough. Let me go, and he won't come back. But give me time to get out of town before you tell my mom.

She'll leave with me, and I don't want her to. She's happy with Garrett."

"Who is Tyde Hall?"

I closed my eyes. There was so much to tell. I went with the brief synopsis. "The biggest mistake of my life."

His grip on my shoulder eased, and he dropped his hand. "Explain the ring."

I opened my eyes, looking down at it beside me on the bed. He wanted the full story. Of course he did. A man had gotten onto his property. Because of me.

"He got one that looked exactly like that out of a gumball machine once and jokingly asked me to marry him. I wore it to be funny. That was before ..." I stopped. I had to get this out. Let him understand before I left. He deserved that much. He was my friend, and I'd put him in danger's way. "Before things went bad. And they went bad fast. When I left, I tossed the ring in a lake. Mom and I were fine here in Ocala for three weeks. Then ... then ... I came back to my suite in Kentucky the night of the celebration party, and there was one on the table. I searched the suite, but there was no sign of him."

"He got this into your suite?" Trev's voice sounded as if he was barely controlling his anger.

I nodded, glancing up at him, then quickly away. I hated seeing him look at me that way. It hurt inside my chest.

"It's why I left that morning. I was afraid to stay any longer. Then, another ring showed up in our camper. It was the first night we came to stay here. I didn't want Mom to see it in the trash, so I tossed it in my bag."

"Was that the last of the rings?" he asked.

I shook my head. "No. Work. It's why I quit. I went on a restroom break, and when I returned, there was one on the counter."

I stood up, and he stepped back, letting me stand this time.

Forcing myself to meet his gaze, I swallowed hard. "He's not mentally stable. I think he's a psycho. He will follow me wherever I go. It's not safe, but it's my problem. Mom is happy here. I want her to be happy. She's sacrificed for me since she was seventeen. It's time she has a life of her own. I can't tell her about this. She'll pack up, and we will be gone. She won't listen to reason. I can go now. While she's in Paris."

"Back to him?"

"No! Did you miss the part where he is a psycho?"

"Is he why you left Miami?"

I nodded.

"Do you love him?"

"No. In the beginning, I thought I did, but it was a crush. If I did feel something, he destroyed it."

"What did he do to you?"

I dropped my gaze to the floor. Seeing the disgusted anger in Trev's normally friendly face was more than I could deal with. "Hurt me."

"How did he hurt you?"

"It started with slapping. Then twisting my arm until it felt like it was going to break. Then hitting. Then shoving me down and kicking."

Trev moved, and I looked up as he planted his fist into the wall beside him.

"Trev?"

He swung his gaze back to me. "Continue."

I looked at the hole in the wall, then back at him. "I, uh, left then. I told Mom, and we left," I whispered. "Is your hand okay?"

"When you lived in Miami, did you live in your camper?"

I nodded, then stopped. "No, not the entire time."

"Where did you live?"

I thought back to the place and wished I had never gone there with Mom. She'd been dating another bad boy on a motorcycle. Granted, he was gorgeous, but he was younger than her. He asked her to move in, and she wanted to. It was a new experience for her. An adventure. So, I went with her. I'd met Tyde there.

"It was a big building with a lot of rooms, kind of like apartments, but everyone knew each other. It was a club. They shared the same kitchen, and there were women who cooked for everyone. Mom was dating a guy who lived there, and we moved in for a while. I got my own room, and I met Tyde there. He pursued me hard. I missed all his red flags."

"Did they all ride motorcycles?"

I nodded. "Yeah, they had, like, some motorcycle club. It was kinda dumb, but when I mentioned it, Tyde got pissed. I never brought it up again. It felt like they were pretending to be on the *Sons of Anarchy*. Even doing the bad things. In the end, I found drugs in Tyde's room, and, well, some of the women who came in there to stay were porn actresses. I think maybe the club had something to do with that too. Tyde had a knife and gun he kept on him most of the time."

"Who did your mom date there?" he asked.

"Micah. But he was a nice guy. Mom found out he was a man-whore though, so that ended. We moved back to the camper, but I continued seeing Tyde."

Trev narrowed his eyes as he looked at me. "Do you remember any of the other names of the men who lived there?"

"Uh, yeah, but they were all nice. I promise. Tyde was the screwed-up one."

"Names," he repeated.

"Tex, Brick, and then there was the president or whatever, but he didn't stay there much. I only saw him twice."

"Name."

164

"Liam ... Walsh I think was his last name."

Trev turned and walked out of the room. I stood there, waiting to see what he was doing when I heard him open the door and close it behind him. He had left.

I let the tears slowly roll down my face as I walked to my bag and began to pack things up. It was time I left. He knew everything now, and he would know who to watch for. Mom would be safe.

Chapter TWENTY-ONE

TREV

Blaise was standing with his arms crossed over his chest at the bottom of the stairs when I walked down them.

"Did you get it all?" I asked him, taking the wire off me and handing it to him.

"Yes," he bit out.

"What's your next move? Call Dad or Liam?"

Blaise ran a hand through his hair in frustration. "I'm going to call Liam. It's his man."

"Just so we are clear, I don't give a fuck that Liam is your father-in-law and that Tyde is one of his men. I'm killing the son of a bitch. Slowly. I'm going to watch him suffer." I was seething. The need to see the bastard's blood on my hands was burning inside me.

"Because you love her or because you care about her?" he asked me.

"I don't love her. She's my friend. I care about her. If any of my female friends had gone through this, I'd want to kill the bastard who did it. She's going to be our stepsister soon. She'll be more family than fucking Liam is."

He nodded. "Good. Don't fall in love with her."

"Not planning on it."

"You put your fist through the damn wall," he said.

"Yeah."

"That's not like you."

"It is now," I replied.

Blaise smirked. "You might have more Hughes in you than I thought."

I shot him a scowl. They all thought I was some pampered brat. Even my own damn brother.

"She's gonna try to run or leave," I told him.

"You have to tell her. She needs to understand that leaving only gives us more to do. It doesn't help us. Fawn will be finding out soon anyway."

This was going to fuck up everything. She might like *The Godfather*, but that was a damn movie. This was real life. One where I was about to kill the son of a bitch who had taken her virginity.

"Fine," I replied.

"Do it soon. I've got to go call Liam. Stay away from down there until I'm with you," Blaise told me.

"Hurry," I growled.

"You fucking hurry," he replied. "I don't want to have to go chase her ass down."

He turned and headed out the front door. I couldn't go back up there and see Gypsi right now. Not while I was this wound up. When she had said she didn't love him, I'd almost shoved her against the wall and fucked her. It was a good thing Blaise had put a damn wire on me.

My hands fisted at my sides as I thought about that motherfucker hurting her and stalking her. I had known she was scared of something. I'd felt it more than once and let it go. He had gotten into her suite. How the fuck had he done that? I needed a drink before I cracked. She did not need me trying to fuck her brains out while I was like this, and it was either that or drink.

I started for the library, but my gaze caught movement out of the corner of my eye, and I looked up. Gypsi was coming down the stairs with her bag. She'd been crying. Her eyes were red. Fucking hell.

"Where are you going?" I asked her.

"Leaving. I'm not staying here. I should have left already," she said to me.

"Go put your bag back in the room. You're not leaving," I said, pointing upstairs. I didn't need to deal with this right now.

"He's dangerous. My being here puts everyone in danger," she argued, continuing down the stairs.

"No one is in danger. You're not leaving this house."

"YES, I am! He will come for me. He's done it before; he got into my hotel suite—"

"NO! He won't! Why don't you trust me?! JESUS!" I shouted, walking up to her and jerking the bag out of her hand.

"Trust you? I do trust you."

"NO, you fucking don't. I am telling you that no one is in danger from that son of a bitch, and you won't listen to me."

She threw her hands up. "Because you don't know him!"

"I know that he won't set eyes on you again."

She shook her head. "He will follow me. He isn't letting this go. He has some sick fascination with owning me."

I knew all about that sick fascination. "I won't let him touch you."

"How are you going to stop him? Trev, you don't know that side of life. You live in a big house. Your life is a fairy tale. There are dangerous people out there."

I laughed. I couldn't stop myself. I fucking laughed. "No, Lollipop, you don't know that side of life. What I know, you can't even begin to imagine."

"You think so? You play video games, have topless pool parties, and get to ride horses all day."

I glared at her. "That's what you think of me? That I'm some rich, spoiled kid who hasn't grown up?"

She stood there, staring at me. "I thought that at first. I know there is more to you now."

"Like a big dick?" I asked sarcastically.

"Yes, but I wasn't referring to your cock size. I meant that you're smart, funny, you work for your dad but show up when you're told to. You're thoughtful, and you listen when people talk. You go buy peanut butter and chocolate snacks because you found out that it's my favorite."

I wanted to tell her that I'd broken the fucker's nose. That I would be slicing him slowly to pieces later. That I wasn't some fucking kid. I wanted her to know I was someone that other men were scared of. My name meant something. I wanted her to see me as a man.

But I couldn't tell her any of those things.

"Go put your stuff up. You're not leaving."

She sighed, her shoulders dropping. "I can't stay here forever."

"I'm not asking for forever. I'm telling you, for now, you're staying."

"Fine," she replied and went to pick up her bag from where I'd dropped it. "Do you want me in your room, or should I go back to the white-and-gold room?"

"My room, Lollipop."

She headed back up the stairs, and I watched her go. I knew there was more shit I didn't know. She'd given me a brief recap. She'd been mistreated by the man who had taken her virginity. He'd pay for it. Until he did, I was going to be on edge.

I went to get my drink and resigned myself to the fact that I was going to have to tell her who I was, who we were. It was time she understood. Blaise was right; if I didn't tell her, she was going to run, thinking it was keeping us safe.

Chapter
TWENTY-TWO

GYPSI

MOM: ARE YOU OKAY?

I read the text, wondering how she always knew when something was wrong. I hoped Trev hadn't said anything to Garrett about Tyde. If Mom found out, she'd demand to come back. I wanted Paris to be good for her.

YES, I'M FINE. GOING TO SIT BY THE POOL TO READ A BOOK.

That wasn't a lie. I had downloaded a book onto my phone, and I was going out by the pool to read it. Something to get my mind off everything. Sitting up here and staring at the wall wasn't helping me. Trev hadn't come back, and it had been over an hour.

MOM: I'M SO GLAD YOU'RE DOING SOMETHING RELAXING. YOU NEVER DO THAT ANYMORE.

I didn't respond to that. Instead, I opened the veranda door and walked outside. Trev was nowhere to be seen, and that was probably a good thing.

MOM: WE WENT TO THE LOUVRE TODAY! I'LL SEND

PICS.

I waited until I took off my cover-up and was settled on a lounger before looking at the pictures. Mom looked like she was glowing in them; she was so happy. She was on her biggest adventure yet.

The door opened, and I lifted my gaze to see Trev walking out with a glass in his hand. It looked like he was drinking whiskey at three in the afternoon. He hadn't meant to join me either. I could tell by his expression when he realized I was out here.

I wasn't sure what to say to him. I wanted to apologize again, but that wasn't enough.

He walked over and sat in the lounger connected to mine, then leaned back, crossing his legs at the ankles before turning his head to look at me. "It's my turn to talk," he said.

"Okay."

"You like the Corleone family," he said.

A small laugh escaped me. "Yeah." Why was he talking about *The Godfather* again?

"Try to keep that in mind," he told me, then looked straight ahead instead of at me.

I watched him take a drink of his whiskey.

His brow was drawn together in a frown. "We aren't just wealthy racehorse breeders."

"I figured your dad owned a lot of things. I didn't think racehorses could afford this lifestyle," I said.

He smirked. "No, it doesn't. And, yes, Dad owns a hotel chain, a hospital, a casino in Vegas, banks, a lot of fucking stocks, and he's the boss of the Southern Mafia." He turned his head back to me.

For a moment, I was expecting him to laugh and say he was joking. The serious expression, however, didn't go away. He was watching me. Waiting on me to say something.

"You're serious," I finally managed to say.

"Very."

I stared out at the pool. My mind reeling over the fact that there was a Southern Mafia to begin with and that my mother was dating the boss. She didn't know. She couldn't. Or did she? Was this another of her adventures?

"In real life, what does that mean?" I asked him.

"Our family started it decades ago. Over the years, it's meant just about everything you are currently thinking. Giving you details, however, isn't something I can do."

I looked at him. "Because you don't know?"

He grinned, but it didn't meet his eyes. "I know."

But he couldn't tell me. His response was extremely vague.

"But you aren't …" I paused, unsure of how to say this. "You don't go and … kill people."

He looked down at his drink. "Some people need to be killed."

I swallowed hard. "Who does the killing?"

He shrugged. "Depends."

"I mean, is it Blaise? Garrett?"

"Whoever needs to."

"You?"

He took another drink, then looked at me. "Whoever needs to," he repeated.

Oh God. He couldn't be serious.

"My mom—"

"Will know before she returns," he said.

So, she hadn't known when she left. I tried to imagine how she would react to this. Mom liked new things. She was a thrill seeker. I had a feeling she was going to find this a thrill.

"Dad is going to propose to Fawn. If she says yes, then you are under our protection. You can't leave and just travel around. You won't be safe. We have enemies and people who would use you to get to Dad. To us. You leave here, and it becomes a problem for us."

I shook my head. That was crazy.

"I'm supposed to live here?" I asked.

He nodded. "You would get to be with your mom."

"Garrett can't tell me where to live."

"Do you like living in a camper? Do you like not having somewhere to call home? Is that really what you want to do? This isn't a bad life." He sounded frustrated.

"The camper is all we had, but we were together. I didn't mind it. I had my mom. That's all that mattered. But I just can't move in here and live off my mom's new husband."

"Then, you can get a job. Dad will give you one. But when he marries your mother, he takes on responsibility for her and her family. That's the way he sees it. You become his responsibility."

I had to stand up. Move. Something. I felt restless. This was overwhelming. How had I gone from worrying about Tyde to now being owned by the Mafia? I was not my mother. I did not like twists and turns.

Pacing back and forth, I tried to think through every aspect of what all this meant. There was still the chance my mom would say no. But seeing the look on her face in the photos, I doubted it. Even if her future husband was a Mafia boss. That was just weird to even think.

"Lollipop, if you don't want fucked, you're gonna have to stop walking back and forth in front of me in that damn bikini."

I stopped and looked at Trev. His eyes were on my body. Problem was, I did want fucked. By him. However, this was not a good time.

"What about Tyde? He's not going to stop trying to get to me."

Trev's eyes snapped up to mine. There was a frightening gleam in them that took me aback. "Yes, he will."

"No, he won't."

"No, Lollipop, he won't. He got caught the last attempt he made to get on this property."

I stared at him, waiting for more, afraid to ask what that meant. He continued to watch me but said nothing. I felt like this was a test, and I didn't like it.

"Does that mean he's … dead?" I asked softly, unsure of how to handle that if he was. I didn't harbor feelings for him, but I didn't want him to die. Just go away.

"Not yet."

Not yet?

"What's that mean?"

Trev stood up, setting his glass on the table beside him. "It means he's caught. Being held until we have all the information from him we need."

Trev took a step toward me.

"Then, he gets … killed?"

"Are you going to beg me for his life, Lollipop? Because if you do, he'll die a much more brutal death. I'm wound up real damn tight right now after hearing him talk about fucking you."

"You talked to him?" I asked, horrified.

What had Tyde said about us? I knew the things he used to call me and accuse me of. The thought that he'd said all that to Trev made me sick.

"Unfortunately," he said, closing the distance between us.

I stared at his chest, afraid to look up and meet his eyes. I didn't want to see anything in them that would hurt.

"I'm not what he says I am. I only ever had sex with him."

"And me." Trev's voice lowered.

His hand touched my waist, and I shivered.

175

"And you."

"Take off the bottoms."

I tilted my head back to look up at him. All I saw in his eyes now was lust.

"I need to get inside you. Get the bottoms off, or I'm tearing them off."

I liked the idea of him tearing them off, but I only had two swimsuits. I quickly took them off, then looked back up at him.

He pointed to the lounger. "Get on your hands and knees."

Having sex right now wasn't what we needed to be doing. I should be asking more questions. Figuring things out. But the demanding side of Trev was making everything else seem unimportant. I walked over and climbed onto the lounger, then looked back at him while he unzipped his shorts and shoved them down with his briefs. My gaze dropped to his full, erect length, and I licked my lips, thinking about how much I loved it in my mouth.

"You can suck it later. Right now, I need to remind this pussy who it belongs to."

My eyes swung back up to his. We both knew my pussy didn't belong to him. At least not long-term. Maybe while this lasted, it did. It made me hot when he said it, so I didn't argue.

His hand came down on my ass hard, and I cried out.

"Do you like to be spanked, Lollipop?"

"Yes," I panted. "More."

He did it again.

"Harder, Trev. Spank me harder," I begged.

"You want me to punish you?" he asked as his palm hit my now-tender butt. "For letting that bastard have this pussy. He didn't fucking deserve it." He was spanking me harder now. I could hear his heavy breathing. "Thinking about him getting

176

to touch you. Fuck you. Makes me so goddamn furious that I want to make him suffer."

Trev's hands grabbed my hips, and he slammed into me with one hard thrust. "FUCK, this pussy is soaking wet. Did spanking do this to you?"

"Yes, and your words," I said, looking at him over my shoulder.

He slid out slowly, then pressed back inside of me, hitting that magical place that I loved. "You got wet because I'm ready to fucking kill a man for touching you?"

Not the kill part, that concerned me, but hearing him talk like that while inside of me was a turn-on. I moaned loudly. What was wrong with me?

He laughed and grabbed my hair in his fist, pulling my head back. "Did he come in this pussy?" His voice was angry.

Why was he asking me that? I didn't want to talk about that with him.

"DID HE COME IN MY PUSSY?!" he roared.

"Yes," I cried.

Trev began thrusting into me hard and fast. "I'm going to fill this cunt up with so much of my cum that you forget anyone else's was ever there."

"Yes! Please!" I begged. "I just want your cum. All of it. I want to feel it filling me up. Over and over again."

"Keep talking with that dirty little mouth," he groaned.

"His dick didn't stretch me like yours. It didn't hit that place deep inside me that feels incredible. I love how your big dick barely fits inside of me. I can feel it pulse." I stopped talking as my climax hit me and cried out, my body shaking with each tremor.

Trev's body spasmed behind me, and then he locked up just before his cock jerked inside me. "FUUUCK! Take it!" he growled.

"Yes. It feels so good. I want to have it leaking in my panties the rest of the day. Give it all to me."

I pressed back onto him, and his fingers dug into my skin.

"Goddamn," he muttered as his dick continued to throb inside of me. Trev ran his hand over my butt gently. "I think I left marks."

"Good."

When his eyes met mine, he grinned. My favorite kind. The Trev grin that had drawn me in the first time I saw him.

"I should have left my teeth marks on it. I owe you several bite marks."

I wiggled my bottom at him while he was still buried inside of me.

His eyes darkened. "I've got to go check on things. Don't start that."

I bit down on my bottom lip, and he pulled out of me with a groan.

"Lie on your back and open your legs. I want to see my cum leaking out of your pussy before I go. That bastard will start talking again, and I need this image in my head to keep me calm."

I turned over, opening my legs for him, then did a little squeeze with my vaginal walls to make the cum seep out. Trev watched as he pulled his pants back up. I slipped a finger down to play with it.

"Jesus Christ," he whispered, then said, "Rub it around."

I took some and coated my lips and clit, then lifted my fingers to my mouth and sucked.

His eyes flared. "Damn, you should come with a warning label."

I laughed, then closed my legs and sat up. If I kept doing this, I would need to get off again.

178

Trev tossed me my bottoms. "Get covered up. I don't want anyone seeing you like that."

His phone started ringing, and his expression immediately changed. "I've got to go. I'll be back later."

Was he going to see Tyde? I wanted to ask, but I was afraid of the answer.

"Okay."

Chapter
TWENTY-THREE

TREV

Stepping down into the underground, I was calmer than when I had left. Gypsi had helped that more than the whiskey had. Gage's evil laugh rang through the tunnel. He loved this shit. There was no way Shiloh, his girlfriend, knew how fucked up he was. She was so damn nice and normal.

I entered the room Blaise was keeping the bastard in and saw his blood had dried on his face. His pallor wasn't good. Probably from all the blood loss. I didn't give a fuck.

Blaise turned to me. "Sax is on his way. This will be good training for him. He needs to see more of this side. We'll wait on him."

Sax was not ready for this, but that wasn't my decision to make. Levi and Gage were both here already. Kye must still be holding Six in a cell for Blaise.

"What did Liam say?" I asked him.

"What about Liam?" Tyde asked with a snarl.

Blaise glanced at him, then back at me. "He doesn't know about the Liam connection."

"Liam will come for me." He sounded so sure that I wanted to laugh.

Blaise ignored him. "He said to do what we needed to. Apparently, Timothy here has been an issue. Liam wasn't happy about what happened to Gypsi."

"What the fuck did that bitch say?"

I stalked past my brother, and this time, he didn't stop me.

I was almost in Tyde's face when Gage stepped up to me, holding out a knife. "This is more fun."

I looked down at it, then snatched it from him and held it to Tyde's neck. "You don't get to talk about her."

"Don't slice his throat just yet. That takes away the fun of it," Gage drawled.

"We are waiting on Sax," Blaise reminded me.

The bastard who had touched Gypsi glared back at me. The hatred in his eyes showed no fear. He didn't care that he was going to die, or he truly thought Liam would save him. I wanted him to know who we were. Who Gypsi would be. Where she belonged now. But I held my tongue until Sax arrived. I didn't trust myself not to react now that I had a weapon in my hand.

"You need some guidance," Gage said beside me. "Watch and learn."

I looked at him as he stepped up to Tyde and got in his face.

"You know where Trev has been?" he asked, smiling. "He left here and went to Gypsi. Made sure to fuck her nice and hard. She was up in that big house, screaming his name."

Tyde yanked on the chains, growling, and then he spit in Gage's face. Gage's maniacal laugh even freaked me out. He

181

wiped it off his face, then reached down and grabbed the guy's balls and twisted while Tyde screamed.

"What part of *we are waiting on Sax* do you two not understand?" Blaise asked, clearly annoyed.

Gage grinned, stepping back and letting go. "Sorry, boss."

"Shit," Sax said as he stepped into the room.

His eyes were on Tyde, and I could see the horror there. I had known he wasn't ready for this. I had at least been exposed to it throughout my life. He hadn't. He didn't live with Garrett.

"Finally," Gage said, walking over to Sax and slapping him on the back. "Come on, Sax. Time for a lesson. Have a seat." He pointed at the stool. "You'll probably need it."

Sax walked over, glancing at me with the knife, then at Tyde. I felt sorry for him. He was too damn soft for this. He was already slightly pale, and I haven't even gotten started.

"This is Timothy. Also known as Tyde. He is a member of The Judgment. He was caught coming onto our property in an attempt to get to Gypsi. He had dated her when she lived in Miami. Thinks he has some claim on her because he took her virginity. During their relationship, he abused her verbally and physically. After she moved to Ocala, he began stalking her. Until he stalked her here.

"Since my father-in-law is the president of The Judgment, I called him out of respect, but Tyde here signed his death certificate the moment he came on my land. However, after verbally attacking Gypsi's character and pissing Trev the fuck off, he now gets a much more brutal death. There. You are caught up." Blaise finished his explanation to Sax but had been watching Tyde's face just to enjoy the moment he found out that Liam was Blaise's father-in-law.

"Trev," Blaise said, "he's yours."

Tyde was still fucking furious as he glared at me. As I looked at Sax's face and the horror in his eyes, it was harder to get my head back in a space to do this. I wasn't Gage. I couldn't just flip a switch. We stood there, staring at each other, while he already had one foot in the grave. I was worried about Sax seeing this.

"Can't let distractions fuck with your head," Blaise said behind me. He knew Sax being here to witness this was bothering me.

"You sure you took Gypsi's virginity? Didn't feel like much of a cock when I grabbed it. Doubt you could have broken a hymen with that worm," Gage said before lighting a cigarette.

"My fucking dick was big enough to make her scream. She craved it! Begged me to fuck her. I couldn't get her off my damn cock; she wanted it so bad. Crazy freak—"

I stabbed his thigh, and he stopped talking and groaned. I owed Gage one. That had been all I needed. Rage had come rushing back, taking over my thoughts as he spewed shit I did not want to hear.

"She's not a freak," I hissed in his face.

"She making you choke her yet?" he asked.

I took the blade and ran it from his chin up to his ear with one hard swipe. He winced and closed his eyes for a minute.

Leaning close to him, I whispered, "While I'm pumping her full of my cum."

He jerked again, but he was weaker. He barely swayed this time. I took the knife and gave him a matching mark on the other side of his face.

"She's leaking my cum right now," I told him, enjoying the way his eyes glared at me with fury.

"He's got a pierced nipple. I can see it through his shirt," Gage said to me.

Taking the blade, I sliced his shirt open, then cut off his nipple while he howled. Had Gypsi liked that? Licked it? Bit it? Jealousy thumped inside my chest. There was no other name for it.

"She loved that thing," he said in a low, strangled voice, as if he had known what I was thinking.

"Can't say I give a fuck," I replied, then sliced off his other nipple.

I reached for my shirt and jerked it off. I wanted him to see the bite marks on my chest. Know that I loved her fucking kinks. I laughed as his eyes flared with loathing.

"Those are just from last night and today," I said, smirking at him.

"You let her bite you." His voice was raspy now as he struggled to talk. "I've got her name tattooed on my back." Then, he sneered at me.

I walked around him and found Gypsi's name in the center of his back in a fancy script and a tiara hanging off the letter *G*. Scowling at it, I tightened my grip on the knife.

"She loved when I called her princess."

"She's not a princess. She's a fucking Lollipop," I growled, then began cutting her name off his body while he jerked, wailing and gasping for air.

Blood was all over my hand when I was finished. I stepped back as his head fell forward, as he was no longer able to hold it up. He was still breathing.

Gage clapped, and I looked over at him. He was grinning with the cigarette in his teeth.

"Fucking badass," he said. Then, his eyes took in the bite marks on my chest. "Damn, Trev. Gypsi has teeth."

"You let her bite you like that?" Levi asked, grinning at me. "I might need to teach you how to use a belt to whip that ass. She's a little firecracker, and firecrackers need taming."

"Trev is a damn freak. Y'all think I'm the psycho, and he's the one choking out his stepsister while fucking her and letting her bite the shit out of him," Gage drawled. "I think he's my hero."

Levi started laughing.

"She's not my stepsister," I pointed out.

"Yet," he shot back at me.

Blaise stepped forward, and I met his gaze.

"You gonna finish it? Or we gonna talk about your sex life?" he asked me.

"They started it," I said, then held out my hand for the gun.

"You can slit his throat," Blaise told me.

"I've got enough of his blood on me already," I said.

He pulled his Glock from its holster and handed it to me. "Then, do it."

The one person who had remained silent and I hadn't looked at was Sax. I couldn't do it yet. He'd just seen a side of me he hadn't known existed. I hadn't known it existed. Things would change now. For both of us. We weren't kids anymore. I'd just stepped off into a dark place I wasn't ever coming back from.

"How many times did she bite you?" Gage asked.

I shot him an annoyed glance, then turned to Timothy Arnold Hall and pulled the trigger.

Chapter
TWENTY-FOUR

GYPSI

I kept my eyes closed when I woke up. Trev's arm was around me, and his front was pressed to my back. He was warm, hard, smelled incredible. The weight of his arm over me gave me fluttery feelings in my stomach. I snuggled closer to him, and his arm tightened its hold on me. Last night, we had watched a movie in his theater after heating up the enchiladas that Ms. Jimmie had left for our dinner.

The Godfather Part II had taken on a whole new meaning for me. I'd gotten so absorbed in the movie that Trev tossed a kernel of popcorn at me. It had then turned into a popcorn food fight before we somehow ended up with Trev's mouth between my legs.

Warm breath tickled my neck, and I opened my eyes just as Trev placed a trail of kisses along the curve of my neck and shoulder. This sleeping together and the snuggling were new to me. I'd never done this kind of thing with Tyde. I liked this. A little too much. I had to be careful to not get attached to it.

Garrett and Mom would be coming home tomorrow. I had to talk to her and figure out what this all meant for me. Would I really stay here? Trev rubbed his stubbled jaw along my skin, and I realized I should be asking if I really wanted to leave. But this wasn't going to last.

"You feel so fucking good," Trev whispered as his hands moved down over my body. "I like waking up this way."

I was glad he couldn't see the goofy smile on my face. "Me too," I admitted.

He kissed my back as his fingertip made a circular caress around my belly button. "You live here, and we can just share a room."

I laughed.

"What? Siblings share rooms. This is a big bed," he said while still leaving kisses on my back.

"Siblings might share a room when they're little. But grown stepsiblings don't," I pointed out.

"We can start a new trend," he murmured.

"When we end this, that would become awkward. You'll want me to have my own room then." The thought of this ending made me feel sick to my stomach.

"I was thinking about that, and I don't see why we can't continue the *steps with benefits* idea. I mean, you'll live here. I'll live here. There isn't going to come a day I see you and don't want to fuck you. We can make it a permanent benefits setup."

I closed my eyes, wishing that it were as easy as all that. But right now, I was feeling things I'd never felt before. It was dangerous territory. We had no future together, and it was only a matter of time before my heart was wrapped up in all this. Trev was easy to like. I was starting to think he might be easier to love. Even if our parents weren't getting married, Trev didn't want a relationship. He was a player. At some point, he'd want to fuck other girls, and I was going to have to deal with it.

Trev rolled me onto my back and hovered over me. His hair was all mussed, and his eyes were hooded from just waking up. My heart beat faster in my chest, just looking up at him. Yep, I was in trouble.

"What's going on in that pretty head of yours, Lollipop?" he asked, shifting so that I could feel his erection on my hip.

"That as nice as that sounds, I don't think it will work," I told him.

He frowned and brushed a curl from my cheek. "You getting tired of me already?"

I laughed. He was so far off; it was funny. A grin tugged at his lips as he watched me.

"Come on, Lollipop. It'll work. We get along. You like me, right? We have fun together."

I nodded. "Yes to all those things. But sex can get tricky after a while."

His thumb ran along my bottom lip. "How's that?" he asked in a husky voice.

"Well, I can't promise you that when you have sex with someone else, I'll take it well. I will try not to get jealous, but I don't know yet. And long-term, that could be a real issue."

A slow grin spread across his lips. "Jealous, huh?"

I slapped his arm. "It's not funny. I am serious."

"I'm serious too," he assured me. "Do you seriously think I am going to have the energy to fuck someone else? You've been keeping my cock pretty damn busy."

I winced. "I'm sorry."

"Whoa. No sorrys. That wasn't a complaint. My cock is available and ready for you anytime you want it. I like that my Lollipop is a nympho."

I shoved against his chest to get him off me, but he laughed, grabbing my wrists and pinning them above my head. My breathing quickened. I liked being held down. His eyes studied me, then dropped to my chest.

"This turns you on," he said, looking back up at me.

I tried to scowl at him. "According to you, I'm in a constant state of arousal."

He smirked. "And I said, I like it. I fucking love it." His hand pushed between my thighs as he checked my entrance with his finger while he continued holding my wrists with his other hand. "So wet already."

"Mmm," was all I could say as he began to play with me.

"You sleep in my bed and give me this pussy like you've been doing, and, Lollipop, I won't need other girls."

I shook my head. "Don't say that. You think it now, but that'll change."

He shoved two fingers inside me. "I've had a lot of pussy," he said through his teeth. His fingers tightening on my wrists. "None have been this fucking good. I just want *you* on my cock."

He began to pump his fingers in and out of me. I couldn't argue when he was doing this. I'd talk about it later.

"Oh, that's good," I panted.

"I got something better," he said in a raspy voice as he moved over me.

I opened my legs and lifted my hips. Trev held himself over me with one hand planted beside my head. The other hand still had my wrists. I watched his mouth go slack and his eyes close as he sank inside me with a low, deep groan in his chest.

"Fuuuck, this is the way to wake up."

"I've never had morning sex," I breathed.

"Me neither."

A laugh escaped me. "Sure you haven't."

He stilled and looked down at me. "If I wake up with a girl in bed with me, I am in a hotel, and I get the fuck gone." He leaned down and brushed a kiss over my lips. "You're the first girl I've fucked on this bed, Lollipop. First one I've woken up to and wanted to fuck again."

He needed to stop this. His words were getting to me. I had to keep sex and my heart separate. I just wasn't sure I could anymore.

"Then, fuck me," I said, lifting my hips to meet his thrust.

He gave me a wicked grin. "Always."

The sun beat down as I walked with Trev to the stables. I had started asking questions about horses over breakfast, and when he found out I'd never been around them, he'd decided that was changing today. I wasn't sure I wanted to ride one just yet, but I didn't tell him that. I was afraid he'd turn it into his mission to convince me otherwise.

He had supplied me with riding boots and explained they were an old pair of his sister-in-law's, and then he'd put one of his cowboy hats on me. I at least looked like I knew what I was doing, going to see the horses. A blonde woman walked out of the stables just as we reached it. She was stunning with platinum-blonde hair, curves, big boobs, and tanned skin.

"Morning, Maddy," Trev said, and she turned to see us.

Maddy was the sister-in-law, and I would be lying if I said I wasn't instantly relieved. I was already doing it. Getting jealous of other girls around Trev. This was a problem, and we'd just gotten started.

She turned her gaze to me and beamed brightly, only making her more attractive. "You must be Gypsi," she said. "I've been wanting to meet you. I met your mom in Kentucky, but you were being kept busy with this one and Sax."

"It's nice to meet you," I replied.

"Maddy loved me first. Blaise stole her away and locked her in his dungeon. It was a tragic tale," Trev sighed.

Maddy rolled her eyes. "Sure it was. And I wanted to be locked in that dungeon."

Trev looked down at me. "Tell her who the better-looking brother is."

I glanced back at Maddy. "Uh ..." I didn't know how to answer this.

"Lollipop, you're letting me down here," he urged.

"Well, it's an awkward question."

His eyebrows shot up. "Are you telling me you think Blaise is better-looking than me?"

I shook my head. "No, but, well, this is his wife, and I just met her. We might all be family soon—"

"Gypsi—or is it Lollipop?" Maddy said, shooting a knowing look at Trev, then turning back to me, smiling. "I'm used to him. He likes to stir the pot. But I'm glad you think Trev is the better-looking one. I'm possessive like that." Then, she winked at me.

Trev let out a short laugh. "You're possessive. Have you met my brother?"

Maddy blushed.

"Blaise's obsession with his wife is borderline criminal," Trev whispered as if she couldn't hear him.

"And I like it," she informed him.

"Because she likes criminals," he continued to whisper.

She cocked an eyebrow at me. "Easy there. I hear you're giving Gage a run for his money."

Trev stilled beside me.

This time, Maddy laughed. "You're a Hughes, Trev. It's okay."

He nodded, but whatever she'd meant by that bothered him.

Maddy seemed to notice it, too, and she took a step toward him and patted his arm. "I've never seen your brother so proud," she said softly.

Trev seemed to relax a little, but he didn't say anything.

"I've got to go get Cree and take him to his first dentist appointment. Wish me luck," she said, then waved before walking out toward a luxury SUV.

"Let's go see the horses," Trev said to me, touching my back and leading me into the stables.

"Jeez," I breathed, stopping inside and looking around.

"What?"

"This isn't what I was expecting."

"Why?"

I turned around, looking everywhere in awe. "It's so nice; I'd live in here."

He chuckled. "The horses who live here are worth a lot of money."

"I can't imagine what their rent is," I teased.

"Come on, Lollipop. I'm starting you out easy. Sunshine isn't a thoroughbred. She's a quarter horse, and she's retired from her barrel-racing rodeo days."

"I thought all you had were racehorses."

He shook his head. "We've got others too. We breed racehorses, but on a ranch this size, you need other horses. Sunshine was bought for Maddy. She doesn't like riding the thoroughbreds."

We stopped at a stall, and Trev whistled. Sunshine turned around to see us, then walked over to Trev.

"She's gentle, but she has excellent bloodlines. You'll get a similar one."

"What?" I asked, looking up at him.

He nodded his head toward the horse. "A horse. You'll get one like Sunshine."

"Why am I getting a horse?"

"Because when your mom becomes a Hughes, you'll be one too. If you're a Hughes, you have a horse."

I shook my head and laughed. This family was crazy.

Chapter
TWENTY-FIVE

TREV

Gypsi walked into the bathroom that night when I was stepping out of the shower.

"Hey, Lollipop. Miss me?" I asked.

She held up her phone and showed me the picture on it.

I dried my hands and took it from her so I could see it better. It was a woman's hand with a diamond the size of a fucking apple on it. Lifting my gaze, I looked at Gypsi. "I'm gonna assume this is Fawn's hand. No other man but my father buys a diamond that damn big."

She nodded, her eyes a swirl of emotion. Did she think this meant anything was going to change? It wasn't.

"Looks like it's official. We get to share a room. I'm not complaining," I replied.

She looked back down at her phone. "It's just that talking about it was one thing… It happening is another," she said softly.

194

I wrapped the towel around my waist and took her phone from her, then put it on the counter. "No, it's the same thing. We are good. Nothing changes."

She blinked several times. "But does she know?"

"About the fact that she's engaged to a Mafia boss? Yeah. He would have told her before putting that ring on her finger."

Gypsi's surprised expression wasn't making me feel better about this.

"I just think ... well, I haven't had much time to think about it all. I mean, we've been ..." She paused.

"Fucking like rabbits," I finished.

She nodded. "Yeah, and it distracted me. But it's real now. Mom is going to marry Garrett. Then, I will be expected to live here too."

I grinned. "Yep. I'll make room in the closet."

She sighed, running her hand through her curls. "Stop joking. I need to think."

"I'm not joking, Lollipop. I mean, yeah, about the closet. You can use the one in the white-and-gold room. Girls have so much shit."

"Stop! You do that thing ... the *make me laugh* thing. It distracts me. Then, you smile, and that's even more distracting. And I forget that I am in this limbo, unsure of what happens next. You haven't even told me what you did with Tyde. You just promised me the stalking was done."

I'd fucking tortured him, then put a bullet in his head. Yep, wasn't telling her that.

"My smile distracts you?" I asked, liking that part of her rant.

She waved a hand at me. "See, you're doing it."

"Doing what?"

She scowled at me. "Being cute and sexy and distracting."

Fuck, I liked when she said stuff like that. Made me stop worrying that she was gonna end our benefits thing. She wanted it as bad as I did.

I let my gaze travel down her body. "I've got better ways to distract you."

"Trev, stop it. I mean it." She turned and stalked out of the bathroom. "And put on some clothes!"

"Hey, you're the one who came storming into the bathroom while I was showering."

"Just cover all that up. I have to think."

Grinning, I looked at my chest in the mirror and touched the fresh bite over my nipple. "Or I could spread your legs open and eat your pussy."

"UGH! Trev!"

Laughing, I went to the closet and grabbed some sweats and a T-shirt. No use in putting on briefs. They'd be in the way. I wasn't letting her think too hard. She might think her way out of living here. And waking up with her in my bed was not something I was willing to give up yet. She smelled so good, and I liked feeling her soft skin against my body. I was keeping that.

She had left my rooms when I came out of the closet. I walked out into the hallway to look for her. Glancing down at the bedroom she was supposed to be sleeping in, I saw the door was open. I doubted she was in there. I turned and went for the stairs.

I heard Sax's voice before I reached the top step. He was in the foyer, talking to Gypsi. The smile on his face as he looked at her made my stomach clench up. I didn't like it. He needed to take a few steps back. Then, she laughed.

Oh, fuck no. I was the one who made her laugh. I started down the stairs, trying not to glare at my best friend.

"Sax," I called out. "Didn't know you were here."

Gypsi turned to look at me, and I winked at her. She blushed, and, fuck, I wanted Sax to leave now.

"Yeah, thought I'd stop by and see you. Heard Garrett put a ring on it."

Was there a fucking challenge in his eyes?

I stepped up and slid my hand around Gypsi's stomach and left it there. "Yeah. Want to have a celebratory drink with us? Lollipop is moving in permanently now. I figure that calls for the good stuff."

"I didn't say I was moving in," she said, staring up at me.

"You are," I replied, not taking my eyes off Sax.

Sax cleared his throat. "So, the stepsibling thing isn't an issue?"

He was here because he thought we were gonna stop fucking. What the hell did he think would happen? She'd open her legs for him next?

"No," I replied.

He nodded. "That's good then. You up for a game of pool?" he asked me then, as if he hadn't just been trying to find out if Gypsi was available.

"Oh, can I play?" Gypsi asked.

Her head was tilted back as she looked up at me.

I grabbed her face and kissed it hard. "I might even let you beat me."

"I'll get the good whiskey. Lollipop, do you still have some bottles of that juice you like in the room?" Yes, I was laying it on thick. Sax needed to know how unavailable Gypsi was.

She nodded, completely clueless to what was going on here, and I was relieved. If she knew, she'd be mad at me.

"Go pick out whatever snacks you want to take up," I told Sax. "All I have up there are peanut butter and chocolate snacks." He needed to know just how thoroughly I took care of her. She didn't need him.

He nodded. "Anything you want me to grab you?" he asked, heading for the kitchen.

"Doritos," I called out.

I turned back to Gypsi with the tightness still in my chest. It wasn't easing. I didn't like Sax looking at her. Thinking about her. This wasn't my normal reaction with females. I might need to be concerned. This was friends who fucked. I didn't do anything but friends. Gypsi didn't know the me that sliced men up. She would hate me if she knew. My throat felt like it was closing. What the hell was that about?

"You okay?" she asked, stepping close to me and touching my arm.

"Yeah, I'm good," I told her, forcing a smile.

She frowned. "You sure? I'm the one who is supposed to be having a crisis. Not you."

That did make me smile.

Leaning down, I kissed her. "You're not having a crisis, but if you try to leave this house, then I'll have a fucking crisis."

"Trev," she sighed. "I wish you wouldn't say things like that to me."

"Why, Lollipop?"

She stepped back from me and looked so damn sad. I didn't like it. "Because we are stepsiblings with benefits."

I needed her to finish that thought.

"And?" I asked.

"And that is it. Don't confuse me."

I wanted to confuse her. I wanted her to need me. To not leave me. To not want another man. I just didn't want a relationship. It was fucking selfish, but I was addicted to her. My actions were no longer my fault.

Chapter
TWENTY-SIX

GYPSI

Trev and Saxon stood there and watched me make my way around the table, sinking four balls before I looked up at them. Trev looked amused.

"I'd let you win, but I'm a bad loser," I told him.

Saxon started laughing, and a grin broke out on Trev's face. It had been tense up here, and this was the first time they both looked relaxed. I was glad I could make them smile. Trev had gotten very possessive when Saxon showed up. My guess was, this was because of Kentucky. But we'd been around Saxon since then. Why was tonight different?

"It's okay, Lollipop. You keep bending over that table, and I'll happily let you win," he replied.

I rolled my eyes and went for the next shot. When it sank in, I glanced back up at him.

"Maybe we should let her finish, then sit out the next game so we get a turn," Saxon suggested.

"Probably the only way we are going to get to play."

I laughed and stepped back. "Fine, y'all can have a turn."

Trev stepped over to me, sliding his hand over my butt. "Who taught you to play like that?"

"My mom," I told him.

"We are getting her and Dad in here. I want to see her beat Dad's ass at pool."

"You two play. I'm hungry," I told him before walking over to the minibar and getting some chocolate peanut butter pretzels.

I picked up my phone and scanned through the pictures Mom had sent me again. Garrett had gone all out. It had all looked magical. The look in Mom's eyes made all the future heartache this would cause me seem worth it. I just struggled with the fact that she hadn't even told me about the *Mafia boss* thing before saying yes. Before, it had been her life, but she was marrying into the Mafia, which apparently included me too. Now, it was our lives.

"I wonder how big that diamond is," I muttered, looking at it.

"Thirty-seven carats," Trev replied.

My jaw dropped as I looked up at him. "Thirty-seven carats? How do you know?"

"Blaise told me. Last wife only got eighteen carats."

Holy crap. How much would that even cost? I wasn't sure I wanted to know.

"Damn," Saxon muttered.

"I didn't know they made diamonds that big," I said in amazement.

"You want to finish this game, Lollipop?" Trev asked me.

I shook my head. "No. It's okay. Y'all go ahead."

I finished studying the images, then went to sit on the sofa to watch them. They were talking now. Not the weird tension from before. I liked watching Trev like this. I liked it even more when his gaze found me. Who was I kidding? I liked all there was about Trev Hughes. I was beginning to understand my mom.

Trev won, and he held his cue stick in the air, grinning at me. He could be such a kid.

"Best two out of three?" Saxon asked.

Trev nodded reluctantly. "Yeah. Okay."

He set his cue down and walked over to pour some more whiskey in his glass. Just watching him walk was a turn-on. God, I needed to get a grip. Mom and Garrett would return tomorrow. There would be no more fucking all over the house. I had to stop acting like his girlfriend and make this stepsibling thing more believable. For my own self-preservation.

Standing up, I stretched, then picked up my juice and headed for the door.

"Where you going?" Trev asked.

"Letting y'all have male bonding without the stepsister in the way," I replied with a grin.

Trev frowned. "No, seriously."

"I think I'm going to the hot tub for a bit, and then I might get a shower. I don't know yet. I'm not running away. Play your game. Have fun." I turned and walked out the door before he could say anything more.

The *hot tub* idea sounded good now that I'd said it.

Deep thoughts were easier had in a massive hot tub with a waterfall view, I decided. Tomorrow, I was going to have a long talk with my mom. If she wanted me to live here, fine. But not forever. As soon as this thing with Trev ended, I was almost positive I'd have to leave. I wasn't sure I could handle it otherwise. But if I could get a job and save up my money, then I could get my own apartment or some place that Garrett deemed safe. He had to own something I could rent somewhere.

My mom was going to be the wife of a Mafia boss. It was something I had to learn to work around. Deciding to have sex with my future stepbrother wasn't the best idea I'd ever had, but I couldn't regret it either. Trev had taught me that there was more to fucking than … well, fucking.

The back door opened, and Trev came walking out alone in swim trunks. They hung on his narrow hips, and the V cut in his lower stomach was one of my favorite places to lick and bite. He had two marks there now to prove it.

"You left me," he said accusingly as he climbed into the hot tub.

"Where's Saxon?" I asked.

"Gone. I won two games," he informed me, sliding over until his body was pressed against mine.

"You didn't invite him out here?"

Trev slid his hand between my thighs and squeezed. "This is our last night before our parents come back. I wasn't sharing."

I laughed. "I'm not leaving tomorrow. As you pointed out, I live here now."

He groaned and pulled me into his lap. "And moving into my bedroom."

I shook my head. "No, I am not."

"I'm a good bed buddy," he said softly as he tugged my top down, then circled one of my nipples with his tongue.

"Yes," I breathed. "You are."

I watched him as he switched from one side to the other.

"Then, say you'll sleep in my bed at night."

"What if I like it too much and don't want to move out?"

Trev looked at me. "Then, you don't."

"You're gonna get bored with me. You say you won't, but that's because it's new."

He grabbed my waist and moved me over his erection. "We've fucked so many times that I've lost count. Does that feel bored to you?"

I shook my head.

His teeth bit down hard on my breast, right above my nipple. I grabbed his arms and cried out. Before I could catch my breath, he moved to the other breast and did the same thing.

"God, I love your tits," he growled.

"You've mentioned that before," I said breathlessly.

"Have I mentioned how much I love your pussy?" he asked, standing me up and sitting me on the edge of the hot tub.

I nodded.

He grabbed my bottoms and pulled them down my legs before tossing them to the side. "You start talking about ending this, and I have to get inside you." He shoved his trunks down and pushed my legs open, then ran the tip of his cock over my clit and down to the tight entrance.

I shifted closer, trying to get him to put it inside. His eyes lifted.

"What do you want?" he asked.

"Put it in me," I begged.

"Do you deserve it? You've been a bad girl today. You won't agree to sleeping in my bed, and I've asked real nice."

He continued rubbing me with it, teasing me with the sight of it so close.

"Trev, please."

"Please what?"

"Please fuck me!"

His hands grabbed my hips, and he pressed into me. I let my head fall back as he started rocking his hips against me.

"It's always so wet for me."

I lifted my head back up and looked at him. "Choke me."

One of his hands wrapped around my throat, gently squeezing.

"Call me names."

His eyes burned into me. I knew this made him hot just as much as it bothered him. I could see it in his eyes.

"You're my little cock slut, aren't you? Can't get enough of it. Dirty little whore wants to ride my dick all the time."

"Yes," I moaned.

His hand tightened on my neck. "You want it hard and dirty?"

"Yes, please. Fuck me hard. Choke me. Make it hurt," I begged.

He began slamming into me. I bent my knees, opening wider, and something about that seemed to snap whatever control he had.

"Fucking hot little slut. Taking my big dick in your pussy. Begging for my cum."

I cried out from the pleasure that bordered on pain. This was what I wanted tonight. I fell apart as the orgasm hit me. Screaming his name as his hand stayed wrapped around my neck.

"I'm gonna come," he groaned. "Fill that pussy up. Make it mine. GAH!" A guttural sound ripped through him as I felt him release inside me.

His hand slid down my chest, and then he pulled me against him. We stayed like that with our arms wrapped around each other as our breathing returned to normal.

"I keep thinking I won't come as hard the next time. But I do," he says with his face buried in my hair. "I fucking do. You've got some kind of voodoo pussy, I swear to God."

I laughed against his chest. "Voodoo pussy?"

"Yeah. Its powers are dark, dangerous, and off the charts. You even get me to say terrible things, and I get off on it. Like right now. We finished. I got my nut, and I can't pull out of the damn thing. I just want to stay in there."

I closed my eyes. He was going to ruin me for all other men.

Chapter
TWENTY-SEVEN

TREV

"You're fucking your stepsister," Dad said as he leaned back in his office chair and put a cigar in his mouth.

"I'm not sure where you got your information." I stopped talking when he took the cigar out and slammed his hand on the desk.

"DO NOT lie to me, Trevor. You were smooth, dodging the cameras. I'll give it to you, but there was one camera you forgot about. I didn't see all of it—thank fuck—but I saw enough to know how that ended."

I winced. I'd been so damn careful about the security cameras. It must have been the one in the kitchen.

"Okay, fine, but I saw her before I knew who she was. And I tried not to do anything about it, but, damn, Dad, you put her up in this house with me. I like her. We get along. She's fun to be around. It's not like we're gonna get in a relationship. It's just sex. She's not my stepsister yet."

Dad was looking at me like I'd lost my mind. "She's a woman, son. Women don't just have sex. They get emotionally attached. They fall in love. They want more." He pointed his cigar at me, held between his fingers. "Fawn can't know about this. I'm in love with that woman. I've never fucking loved someone like I do her. She's everything I wanted and could never find. You won't fuck this up. I won't let you send her packing. That daughter of hers is a replica. I get it. Hell, I can't keep my damn hands off Fawn. But you using her daughter as a fuck buddy won't work. Keep your dick in your goddamn pants."

There was no way in hell I could do that. My dick was addicted to Gypsi.

"You sliced the fucker up who had been stalking her. I'm proud of that shit. To hear Blaise tell it, you've got more fucking Hughes in you than he does. But that doesn't mean you get to fuck her. She doesn't deserve to be used. She's a Hughes now. They both are. We treat them like the fucking queens they are. Do you understand me? Protect her. But go fuck some other bitch. Gypsi is off-limits."

Fucking hell! I didn't want another woman. I wasn't even sure I could get a damn hard-on for anyone else. "Dad, I can't just push her away. We've become friends. We play pool together. I'm teaching her to ride. It's not just fucking."

"You can do all the other shit. Fawn is worried Gypsi is going to want to move into her own place. I've sold the goddamn camper, and their stuff arrives here today. I hate that damn thing," he muttered. "Point is, you make her want to stay here. Don't fuck her, make her get emotionally attached, then run the hell off once she sees one of those sluts bouncing on your dick at your pool parties. Be her brother. Be her friend."

He was asking the impossible. I wanted to fucking shout how this was fucked up and I wouldn't do it. Gypsi would want me, and I wasn't going to be able to turn her down. She'd thought I was joking about the voodoo pussy, but I'd been serious.

"I'm not her brother," I snarled.

"But you're going to be. She wants to ride? Go take her to buy a horse. Give her a reason to stay here. I want Fawn so damn delirious with joy that she can't stand it."

"What do you mean, go buy her a horse?" I asked, praying he meant I was being told to take Gypsi on a road trip.

"Do some fucking research, find some horses for her, take her to see them. Buy her a goddamn horse. Make her love horses and forget about your damn dick."

Was he seriously this delusional? He thought we could just turn it off like that. Told me to stop fucking her, then sending me on a horse-buying trip with her. This man was supposed to be a Mafia boss. He was losing his skills. It was time he retired and handed it to Blaise if he thought I was going to be able to take Gypsi off alone and not fuck the hell out of her.

"Yes, sir," I replied, standing up.

"Go talk to her. Fix this shit. Stop it. Make sure Fawn doesn't find out. And stop calling her Lollipop. It sounds dirty."

I nodded and turned around, keeping a straight face because of all the fucking cameras in this room.

Blaise was waiting on the other side of the door when I stepped out and closed it behind me.

"I didn't tell him shit about Gypsi," he said. "You fucked that up with the camera in the kitchen."

I nodded. "Yeah. I figured that one out."

"It's for the best in the long run. Might not seem like it now, but Garrett loves this one. She's not going anywhere. He even mentioned semi-retirement."

Fuck. That would mean Blaise would step up.

"I need to go handle some things," I told him before heading for the stairs.

This morning, I'd gotten to wake up to her in my arms again. Giving that up was gonna be painful. I wasn't sure I could. We needed to go on that horse shopping trip fucking soon.

Gypsi had left to go shopping with her mom. She hadn't texted me to tell me. I'd heard it from Ms. Jimmie. It bugged me that she hadn't thought to tell me. I didn't want things to fucking change. My fist connected with the punching bag in our gym over and over while I tried to control the shit running through my head.

She'd crawled on top of me this morning and ridden me, looking like a goddamn goddess. Her hair all messy from sleep. Saying filthy shit with her husky, sleepy voice. Now, I didn't even get a fucking text that she was leaving. And fucking Kye had driven them. He was the one keeping them safe. I didn't like it.

"You beating the shit out of that bag have anything to do with your dad coming home?" Sax asked.

I turned to see him leaning against the wall with his arms crossed over his chest, watching me.

"Yes," I bit out. "What, did he summon you to talk about your new role in the family business?"

Sax shook his head. "No, I came to talk to you. Figured with the parents home, I'd be able to get you alone. You know, when your head isn't on getting rid of me so you can have Gypsi all to yourself."

I started punching again. If he was here to piss me off, today was not a good day.

"Not in the mood, Sax," I said.

209

"Then, get in the mood. We've been best friends all our lives. This needs to be cleared up."

I stopped and turned back to him. "She's off-limits."

He nodded. "Yeah, I know. I'm not after her."

"Then, what the fuck do you want to talk to me about?"

He raised his eyebrows. "About the fact that I don't intend to ever make a move on Gypsi. And that you're fucking lying to yourself if you think what you're doing with her is some benefits bullshit."

"We're friends too," I said, feeling less angry toward him now that I knew he wasn't after Gypsi.

"I watched you torture a man with a knife, then kill him with a shot to the head, and you never even flinched."

"It was a job. It's what we do."

"You'd never done it. And for a moment, I saw you freeze up. You weren't going to be able to. I saw it on your face. In your eyes. But he started talking about Gypsi, and something came over you. I'd never seen you like that before. The more he talked about her, the more insane you got. I know you better than anyone else. And you wouldn't have done that for someone you didn't love. Fuck, I'm not sure you could have done that for me."

I stood there, staring at him. What was he fucking saying? That I loved her? That was shit. I was in love with her fucking pussy. That was for damn sure.

"I care about her, but I am no longer allowed to fuck her."

Sax shrugged. "Whatever the case may be, you need to look at how you feel about her and accept it."

"I don't love her, if that is what you're saying. She's a friend. I like to fuck her. That is it. There's no future in this. She's not special to me. She's gonna be my fucking stepsister. End of story. We will end this, and I'll go fuck someone else." Just saying it made me sick to my stomach. That was a warning

I should have paid attention to before now. I didn't want anyone else's pussy, and that was not normal. Maybe Gypsi had gotten in my head and messed with it.

Sax walked over to the weight bench. "That's all I'm going to say about it."

"Good."

Chapter
TWENTY-EIGHT

GYPSI

"I don't love her, if that is what you're saying. She's a friend. I like to fuck her. That is it. There's no future in this. She's not special to me. She's gonna be my fucking stepsister. End of story. We will end this, and I'll go fuck someone else."

Those words kept replaying in my head as I sat in the bedroom that was now mine. I'd been told to decorate it however I wanted. There were clothes in my closet with ridiculous price tags. Cocktail dresses and formals. More things than any one person needed. Mom had insisted Garrett wanted me at all the events they went to and I had to dress the part.

All I wanted to do was go get our camper and leave this town. My heart felt like it was shattering over and over again. I'd been so stupid. Knowing that what I'd heard was exactly what he had said in the beginning. Hearing it had hurt so bad because it was then I realized I loved him. I'd let this go too far. He had charmed his way into my heart, and I had never had this kind of pain before.

My phone dinged, and I glanced down to see a text from Mom.

WE ARE GOING OUT. MS. JIMMIE HAS SET UP A DELICIOUS TACO BAR IN THE KITCHEN. GO EAT SOMETHING. LOVE YOU!

I had no appetite. I set my phone down on the bed and pulled my knees up to my chest. This was what I'd asked for when I decided friends with benefits was something I could do. Trev hadn't even texted me today. I'd left his room after waking up and having sex with him. I'd let myself believe that I was special to him. That he had meant all those things he said to me. He had just been sex talking. I was too naive to know the difference.

There was a knock on my door before it opened, and Trev walked in. He was sweaty from his workout, wearing a sleeveless shirt and athletic shorts. That smile of his made my heart squeeze. He wasn't mine. He never had been.

He leaned against the doorframe. "We got a trip to plan," he said.

"A trip?"

"Dad has given me the order to take you horse shopping."

I stared at him, confused. What was horse shopping?

"You, me, and a road trip. I say we stretch it out. You need to be picky." He winked at me, shoving off from the doorframe and walking over toward me.

I tensed. I had to end this. I held up my hand to stop him. Watching the confused frown mess up that sexy smile made me feel guilty. I liked seeing him smile. I liked hearing him laugh.

"What's wrong, Lollipop?"

I couldn't lie to him. Hurting him, even though I wasn't sure I had that power, I couldn't do it. "We have to stop."

"Why? Because our parents came home? We'll be careful."

I shook my head. "No. That's not it."

He took another step toward me. "Then, what is it? I thought we talked about this going on for a long time."

We had. Then, I'd gotten feelings.

He reached out and touched my waist.

I backed away from him. "No."

"I get it. They're home. It feels real now. But steps with benefits is something we are inventing. It'll make us famous," he said, tilting his head with that wicked grin.

"Trev, it's ... we need to ... I don't think I can—" I stopped and covered my face with my hands.

This was too hard. Was this what true devastation felt like?

"Lollipop, I'm real close to putting you over my knee and spanking your ass." He smirked. "You'd fucking love that."

Yes, I would, and the fact that it wasn't going to happen made me literally ache.

"I'm in love with you," I blurted out.

His face paled, and he stepped back. He looked horrified. Watching him stare at me as if he might be sick was painful. Part of me wished I could take it back.

"You can't. I mean, we didn't agree on that."

I laughed. It sounded harsh. Bitter. "As if I can control that. I'm sorry that my heart had other ideas."

He ran a hand over his face. "We haven't known each other that long. You can't love me. That's not normal. Fuck, Gypsi," he muttered. Not Lollipop. It was like he'd taken a knife and shoved it into my chest. "This messes it up. Doesn't it?" His eyes searched my face for something I couldn't give him. A way to work around this.

"Yeah, Trev, it does. I can't keep doing this with you and knowing I'm not special to you."

He shook his head. "That's not true—"

"I heard you. Just please don't. Don't lie to me. I can't take that."

I watched him try and figure out what I'd heard, but it didn't take him long.

Realization dawned on him, and he winced. "Goddammit."

"Let's just get some distance. Some time. Then, *maybe* we can do the friends-stepsiblings thing. I just need to work through this."

Trev stood there, staring at me like he wanted to get the hell away from me. Me and my honesty. If only I were better at lying. Baring my soul wasn't always easy.

When he turned and walked out of the room, not looking back even once, I knew that this was completely one-sided. Part of me had hoped he'd admit to lying to Saxon and saying he felt something for me too. But he hadn't. I shouldn't have expected more.

I lay down on the bed, curled myself into a ball, and let the tears come.

ONE DAY SINCE TREV WALKED OUT OF MY ROOM

"Why are you showing me the third floor?" I asked Mom when the elevator I hadn't even known was in this house stopped at three instead of four.

The entire fourth floor was the master suite. I'd thought we were going up there so Mom could show me after she gushed about it over breakfast.

Mom gave me her beaming grin and waved her hands out as she spun in a circle. "Because I am supposed to redecorate this entire floor and I want your help."

I glanced around. It was as elegant as the rest of the house. "What needs redecorating?"

"I know it looks fabulous already, but Garrett wants things changed. No one uses these rooms anymore. He wants Cree to have a room up here and to add a master suite if Blaise and Madeline ever want to stay here. He had a former stepdaughter who stayed here, even after he divorced her mom—Gina, I believe her name was. Anyway, she is no longer in the family." Mom lowered her voice as if someone could hear her. "She handed Madeline over to men who abducted her on purpose. To get rid of her."

"Oh my God." I was whispering now, I realized.

Mom nodded. "Right? But come to find out, it was actually Madeline's real father. And the people who took her weren't bad people. But Blaise couldn't forgive Gina and sent her away."

"It's weird that she stayed here after her mom divorced Garrett," I pointed out. That seemed creepy.

"Well, there's a reason. The other person who had a room up here was a girl named Angel. She was very close to Blaise, growing up, and then she was in a car accident. It killed her parents and left her with permanent brain damage. Her parents were very close friends of Garrett's, so he took her in. Gina helped take care of Angel."

That was less creepy. I relaxed somewhat. "What happened to Angel?"

Mom cut her eyes at me as I followed her into the first room. "Well, Angel loved Blaise before the head injury. She remained attached to him, and he seemed to be the only person who could calm her. In her head, he was hers. Then, Madeline came along, and they had issues, but with Angel being here, it gave them some space.

"When Cree was an infant, he was in the nursery Garrett has for him on the second floor. Angel took him from the crib and brought him up here. Thanks to the security cameras,

Ms. Jimmie was alerted right away, and she came to get Cree. Blaise was in the house at the time, and he heard the alarm in the nursery, but he arrived after Ms. Jimmie. Ms. Jimmie had Cree back safely in her arms and was scolding Angel.

"Blaise came in the room and took Cree from Ms. Jimmie. Angel then began screaming and clawing at Blaise. Anyway, after that, Garrett had her moved to live with an older couple he trusts, who wanted to take her in. She's better there. Being near Blaise, seeing his wife and child was making her get more hysterical."

I stood there, staring at Mom as she walked around the room, looking at things. That was so sad. All of it.

"Wow, that's dark," I replied.

Mom looked at me and shrugged. "I guess every family has their dark stories."

This was my moment. She'd not brought up who Garrett was to me yet. I'd thought this *going to the master suite* idea was her way of getting me away to talk to me. But here we were, on the third floor, talking about redecorating.

"Especially in a Mafia family," I replied.

Mom stilled with the vase she'd picked up in her hand. Her head turned to me, and I saw the apology in her expression before she even spoke.

"You know," she whispered.

"Yes, and I've been wondering when you were going to tell me. Seeing as Garrett being a Mafia boss affects my life too. Apparently, it's not safe for me to live on my own or to have a normal job. Kye taking us shopping was for security, Mom. He wasn't just the driver. I was aware that he was following us as we shopped. Driver's don't do that."

Mom set the vase down and sat on the edge of the bed. "I'm sorry, Gypsi. I didn't know how to tell you. I was going to, obviously, but, well, it was a lot for me to process. I like crazy adventures; you don't. I worried you wouldn't be able to accept it since you're not the one in love here."

I wanted to laugh. She had no idea. My chest ached, just hearing the word *love*.

"So, it's true. I have to live here. I can't go back to the camper?"

She gave me a tight smile. "Honey, the camper has been sold. All our things from it are in boxes. I was going to have your things brought up to your room as soon as I got the nerve to explain all this to you."

Sold. The camper we'd lived in most of my life had been sold. My eyes stung, and I had to turn away from her for a moment. I needed to digest this. Sure, I had known she no longer needed the camper, but it was all I'd known.

"Oh, Gypsi," she said, getting up and walking over to me.

She pulled me into her arms, and I went. I needed that more than she knew. Not just because of our camper or because our life was completely changing. I needed it because my heart was broken and no one knew. I couldn't tell anyone. I had no one to share it with. My mom had been my best friend my entire life. I'd told her everything.

But this I couldn't tell her. That made the hurt slice even deeper. I was alone. I knew she'd be there. She was my mom, but she wasn't all mine anymore. She was going to be some-one's wife.

"I know this is a lot for you. The change. The lifestyle. I want you to enjoy this. As happy as Garrett makes me, I can't do this if you're miserable. You're my number one. You always have been."

A tear ran down my cheek, and I bit my lip hard, try-ing to stop any more from falling. I was grown. Mom had given up everything to be the best mom a girl could ask for. But she was done raising me. I wasn't going to stand here and ruin this for her by falling apart because my heart was broken over a guy. One who had made it very clear that what he wanted from me was sex and friendship. It might have been slightly easier to handle if I hadn't heard him say I wasn't special to him. Couldn't a friend be special? Was it because I was a freak? Did the kinks that had made Tyde so angry with me make it impossible for Trev to think of me as anything but a slut?

Mom pulled back and looked at me. "Listen, I will get Garrett to buy the camper back. We can park it somewhere on the ranch."

"Mom, no. That's silly. It's not even that. Not really. I just need time to adjust to all this."

She cupped the side of my face. "I love you, Gypsi Lu. You know that, right?"

I nodded. "I love you too, Mom."

She pulled me in tightly for another hug. "Oh, and one more thing. It's not a big deal, but I don't want you to be blindsided by it. Do you remember who Liam Walsh is?"

I nodded, stiffening. Was this about Tyde? My stomach knotted.

"Well, he's Madeline's father. The MC are the guys who took Madeline that time. She had never met her dad. They are close now, and all is well. Garrett knows about Micah. I don't want secrets between us. He also knows about Tyde, and we don't have to worry about him anymore. Liam has disassociated from him. He is no longer in the MC. Garrett said he won't ever come here."

I stared at her, wondering if there was any more news that was going to shock me. Trev had already promised that Tyde was gone. But the Liam thing—I hadn't seen that coming.

"Tyde got on this property. They caught him. What did they do to make him stop stalking me?" I asked her.

She frowned at me. "I'm not happy about you not telling me about the stalking. I could have protected you. That little shit was screwing with the wrong woman's daughter."

"Mom, he is a psycho. What were you going to do? Hit him with a frying pan?"

She shrugged. "Or a baseball bat."

"I'm sure that would have sent him running."

She smirked at me, and then a laugh bubbled out of her. "Well, he's gone now."

"But how? Do you know what they did to him?"

She looked down and then lifted her eyes back to me slowly. "In this family, there are some things you don't want answers to."

"They wouldn't have killed him, right?" I asked, not sure again how I felt about that.

"Who knows what they chose to do?" She turned back to the room and looked around. "Now, what do you think about bold colors? Maybe an emerald green."

This was an answer I wouldn't be getting. Maybe she was right. Maybe I didn't want to know.

Chapter
TWENTY-NINE

GYPSI
THREE DAYS SINCE TREV WALKED OUT OF MY ROOM

Mom and Garrett were both at the dining room table when I came down for breakfast. It had just been Mom the past couple of mornings. Trev was MIA. I hadn't seen him in three days. I'd run him off from his home with three dreaded words—*I love you.*

"Good morning!" Mom said brightly as she put her cup of coffee down. "Did you sleep well?"

"Yes," I lied.

I had tossed and turned most of the night. When I had slept, I dreamed of Trev, and I would wake up sad, alone, and broken.

"Ms. Jimmie made a lovely spread today," Mom said, waving her hand at the food that went down the center of the table. It was all placed attractively on fancy silver serving trays.

I picked up a plate and began to put some fruit on it, then moved to get what looked like tiny pancake towers, layered with whipped cream and strawberries, before taking a seat.

"Your mom tells me you would like to work," Garrett said.

I looked up at him as he set the *Wall Street Journal* that had been in his hands down on the table beside him.

"Yes, sir. I don't think I can just do nothing. I like working, and I want to make my own money," I explained.

He nodded. "I respect that. She also mentioned you enjoy photography."

"Yes."

"The ranch—the horse racing part of it at least—has its own social media. Madeline convinced me it was needed once she started working here. She does what she can with taking photos and keeping it updated. The horses, the races, that sort of thing. It helps bring more potential customers to us. However, Madeline will tell you herself that photography isn't her strong suit. She also struggles with balancing that with all the other jobs she has in the office and having time with Cree. If you would be willing to take over the social media part of the stables, go to the races, take photos of the day-to-day operations at the stables and the work put in with the horses, I will supply you with the equipment you would need. It would be salary based since hours could be heavier on some weeks and lighter on others. One hundred twenty-five thousand a year. With bonuses."

I sat there, silent, staring at him. He was offering me a job I would have never dreamed of getting without a college degree. There was no way I could accept that salary. It was entirely too much when I was already living in his home and eating his food. The clothes in my closet he'd purchased for me were more than I could ever repay him.

"If you want to attend college, I can arrange for you to do so in the fall. It would be safest for you to attend the private college a little over an hour from here. You can do many classes online, and the days you need to be on campus, I can send one of my men with you."

College? I turned to look at Mom, who was watching me with that hopeful look in her eyes. She wanted this for me. She had sacrificed for me since she had been a teenager. Now, she was able to do this, and I knew it was important to her. Accepting it was hard for me though. Garrett wasn't my father. He didn't have to do any of this for me.

"I ..." I paused. I wasn't sure what to say. How to say it. I didn't want to be any more tangled up with this family than I already was. But did I really have a choice anymore? The reason I wanted to stay didn't want me. "Thank you. The job sounds amazing. I can't accept that kind of salary though. Not with everything you're already giving me. It's too much. But I would like the job. School ..." I paused and looked at Mom again. I didn't want to let her down, but I had to draw some lines. I couldn't give up my independence completely. "I think I need to save for that. Pay my own way. You aren't responsible for my education. But I do appreciate the offer. That's very generous of you."

Garrett's eyes were on my mother now. He was waiting on her cue as to how to proceed. I liked that. He wasn't taking control. He was letting her lead this.

Finally, he looked back at me and nodded. "Okay. If that is what makes you happy. We can lower your salary to one hundred thousand, but that is as low as I will go. If I hired anyone else, that would be their starting salary. I'm not going to pay my stepdaughter less."

With that kind of money, I'd be paying for my college within a year.

I nodded. "Okay. Thank you," I replied.

He smiled then, looking relieved. "Good. I'll get Madeline to order the equipment you'll need. Give her a couple of days.

She will contact you when she's ready for you to report to her office in the stables."

"Yes, sir."

He stood then and walked over to Mom, bending down to kiss her. She touched the side of his face with her hand, the massive rock he'd put on it flashing at me. I turned my attention back to my food. I had a job. I had a plan for college. This wasn't so bad. It would be perfect ... if I didn't miss Trev. If his absence wasn't breaking a little more of my heart every day.

TREV
FIVE DAYS SINCE GYPSI FUCKED WITH MY HEAD AND RUINED EVERYTHING

"You've been drunk for four days. Laid up at the house, worrying Trinity and Shiloh. Now, I've got you at a damn strip club, and you still look fucking miserable. When are you gonna tell me what the hell is wrong with you?"

Levi's gaze was locked on me as he waited for an answer while I watched the dancer do things to the pole that should be turning me on. It wasn't.

I reached for the beer he'd put in front of me. "My stepsister," I snapped.

He laughed. "No shit. I have that much figured out. But, dude, you knew when you started fucking her that Garrett was serious about her momma. I don't see how this engagement should send you into a downward spiral."

I shot an annoyed glare at him and took a drink of my beer. "Let me just watch the naked women and not talk about Gypsi."

"I would, but you're glowering at them like you would rather throw darts than dollar bills. You need to talk and get this shit out of your head. You're too young for this kind of thing. Don't get all fucked up on a girl at your age. Gage did that, and look what happened to him. Fucking Marines."

Yeah, but Gage had his girl now. She was in his bed. Same damn girl he had been in love with at twenty-two. Even after five years of not seeing her. One look at her, and he had been done. That shit was scary. No one should have that kind of power over you.

"It's not that. I'm not like Gage. This is a different situation," I grumbled, annoyed that he wouldn't shut up about it.

I was struggling to get a hard-on as it was. He wasn't helping by talking.

"Doesn't look like it to me. You carved a man up over her. Looks exactly like Gage's situation."

I slammed my beer down and glared at him. "It was about fucking. That's it. We got along. We had fun. I liked being around her. I loved fucking her. She was the hottest damn fuck of my life. I wasn't in love or obsessed, like Gage was."

"She ended the fucking when the parents got engaged?" he asked me.

I shook my head. "No," I replied through clenched teeth.

"Well, why the fuck are you drinking all day, laying up at our house, slamming around like you're angry at the world?"

"Because she told me she fucking loved me. Ruined it all. It was so damn good too. Fucking epic. Then, she had to go and say that stupid shit."

Levi let out a low whistle, leaning back in his chair. "Damn," he muttered.

I tossed back the rest of the beer and tried to pay attention to the girls currently groping each other onstage.

"You just need to fuck someone else. A professional. Someone who can remind you that there is no magic pussy. They're all pretty damn magical," Levi told me.

He leaned forward and motioned for one of the strippers on the floor. She was blonde with big tits, and I could tell she knew Levi by the way her lips curled as she made her way to our table.

"Pandora, I'd like you to meet Trev Hughes. Blaise's younger brother. He's had a bad week. Thought maybe you might break one of your rules since he's a Hughes and my friend. Take him back to a room. Help him forget the shit week he's had."

The blonde's eyes lit up at the sound of my last name. "A Hughes. I'll break any rule for a Hughes," she purred and walked over to me, running her fingers through my hair. "You're as pretty as your brother," she said, then bent down. "Come with me," she whispered in my ear.

I glanced over at Levi. He held up his beer to me and took a drink, then winked. What the fuck? Maybe this would work. I sure as hell needed something to work. I was killing my damn liver with the nonstop drinking.

When I stood up, she slipped her hand in mine and led me through the crowd. The hall of rooms—as Levi had called it the first time he brought me here a year ago—was one I had never been down. Paying for a blow job or sex was dumb. I'd get that shit for free. But right now, I needed something other than Gypsi on my mind.

I followed Pandora into a room with red walls, a black leather sofa, and some other shit I had no idea how to use. She closed and locked the door, then pointed at the sofa.

"Go get comfortable," she told me.

I looked at the sofa, and the image of old, fat men, who had paid to fuck a hot piece of ass, sweating on that thing turned me off.

I glanced back at her. "What is it that you're planning on doing to get me in a better mood?" I asked.

She squeezed her tits as she walked over to me, then ran her long, sharp red fingernails down my chest until she was gripping my cock through my jeans. "What do you want? I'll do dirty things for a Hughes."

I bet she would. Except when she said the word *dirty*, it reminded me of the shit I'd said to Gypsi when we were fucking. Maybe she just didn't need to talk. I knew this was supposed to get my mind off Gypsi, but she was blonde. On her knees with my cock in her mouth, shutting her up, I could pretend.

"On your knees," I said as I started unbuckling my belt.

I was barely holding on to a semi-erection right now, but if a woman's mouth took my dick, it would get hard. It was a dick. She grinned and watched me as I shoved my jeans down, freeing my cock.

Her hands were bigger than Gypsi's, and she didn't have the curls. But I could work with it. She began to lick it, and like I knew it would, the damn thing jumped to attention. Grabbing her hair with my hand, I pushed it into her mouth.

"Suck it," I growled.

Her nails bit into my thighs as she took my cock deep. I closed my eyes and brought up the image of Gypsi on her knees in front of me. My cock shoved in her sweet mouth. FUCK, I missed that.

"That's it," I moaned. "Take it deep, Lollipop."

She gagged as I shoved harder into her.

"You love to gag on my big dick, don't you?" I asked.

She pulled back, letting it come out of her mouth. "Yes! Fuck my mouth," she panted.

Wrong voice.

My eyes snapped open, and the stripper on her knees looking up at me wasn't what I wanted to see.

"Don't talk!" I barked. Then closed my eyes again and tried to pull the image of Gypsi back up before I lost my fucking hard-on. Those insane sunshine-and-honey eyes staring up at me. Loving how I took her mouth. God, she was gorgeous.

"That's it, Lollipop. God, I need this."

Fingers slid up my thighs toward my chest and stopped. I felt the sharp nail circle around something, and my eyes snapped open on a growl. She was messing this up. Looking down, I saw her staring at one of the fading bruised bite marks Gypsi had left on me. Seeing her tacky nails touch it, where Gypsi's mouth had been, sent a blinding rage through me. I shoved her back and walked away from her, pulling my jeans up.

"This isn't going to work," I said, buckling my belt. "Sorry for wasting your time." I didn't even look back at her as I made my way to the door.

This was fucking Levi's fault. I didn't need a damn stripper. I needed Gypsi.

"Trev." Pandora called my name.

Gritting my teeth, I turned back to see what she wanted. I had just gagged her with my cock and then shoved her off me. It wasn't my best moment.

"Yeah?" I snarled. I couldn't help it. I was angry. She'd touched Gypsi's bite mark. That wasn't hers to touch.

"Whoever she is, this Lollipop, go get her. Fix it."

"I can't fucking fix it!" I snarled. "She loves me. I can't fix that."

Pandora raised her eyebrows at me. "And you don't love her?" She laughed. "You're either in denial or scared. Whichever it is, get over it before you lose her."

I jerked the door open and stalked out of there. This fucking strip club was not what I needed. I needed to fucking see Gypsi. What was so wrong with her loving me? That wasn't so bad. She loved me, and I wouldn't have to worry about losing her. I wouldn't lose her to another man. I mean, she would know I didn't love her, but she was special. I had to fix that. I hadn't meant it when I said it to Trev. I was angry, and it had just come out. Gypsi was fucking special. That was it. I could love her, and she could be special to me. We'd get along great. It could work. I fucking needed it to work. I'd tell her how special she was, and things would go back to the way they had been.

Levi was frowning when I got back to the table.

"That was a fast fuck," he said.

"We didn't fuck. We're leaving."

"Ah, man, please don't tell me you couldn't get it up."

I scowled at him. "She sucked my dick. Of course I got hard. It was just the wrong mouth. We need to go."

"The right mouth being Gypsi's?" he asked, standing up.

I nodded. "It's time I go home."

Levi chuckled. "You might want to go wash the smell of strip club off your body first."

Good idea.

Chapter
THIRTY

TREV

The Rolls-Royce and Mercedes G-Wagon in the driveway meant Dad had company. At least he would be distracted and I could get Gypsi in my bed without him noticing. His *no fucking* rule was not going to work. I'd deal with him later.

Right now, I needed to go make sure Lollipop knew she was special. Real fucking special. And she could love me all she wanted. Why had I freaked out before? I'd gotten it in my head that her loving me meant we couldn't do this because she would think it was more than sex. But it would keep her with me. It wasn't a bad thing. It was security.

Yeah, it was my security. I liked that. It meant I had her. No one else did. Besides, if a girl was gonna fall in love with me and possibly get obsessed, then Gypsi was the one I wanted to do it. The idea of her being clingy made me smile. She could be crazy-obsessed girl all she wanted. I'd keep her safe. I was also so damn hard, thinking about it, that my cock was throbbing.

Stepping in the side entrance to be sure to miss whoever Dad had over for the evening, I started down the hall to get to the back staircase. Hopefully, Gypsi was in her room and not being forced to play stepdaughter to the guests. As I passed the theater, I heard voices. I stopped when Gypsi's voice hit my ears, and I turned to go back to the door and listen. The other voice was male. I started to shove the door open, and I paused, taking a deep breath.

This was Gypsi. She wasn't going to be on some date with a guy five days after telling me she loved me. It was probably one of the guests. Dad more than likely was having her entertain the son of one of his friends. Which made me want to put my fist through another fucking wall, but it wasn't Gypsi's fault. That was mine. I'd left her here.

I pushed the door open slowly. There was some movie I didn't recognize playing, but my gaze went to Gypsi. Townes Hoagan, the son of the senator two states over, was looking at her like she was his last meal. Her blonde curls were pulled up, leaving her neck bare. Her shoulders seemed tense. Like she was uncomfortable, but her musical laugh confused me. Was she faking? Surely, she didn't like this guy. He was a prick. Talk about rich, spoiled kid. He was your typical frat boy.

I took another step inside, and then he leaned in, cupped her face with his hand, and kissed her. She didn't push him away. He was kissing her, and she was letting him. I turned and left the theater, unable to watch it. If I ripped Townes's arms off his body, my dad would be upset. Besides, she hadn't been pushing him off. She'd let him.

Five days ago, she had been in love with me. That didn't look like she loved me. That looked like she was willing and ready for the next guy to come along who would fuck her brains out. She was a sex addict. I'd taken my dick away, so she was shopping for a new one.

Slamming through the house, I went to my room, shaking with rage. The pain in my chest and sick rolling in my stomach didn't help. I grabbed the first thing I came to, which was a lamp, and threw it against the wall. I seethed as I watched it shatter and fall to the floor. My gaze swung to the snacks I had in here for her. Those needed to be gone. I wanted all fucking memories of her out of here. Shoving the snacks into the closest garbage, I tied it up and set it outside my door. I'd take it down later. For now, it had to be out of my sight.

Reaching for my phone, I scrolled through my Contacts until I found Bea's number. This time, I wasn't going to picture Gypsi. I was going to get her the fuck out of my head.

GYPSI
SEVEN DAYS SINCE TREV WALKED OUT OF MY ROOM

Mom and Garrett had left before sunrise to go to New York. Garrett had set up appointments for her to meet with wedding dress designers. The next Mrs. Hughes had to have a one-of-a-kind wedding dress.

Today, I was supposed to meet with Maddy at the stables and start my new job. If it wasn't for the fact that I knew Trev had come home—because I'd heard Garrett mention it yesterday—and I still hadn't seen him, I would be more excited about today. Knowing Trev was hiding from me was difficult. I hated that this was what we had turned into.

When I stepped into the dining room for breakfast, Trev was sitting at the end of the table. He lifted his gaze to mine and then picked up his cup of coffee. I stood there, staring at him like an idiot, but no words came. Just seeing his face again made my chest warm. It eased some of the pain.

"Excuse me," a female voice said behind me.

I stepped out of the way automatically, and Bea—topless pool girl—walked past me, wearing only one of Trev's shirts.

"I couldn't find the Splenda," she told him.

"I'm sorry," he replied, smiling at her. "Do you want me to go look?" Then, he shifted his gaze to me. "Do you know where the Splenda is, Gypsi?"

I shook my head.

He turned back to her. "I can go look," he told her.

"I don't have to drink coffee," she said, then leaned down to kiss him.

Numbly, I stood there as he ran his hand under the shirt she had on and grabbed her ass. She was here the morning after. This wasn't a hotel room. She had slept in his bed. She had woken up with him. He was having breakfast with her. Everything he had told me was a lie.

I turned and ran. I headed for the front door. I had to get out of this house. Away from that. If I'd had anything left for Trev to break, he'd just crushed it into a million pieces. Opening the door, I headed outside. A sob escaped me as I made my way to the stables. I couldn't go into Maddy's office like this, but I wasn't about to go in that house.

Why was it that when I finally fell in love, when I let myself feel something, that it was tragic?

"Gypsi?"

I lifted my eyes from the ground to see Maddy standing outside the stables. She was walking from her car. I was too early. The concerned look on her face as she looked at my tear-streaked one was embarrassing. I came to a stop and wiped at the tears on my cheeks.

"Sorry, I, uh, just needed some air. I'm not rushing you. I will just walk around a bit," I told her.

She glanced up at the house, then back at me. "You can come with me to the office and tell me what my brother-in-law did."

I shook my head. "No. That's okay. It's nothing. All my fault."

Maddy put a hand on her hip. "I love Trev. But I also know him. He means well, but he's not the best when it comes to handling girls."

I wasn't going to do this. By talking to one of them, it would feel like I was trying to get his family to side with me. I wouldn't do that.

"No, really. Trev was honest with me from the very beginning. Very honest. He made no promises. The thing we had, it's over. We will be family soon. I just ... it's just hard to see him with someone else. And that is all on me. Not him."

Maddy scowled at the house again. "You are telling me he has a girl up there this morning?"

"Yes, but it's his house. He can have over whoever he wants." I was defending him. What had this man done to me? I could hardly believe my own words.

"I don't know much about what went on with the two of you. It isn't my business. But I do know that Blaise thinks it was serious because of some things he saw from Trev. That being the case, Trev having a girl over this soon is cruel. He needs to be slapped."

Why did I run down here? I could have gone to my room and cried. But, no, I'd had to be dramatic and run out of the house like a lunatic. I wouldn't even be able to look at Trev again. I'd tossed my pride out the window with that reaction.

"Please, if you could, just keep this between us. I've already embarrassed myself in front of him. My reaction was pathetic and humiliating enough. I'd like to let it go and move on with my life. Don't say anything to him or anyone. If I could just start working today, that would help."

Maddy nodded. "Of course. I understand," she said gently. "But if you need to talk or vent or cry, I'm here. I'll listen, and I won't say anything."

I sniffled. "Thank you."

"Of course. Now, let's get you working and too busy to think about this mess," she said before heading into the stables.

Chapter
THIRTY-ONE

GYPSI
EIGHT DAYS SINCE TREV WALKED OUT OF MY ROOM

Tonight would be my first event at a fundraising gala as Garrett Hughes's future stepdaughter.

Stylists arrived at the house, and they styled our hair, did our makeup, and chose our clothing. Mom loved every moment of it. When Garrett came in to see how things were going, she jumped up and threw her arms around his neck. He looked at her with that worshipful expression.

Trev had disappeared again, and I hadn't seen him since the dining room with Bea. This time, I was avoiding him too. Seeing him was the last thing I wanted. My emotions were a fragmented mess. How long would this last? Did you eventually get over the devastation? Move on and feel again for someone else? I wasn't sure I wanted to ever give my heart to someone again. But then I'd remember how it had felt to wake up with Trev. How laughing with him and cuddling in his arms had given me that deep-seated joy. I'd like that with someone who wanted it with me too. Who thought I was special. Who could love me in return. One day, maybe. If I ever put myself back together again after this.

These were things I would have asked my mother, if it wasn't Trev who had caused the damage. She was high on life today, watching me get fixed up. Looking in the mirror, I had to admit they had done a good job. I almost felt like I might fit in at this thing.

I just wished someone had warned me before I climbed into the limo. Trev was sitting in the far back corner. Our eyes locked for only a moment, and then he dropped his gaze back to his phone, as if the sight of me bored him. Nothing could have prepared me for that greeting. I wasn't sure I could breathe; my chest constricted so badly. I'd warned him that the day would come that I bored him. It was here, and all it had taken was my telling him I loved him.

I slid in to sit across from my mom and Garrett. The massive rock on her hand caught the light and sparkled.

"I've always put you in pink because you love it, but, wow, we should have tried gold on you. It brings out your eyes," she told me.

"You look incredible in gold," I told her.

She should be wearing this dress, but they'd put her in a shiny silver dress that clung to her curves.

"I copy-pasted with you, honey," she replied. "What looks good on me will always look good on you."

I shrugged. Mom was a level of beautiful I wasn't, but I wasn't going to argue that with her. She was my mother, and to her, no one could compare to me.

"Maddy brought me your recent photos to look over. They're impressive," Garrett said. "You have a real eye behind the camera."

"The camera you supplied me with has a lot to do with that. I don't think it makes a bad picture," I told him.

That was the truth. The camera had every bell and whistle made.

"It takes talent to produce those kinds of photos," he replied, and then his gaze shifted in the direction of Trev. "You going to look at that phone or be social?"

I didn't look at him.

"I'm sorry. Did someone need me?" he drawled.

"When we are together as a family, then I expect you to act like it."

"This isn't my family. It's yours," he replied.

I stared down at my hands as if my new nail color was fascinating.

There was an uncomfortable silence. I knew Mom wasn't going to like this. It would upset her. Then, Garrett was going to take it out on Trev.

"He's busy with his phone. Most likely texting that girl who I've seen around the house the past two days. He has his father's good looks. There must be a line of girls after him," Mom said in her pleasant way. Using her musical voice that no one could be annoyed with.

I lifted my eyes to stare out the window. I wouldn't look at any of them. I couldn't. They'd be able to see it on my face. The heartbreak, loss, longing.

"It's a never-ending line," Trev replied with amusement in his tone.

"I have no doubt," Mom replied. "Be picky."

He chuckled. "I will."

Please stop, Mom. Please, please, please. I closed my eyes a moment and managed to keep from tearing up.

"Don't be as picky as Gypsi though. I was sure she and your friend Saxon were going to possibly date, but no such luck. But the senator's son that came over the other night ... what was his name?"

"Townes," Garrett supplied.

"Yes! Townes. He seemed very taken with you, Gypsi. He got your number, didn't he? If he calls, please give him a chance. He was a nice young man."

"Townes is a spoiled prick," Trev said.

"Son." Garrett's one word held a warning.

"Well, if he is a prick, then Gypsi needs a heads-up," Mom said to Garrett. "I don't want to push her into anything where she gets hurt. She's not got much experience with guys. Her one time she decided to finally date, he ended up being abusive."

Please, Mom, just stop.

"Townes isn't a prick," Garrett said. "I wouldn't have invited him if he was. I'm choosing the men I put in Gypsi's path carefully. I promise."

Oh God. He had invited Townes on purpose? Townes was a prick. He was too aggressive and touchy. He even kissed me. He was a sloppy kisser too. It had made me sick to my stomach.

"I didn't realize marrying her mom made you Gypsi's matchmaker. Does she require that much help, finding a man?"

Trev's words made my gut twist. I wanted out of this limo. I wanted my camper. I should have told Mom yes to having Garrett buy it back. I could live on the property in my own safe haven. Away from girls walking around in Trev's shirts after climbing out of his bed. The one he'd told me he didn't let other girls sleep in.

The limo came to a stop, and I almost cried in relief.

"Trev, you'll come directly home and meet me in my office after this." Garrett's tone reminded me of ice-cold granite.

The door opened, and I climbed out first since I was closest. Kye took my hand and helped me out. I thanked him, then stood to the side, waiting on Mom and Garrett. Mom stepped out next, and then she was followed by Garrett. He held his elbow out to her and slid her arm around it. I started to follow behind them when Trev was at my side. I didn't turn to look at him. What was he doing so close?

"Take my arm, Gypsi," he whispered. "I have to escort you in here. You don't get a say in it."

I looked down at his arm he held out to me. I was supposed to touch him. How was I going to survive that? He was already so close that I could smell him. That was hard enough.

"Gypsi." He said my name again. Just hearing him use it made me want to cry.

To think I hadn't liked the name Lollipop in the beginning. I'd give anything to hear him say it again. It would more than likely crush my soul, but still.

I slipped my arm inside his and tried to think of something other than him. The pictures I had taken today. How nice the new camera was. Anything but how delicious Trev smelled or how hard his bicep was under my hand.

"You should probably smile. I know I'm not Townes fucking Hoagan, but you're an excellent actress," he said between clenched teeth.

I turned to look up at him for the first time. "Why would you say that? You're right. Townes is a prick. And pushy."

Trev's arm flexed under my touch as his eyes locked on mine. I jerked my gaze away. I couldn't look at him. That was not good for my mental health, and right now, it was hanging on by a thread.

"I need you to explain that comment further," he told me.

I shrugged. I didn't see how that needed further explanation. "It's what I said. He didn't take hints. He made up reasons to touch me. He talked about himself to impress me. It was a very long, draining evening I don't want to repeat."

240

I took a quick glance at Trev, and the veins in his neck were standing out. His jaw appeared to be clenched tightly. Was Townes actually his friend? Had I insulted him?

There were no more questions. We entered the ballroom full of extravagant decorations, beautiful dresses, and men in tuxedos. None of them compared to Trev in a tuxedo, but I wouldn't be appreciating that view tonight. My goal was to not look at him at all.

Garrett was stopped by a group of people, and he began introducing Mom. When he turned to me, Trev released me, stepping away, and I moved to stand beside my mother. Smiling and trying my best to appear happy to be here. I was tempted to look around the room for Trev, but I couldn't bring myself to do it. Not while keeping a smile on my face.

Chapter
THIRTY-TWO

TREV

My eyes stayed locked on Gypsi as she charmed every damn person my father introduced her to. The smile wasn't genuine, and it was fucking killing me. I was ninety-nine percent sure I had fucked up. The look of disgust in her eyes when I'd mentioned Townes, that hadn't fit with what I'd seen in the theater.

If I was wrong and she hadn't kissed him back …

If I'd walked out of that theater too soon and she'd pushed him away …

Jesus Christ, how was I going to live with myself after what I had done to her that morning with Bea? I'd set it up. Knowing she would come down to breakfast and our parents were gone. I wanted to hurt her like she had hurt me, but when she ran out of the room, I felt fucking sick. I'd taken it too far.

Youngstreet was almost thirty years old! What the hell was he looking at Gypsi like that for? He reached down to whisper something in her ear, and that was it. I couldn't stand here and watch. I needed to talk to her. Alone. Dad could get the fuck over it.

She wasn't comfortable. He was too close, and she was tensing up. Did my dad not see this? I reached her just as Youngstreet leaned close to her again and wrapped a hand around her arm. She jumped, startled by the touch, as her eyes swung up to meet mine. Confusion swirled in the honey gold that was in every damn dream I had.

"Excuse us. I need to introduce Gypsi to some friends. If you don't mind," I told Youngstreet, then sent my dad a pointed look before leading Gypsi away from that idiot. I kept walking though. I saw several people I knew, but I hadn't taken her away to introduce her to anyone.

"Trev?"

Just hearing her say my name made my cock twitch.

Glancing back to make sure my father was preoccupied, I pushed Gypsi through a side door down a small hallway, then yanked open the first door I came to. It was a walk-in closet with shelves of linens. Pulling her in with me, I turned and closed the door behind us.

"Why are we in a closet?" she asked softly.

I turned on her and made sure her eyes were locked on mine. I had to see them when I asked her the next few questions.

"Did you kiss Townes in the theater?"

She scrunched her nose. "He kissed me. It was awful."

Fuck. Fuck. Fuck.

I closed my eyes and took a deep breath. "You didn't make out with him or any other guy my dad has thrown at you?"

"No," she whispered.

I opened my eyes and saw the pain reflected in hers. I'd hurt her. Maybe beyond what I could repair. Me and my goddamn jealousy.

"Why are you asking me this?"

I ran a hand over my face, feeling like a caged tiger. Ripping something apart right now would help. "Because I came home, wanting to see you. After five fucking days of drinking myself to death, I decided that you loving me wasn't a bad thing. I care about you. I want you more than I want to fucking breathe. I had freaked at first but then realized if you loved me, then I could keep you. I wouldn't have to worry about you leaving me. Moving on. But I walked in to see you kissing that dipshit, and it didn't sit well."

"You could have asked me," she said softly.

I spun around and looked at her. "Yeah, but I'm not sane when you're involved. I lose my damn mind. I can't think straight. I was so sure you didn't love me and had moved on. That you weren't going fucking crazy, missing me like I was you. So, I called Bea."

"Please. Stop." She held up her hand. "I don't want to hear this part."

There was so much hurt shining in her beautiful eyes, and I had put it there. I hated myself.

"I have to tell you. Because what you saw isn't what you think. I set you up. I wanted you to hurt like I had when I saw you kissing Townes." I walked over and took her hands in mine. "I didn't sleep with her. I couldn't even fuck her. She came over several times, and I was trying to make sure you saw her, but you didn't. So, I set it up—her wearing my shirt first thing in the morning. I invited her to breakfast. Gave her a time. Told her we would swim after. She got there. I had her take her sundress off and put my damn shirt on."

Gypsi chewed on her bottom lip as she listened to me. "Really?" she asked, sounding scared to believe me.

That was my fucking fault too.

244

"Yes. I won't lie; the first night I was going to fuck her. But she wasn't you, and I couldn't."

Gypsi let out a long breath. "Wow. I wasn't expecting all that."

I cupped her face in my hands. "I'm sorry. I will apologize for the rest of my life if I need to. I just need you to forgive me. I want my Lollipop back."

Tears filled her eyes, and that gutted me. What did it mean? Was she about to tell me that ship had sailed?

"Don't cry on me. You're scaring the shit out of me."

She sniffled. "I'm sorry. I just ... I didn't think you'd call me that again," she said, reaching up to wipe the tears off her face.

I moved her hands and did it for her. "We can't mess up your makeup. Dad will be even more pissed at me than he already is."

A soft laugh escaped her then, and all I wanted to do was wrap her up and take her to my room and keep her.

"She didn't sleep in your bed then?"

I shook my head. "Only you, Lollipop."

She smiled up at me then, and my heart began to pound against my chest so hard that I was sure she could hear it.

"Am I forgiven?"

She nodded.

"I want to kiss you, but if I let myself, I'm going to fuck you. Dad is going to notice we are missing soon. I've got to get us back in there."

A small frown touched her face. "I don't know if ... if we should ..."

"Fuck?"

She nodded. "This was hard. Really hard. And the *loving you* thing didn't just go away. I guess ... I don't need you to love me. That's not what I am saying. But to be intimate with you and love you, I at least need to be special—"

"Stop." I put my finger over her mouth. "Listen to me." I leaned down, caging her in with my arms, and looked her directly in the eyes. "What you heard was me struggling with my dad telling me I couldn't have you anymore. That I had to end things with you. I was angry. I wanted it to be true. I wanted it to just be about the sex. But I knew it wasn't, just like Sax knew I was fucking lying. You are special to me. So very, very special. I swear it, Lollipop. You don't know the lengths I would go to in order to protect you." Like torture and kill a man.

She blinked several times. "I am?" she asked me quietly.

"Yes. I swear to God."

She smiled then. "Okay. That's enough."

Chapter
THIRTY-THREE

GYPSI

The rest of the night felt like one of my dreams, and I was afraid I would wake up in my room, alone. Trev never left my side. He introduced me to people. He stayed with me when Garrett wanted to take me around. When it was time to eat, he made the man who had been assigned to the seat beside me change places with him. Garrett's scowl did not go unnoticed, but Trev didn't seem to care.

Several people made comments about having me under the same roof with Trev and how that was a temptation for him.

Trev would laugh and say things like, "You have no idea," and, "I'm just glad they're getting married so I get to keep her around."

Mom would laugh, but many times, her eyes would meet mine with curiosity. The ride back in the limo was a very different experience. Trev didn't sit in the corner on his phone, but he wasn't pressed up against me either.

I was going to get questioned by Mom soon. She didn't seem bothered by it though, just confused.

"That was a fun evening," she said, smiling.

"I'm glad you enjoyed it," Garrett said to her while holding her hand in his. "Did you have a nice time, Gypsi?" Garrett asked.

"Yes, thank you. For everything. The hair, makeup, dress, all of it."

He nodded with a pleased smile on his face.

"You were a charming gentleman tonight, Trev," my mom said to him.

She was feeling him out. I could see it in her eyes.

He shrugged. "I can be when I have the proper motivation."

She laughed softly, but her gaze flicked to mine for a moment. "We all need a little motivation sometimes. But tell me, was that motivation my daughter?"

I tensed. She was doing this here. Going for the jugular. *Thanks, Mom.*

Not what I wanted to happen in the limo with her and Garrett.

"Yes, as a matter of fact. It seems Gypsi and I had a misunderstanding. It was my fault, and once it was cleared up, I had some making up to do."

Mom raised her eyebrows in surprise. "I see. And this misunderstanding was about what exactly?"

"Mom," I said, begging her with my eyes to shut up.

She tilted her head and gave me a knowing smile. "Honey, I am your mother. I want to know if Trev and you are having a thing or whatever. Is this friends, or is there more to it?"

"I've already spoken to Trev about it, Fawn. He knows not to cross that line," Garrett assured her.

She looked up at Garrett. "Is that a line you drew or that Gypsi drew?" she asked, turning back to me.

He frowned. "I drew it for you," he said.

Mom shook her head. "It's not my line to draw. Gypsi is an adult. I don't draw lines for her."

Garrett cleared his throat. "I see. I just ... well, I realize they're adults, but we will be family. We are family, and that can get messy. Trev isn't one for relationships. I don't want to make things awkward for everyone in the future."

Mom swung her gaze to me, and we looked at each other for several moments, having a silent conversation only a mom and daughter who had grown up together could have.

"I think that Gypsi is able to make those decisions. She's not dramatic. She forgives easily. If everything is out on the table, there are no hidden agendas, then telling them what they can and can't do will only make it all the more tempting."

"Not sure that's possible," Trev said, and my widened as I gaped at him.

Mom's musical laughter filled the limo, and Trev shrugged when his eyes met mine.

Garrett shifted in his seat. "Very well, Fawn. I just want you happy. This is in your hands. I will stay out of it."

She leaned into Garrett and pressed a kiss to his cheek. "No, love, it's in their hands. Not mine."

We arrived at the house and all exited the limo. Mom whispered things to Garrett, and his chuckle followed them up the stairs to the house.

Trev held my elbow, keeping me back until they were far enough away, then looked down at me. "My room tonight, Lollipop," he said softly. "I'm going to handle something quickly with Kye. But be in my bed when I get there."

"Okay," I replied.

He released me, and I climbed the stairs. Mom was waiting at the door for me when I reached it. Garrett was already up the left wing stairs. She closed the door behind me, then took my arm.

"Did I do the right thing? Is that what you want?" she whispered.

I nodded.

She looked at me with her *worried mom* frown. "Don't get hurt. I know I talked a big game in that limo, but I am worried. Trev does look at you like you're the precious jewel you are, and that's why I did it. I watched him tonight, and he won me over with the way he couldn't see anyone but you. It's just that you've been hurt already, and I feel like that was my fault. Is Trev why you aren't seeing Saxon?"

I nodded. "It's been Trev all along. Since day one."

"Oh, honey. If anyone can tame a playboy, it's you. I have faith in you."

I laughed. "Thanks, but I'm not trying to tame him. It's a *friends with benefits* thing."

She raised her eyebrows. "The way he was looking at you was not friendly."

"That's the benefits thing."

"Not so sure about that."

I reached up and kissed her cheek. "Stop worrying, and thank you. Garrett had put the hammer down on Trev. This helps. We've had a rough week. I'll tell you about it later. I'm just glad it's all cleared up. I missed him."

"So, it wasn't my engagement that had you so sad. You like it here?"

"I like it here. And I'm happy about your engagement. If it falls through, we can sell that ring and live the rest of our lives on the profit."

Mom laughed and shook her head. "I love that man. This isn't falling through."

I believed her.

Chapter
THIRTY-FOUR

TREV

Gypsi was asleep in my bed when I got back. It had taken longer than expected with the new security guy we had in place. I watched her sleep while I took off the tux and kicked off my shoes. Seeing her there was right. It made every-fucking-thing in my life feel like it was going to be okay. She made it okay. She made it perfect.

Pulling back the covers, I paused when I saw her naked body and thanked whatever gods there were for that view. I moved over to her and rolled her onto her back. She made a noise, but her eyes didn't open. Pushing her thighs open, I stared down at the pretty pink folds. I should let her sleep, but I had missed her too bad.

I leaned down and began to lick my favorite spot in the world. She moaned and jerked lightly. Lifting my eyes to look up at her, I was met with her sleepy smile.

"That's the best wake-up I've ever had," she breathed.

"I've been missing this pussy. I needed it on my tongue," I told her.

She opened her legs wider and buried her fingers in my hair. "So good," she mumbled.

I played with her clit, and she made sexy little noises, making my dick throb harder.

"It makes me crazy, thinking about someone else touching this. Tasting it. I'm fucking jealous. It makes me do stupid shit," I told her.

She lifted her hips to meet my tongue. "That turns me on," she panted.

"You want me jealous?" I asked, sliding a finger into her tight hole.

"YES!"

Grinning, I watched her pleasure as I plunged two fingers inside her while licking at her sweet juices. "So fucking sexy."

"Trev?"

"Yeah, Lollipop?"

"Please fuck me now."

I took one last lick, then climbed up and over her. I wanted her like this. Face-to-face. After the shit week without her, I wanted to see her. Feel the connection when I was deep inside her.

Her wet, slick entrance squeezed me as I sank all the way in, hitting the back spot that drove her crazy. Her hands grabbed my arms, and she held on to me, lifting her hips to meet my thrusts.

"There is no pussy that compares to this. I swear, Lollipop, my cock only wants you."

Her eyes looked up at me with so much emotion that it almost undid me. I had to clench my damn ass to keep from unloading inside of her already. No one had ever looked at me like that. As if I was all they wanted. I met all their needs.

Damn, the fucking rush in my chest was overwhelming. I leaned down and kissed her on the lips. Her mouth opened for me, so hungry and desperate for a taste. I slid my tongue over hers in a gentle caress. The longing to get lost in this. For everything else to fade away until it was just us.

Her little licks and soft moans sent jolts of pleasure straight to my dick. I wasn't going to last much longer. Although I wanted it to never end.

"Lollipop, come for me, baby. All over my cock," I pleaded.

Her eyes held my gaze, and her mouth fell open as the first tremor ran through her body. The cry that tore from her was my name, and that was all it took. The hard surge that crashed through me sent my release pulsing into her.

"OH GOD! TREV!" She shook as a second orgasm hit her. Making her cunt continue to suck me.

"Damn, Lollipop, don't stop. That's fucking heaven," I groaned as my length was being worked over, still deep inside her.

"Oh, oh," she panted, then slowly began to ease beneath me. "That was—" She stopped, still trying to catch her breath.

"Earth-shattering," I finished for her.

She nodded and smiled up at me. I held those pretty eyes with mine, wondering how I'd thought I could end this. Walk away from it. I should have been on my knees, begging her. Promising her everything. Whatever the fuck she wanted.

I bent my arms and held myself over her just enough so she could breathe. "I don't want to pull out of you yet," I told her.

She wiggled her hips. "Then, don't."

I leaned down and kissed her. "Do you want to come again, Lollipop?"

"Yes," she said, kissing me back.

"This sweet little pussy missed me," I said, grinning.

"Yes."

"We might fuck all damn night," I told her, feeling myself start to slowly harden again.

"Please," she breathed, pressing her hips up when she realized I was growing inside her.

I pressed a kiss on the tip of her nose, her eyelids, then went to her ear to whisper, "You own this cock, Lollipop. You use it any way you want to."

"Then, let me ride you."

I rolled over, taking her with me, not wanting to leave her tight sheath. She straddled me with her wild blonde curls all over the place and that sexy grin on her face as she began to rock against me. The sight made my chest so damn tight that I struggled to breathe. It didn't get any more perfect than her. At least not for me. I stared up at her as it dawned on me what this tightness was. The warm rush that I didn't understand. The insane jealousy and possessiveness. The uncontrollable rage when I thought someone was taking her from me. Or hurting her ...

Holy hell.

I fucking loved her.

Chapter
THIRTY-FIVE

GYPSI

The lighting was perfect. Kye had Iron War out in the straight track, working with him. Moses Mile had originally owned Iron War, but Maddy had said he'd been difficult. He had some emotional damage, but he had excellent breeding. Garrett had brought him over to have Blaise work with him, and he was now ready for the track.

Kye, in a cowboy hat, on top of a thoroughbred as impressive as Iron War, made for excellent photos. I had spent the past thirty minutes moving all over to get the best shots. Once, Kye came close to where I stood and smirked at the camera. Women were going to love that picture.

Standing to move one more time, I looked down at the photos I'd already taken. I was sure I had enough, but that horse was beautiful. The sounds of the horses' hooves got closer, and I looked up to see Kye headed toward me.

He pulled to a stop beside me. "You get what you need? Or do I need to take him out some more?"

"I think I have enough, but maybe one more, if it's okay. That time you got close and smirked at the camera—could you do something like that before we lose the lighting? I think it will be a big draw for females. Just to get more follows and likes."

He laughed. "Okay. Yeah, I can do that. What about winking?" he asked and gave me a wink.

That could work.

"What the fuck are you winking at Gypsi for?" Trev called out from behind me.

"Shit," Kye muttered.

I looked back at him, thinking he was kidding but the scowl on his face was serious. We'd had a great week. Trev had even began teaching me to ride. We had started looking at horses online, and Trev had made calls to decide where we were going to go look for my horse. Seeing him angry was startling. He'd been all smiles until now.

"I'm fucking serious, Kye," he said with a snarl when he reached us. "Why are you winking at her? She's taking photos; she's not out here to flirt with your ass."

Trev's hand slid around my waist, pulling me against him. I stared up at him in confusion.

"Trev," I said, and his face softened as he looked down at me, "I asked him to do something flirty for the camera. It will go over well on social media. He was asking me if a wink would work."

Trev glanced back in Kye's direction.

"Truth," Kye said, holding up his hands.

Trev nodded. "Okay."

He didn't apologize, and he didn't let me go.

Kye's gaze dropped to Trev's hold on me. "You gonna let her take this picture, or are we done?"

Trev's fingers flexed as they tightened on my waist. Okay, apparently, we were done.

I turned to Kye. "I have plenty. It's good. Thank you," I told him.

He nodded, then gave Trev an amused grin before turning Iron War and heading for the stables.

"You want to explain that?" I asked Trev when he was gone.

Trev smiled at me like he'd just won something. "Let's go somewhere. It's the weekend. What about the Virgin Islands? We have a house there and a yacht."

"What?" I asked, trying to decide where this was coming from.

"Have you been to St. Thomas? You'll love it. I can take you to my favorite restaurant."

"Just the two of us? Go to the Virgin Islands?" I asked incredulously.

He grinned. "I don't like to share, Lollipop."

I rolled my eyes. "That's not what I meant. That sounds … I don't know. It's not work-related. It's not a family thing. It just feels …"

I did not want to say *relationship* because I was afraid he'd go into hiding for a month. Things had been perfect all week. I hadn't said the L-word again. I hadn't put any pressure on him. It was Trev who had instigated the movie nights. Trev who had started making time for my riding lessons. Not me.

"It sounds like what?" he asked, leaning down to brush a kiss across my lips.

"Trev," I whispered. "We are in the wide open. Anyone can see you."

"Good."

I grabbed his face with my hand. "Did you hit your head?" I asked.

He chuckled. "No. I kiss you all the time."

257

"Yes, but not out like this."

"I need to fix that," he replied, then leaned in, his tongue flicking a little along my bottom lip.

"I am going to drop this expensive camera if you keep that up," I warned him.

"I'll buy you a new one," he said softly.

"Trev."

"Hmm?" he murmured as he trailed kisses along my jawline.

"I need to put this camera in its bag," I sighed.

"Tell me you'll go to St. Thomas with me this weekend," he urged.

"Yes, if that's what you want."

He stopped kissing me then. "Put your camera up, and let's go get packed although you really just need that white bikini with the pink piping on it."

"You want to leave today?" I asked as I put the camera up.

"We can leave in the morning if you don't want to go tonight."

I put the bag strap over my shoulder, then turned back to him. If he realized this was him acting like more than friends with benefits, he was going to panic. Someone was going to tease him about it. I knew the guys, and they would say something. Then, Trev would go missing. I wasn't sure I could recover from that again.

"You're frowning, Lollipop. I don't like it when you frown," he said with his own frown this time.

I sighed and tried to think of how to say this and not upset him. It was a fine line with Trev Hughes. One I thought had gotten easier this week, but still.

"It's just … us going to St. Thomas together. Just the two of us isn't very friends with benefits."

His frown deepened.

258

Well, crap. I'd done it. Why hadn't I just shut up? When the guys started teasing him about it, I'd have to deal with him acting weird again. Now, I had just sped the process up.

"Okay, now, before you go and get weird, or run off to prove something, or whatever, I did not say the L-word. I did not say *relationship*. I am just warning you that the guys will say something about this and tease you. I need the reassurance that, when that happens, you won't go MIA on me and repeat the last time. I didn't like that, and I don't want to do it again."

Trev reached out and took the bag off my shoulder, then put it on his. "You worry too much, Lollipop. Come on."

He draped his arm over my shoulders as we walked back to the stables.

"You still liking the job?" he asked me like I hadn't just broached a deep subject.

"Yes. I love it," I replied.

"You're great at it. Dad's impressed, and that's hard to do."

A smile tugged at my lips. I was glad I hadn't disappointed Garrett. Not after what he was paying me to do this.

We stepped into the stables, and I went to put the camera bag away and lock up. Maddy had left an hour ago. The horses were all put up for the night. Kye was brushing Iron War. I waved at him as we passed on our way out, and he nodded his head.

Trev ignored him. He was still being ridiculous about that wink. I started toward the house when Trev grabbed the back of my jeans and tugged me back.

Glancing over my shoulder, I frowned. "What are you doing?"

"We aren't going to the house just yet."

"I thought we were going to pack."

He licked his bottom lip and distracted me. I watched his tongue slide in and out of his mouth slowly.

"We will, but I want to take you somewhere first."

I nodded. I was willing to go wherever he wanted to take me. The stone path that led behind the main stables turned into a dirt path that led into some woods. Trev held my hand, walking in front of me. It wasn't very far before the trees cleared, and there was a rushing stream. It was beautiful. I hadn't even realized it was hiding back here.

Trev kept going until he got to a massive live oak tree. He tugged gently on my arm and then pushed my back against the tree. I stared up at him. Those gray eyes were hooded as his gaze dropped to my mouth. Maybe he hadn't brought me to see the stream, but make out instead. I was good with that.

"I've had you in my bed all week," he said in a husky whisper, brushing his knuckles over my lips. "I've been buried deep inside you more times than I can count."

I was starting to pant. When he talked in that deep, raspy voice and looked at me like that, it got to me.

"But there's this thing that's been bugging me," he said, leaning down to press a kiss on my neck. "I keep waiting. Been real patient. Trying to make you so fucking happy that you can't see anyone but me."

I laughed. "Uh, Trev, that has never been an issue."

He lifted his head, and his eyes met mine again. "What? That you just see me?"

I nodded. "I have made that clear."

"I need you to make it clear again," he whispered against my lips.

I tilted my head to capture his lips, but he pulled back.

"What?" I asked, ready to beg.

"Tell me why you don't see anyone else, Lollipop." He wrapped a finger around one of my curls.

What was he wanting from me? I was too turned on to understand. Did he want me to talk about his dick being big? Was this him trying to get me to dirty talk?

"Trev, just tell me what you want. I don't understand."

He slid his knuckles under my chin, and I didn't miss the pleading in his expression. I just wanted to give him whatever it was he needed.

"Lollipop, I need to hear you say it."

I started to ask what, and he pressed his palm against my heart. Was I understanding him correctly? If I was wrong, this could be bad. I bit down on my lip hard. He shook his head slightly and tugged my lip free.

"I'm afraid I'm wrong, and if I am, it will be an issue. I don't want issues."

He rested his forehead on mine. "Say it."

"I ... I don't ... see anyone else but you because ..."

"Because why?" he pushed.

"Because I love you."

Trev's mouth slammed against mine so hard that it took my breath away. He tasted me as if he needed to savor the flavor. His hands gripped my waist and held me against him. It was clear I had said the right thing. If he had wanted to hear me say that again, he'd just had to ask. I'd thought my not saying it was easier on him. Not having the reminder.

I slipped my hand into his hair and held on to him while the dark, sweet, erotic tangle of our tongues made me lightheaded. When he broke the kiss, I let out a cry, not ready to end that.

"Look at me," he said in a soft growl.

I opened my eyes and met his gaze.

"I love you. So fucking much that it consumes me. It took me a little longer to figure it out, but when something gets this damn strong, it's hard to deny."

I felt tears well up in my eyes. These were not words I had expected to come out of Trev Hughes's mouth.

"Lollipop, if you start crying, I'm gonna fuck you right here until the only crying you're doing is saying my name while you orgasm."

I laughed, then sniffled. "That's not a threat, Trev."

A wicked grin spread across his face. "No, I guess not."

I slid a hand from his hair to touch his cheek. "You love me?"

He turned his head to kiss my palm. "Yes. I love you. Everything about you. Not just your hot little pussy, but it did start this thing. That, and your dirty mouth that bites."

I laughed, burying my face in his chest.

"Don't go getting shy now. I've got bite marks all over my chest, and those filthy words coming out of that mouth make me come so hard that I see stars."

I lifted my face to his and smiled. "Can we do that now?"

He groaned, picking me up. I wrapped my legs around him, and he walked us over to a grassy patch farther down.

"Yeah, Lollipop," he said, kissing me. "We can do that now."

"You're sure you love me? This isn't just the sex talking?" I asked him as he put me down on the grass. The fear that I was going to wake up and this was going to have just been a dream began to take root in my thoughts.

Trev grinned as he looked down at me. "Truth be told, I may have fucking fell in love with you when you laughed at my pickup line. I just didn't realize the things you made me feel that confused me were things that came with falling in love. I'd never been in love. I'm sorry it took me longer to realize what this was. I just assumed it was your voodoo pussy making me unhinged."

I laughed as I gazed up into his gray eyes. "I make you unhinged?"

He sighed and brushed hair out of my face. "Lollipop, you have no idea the levels of unhinged you've brought me to."

Please don't let this be a dream. My heart was so full. This was happiness. The pure kind. Untainted and real.

"Do we worry about the future?" I asked him.

He frowned. "What about it? The fact our parents are going to make us step-siblings?"

I nodded.

He leaned down and pressed a kiss to my cheek then another to the corner of my mouth. "There's nothing to worry about. Nothing changes for us," He whispered.

Closing my eyes, I shivered as his lips trailed down my neck. "If this ends," I hate the way saying those words make me feel but I don't get to finish that sentence.

"It won't. Ever. If you try to leave me, I will lock us in my room and we will live there for the rest of our lives."

I start to giggle and he lifts his head, his lips curl into an amused grin. "What? You think that's funny?" he asked grabbing my butt and pulling me against him. "I'm fucking serious, Lollipop. No one else. Just you. This is for keeps."

For keeps. Those two words were almost as beautiful as hearing him tell me he loved me. Trev wasn't what I expected and every time I thought I knew what he was going to do next he surprised me. Making me only love him more. My mom loved adventures the way I loved stories. Somehow while she was living her wildest adventure yet, I'd found my favorite story. The one that belonged to us—mine and Trev's.

Whiskey Smoke Teaser...

Chapter ONE

ASPEN

Blinking I sat up as the roar of motorcycles grew louder. The light from the television was all that lit the darkened living room. I reached for my cell phone to check the time. It was after two in the morning. Irish, my older sister, wouldn't be home from work for another two hours. I hadn't meant to fall asleep on the sofa watching *Dawson's Creek* but since Irish introduced me to it I had gotten addicted. Television was something I hadn't realized was missing from my life.

Stretching I stood and picked up the remote to turn it off wondering if Gran had ever watched anything on a screen a day in her life. She had believed it was evil so probably not. It made me sad to think of all Gran hadn't experienced in life. Death came for all of us at some point and I wanted to soak in every adventure I could until that day came. Irish lived her life that way. Although Gran died thinking Irish was headed straight for Hell, I disagreed. I believed Irish was making sure not to waste a moment. God had to respect that.

A knock on the door startled me and I stared at the door unsure what to do. Who would be knocking at this time? Irish hadn't told to expect anyone.

Quietly I walked over to the window beside the door and peeked out. There were two motorcycles in the driveway. A man was on one of the bikes but the other one sat empty. I shifted the curtain to see if I could get a glimpse of who was at the door. Black leather jacket, light brown hair pulled back in a man bun was all I could see. It was intriguing. Very *Sons of Anarchy*. Another binge watch Irish had put me on to since I'd moved in here with her.

Irish had interesting men in her life. Living vicariously through her stories had been what got me through some of my darker times. Being the younger, sickly sister had caused me to miss out on a normal high school life. There had been no going off to college and frat parties for me either. Unable to help my curiosity, I moved to the door and unlocked it then opened it to face the man on the other side.

With the porch light illuminating his face I sucked in a breath. Hazel eyes stared at me under thick dark lashes. He had a short beard, just enough to be sexy and lips that made you want to stare at them. It was tempting to reach out and touch them.

"You're definitely not Kitty," he drawled in a deep husky voice that made me shiver.

Kitty was my sister's stage name. I shook my head as I soaked in the sight of the man in in front of me. "She's at work," I replied softly.

He raised an arm and leaned on the doorframe as his eyes raked down my body with what I thought was approval. I had very little experience with men except for the romance novels I read and I didn't think those were very accurate. According to Irish real men were nothing like the ones in books. Although this one sure looked like one of the guys in the books I read.

"I'm gonna need a name, darling," he said as his eyes locked back on mine.

My face felt warm and I knew I was blushing. Sure, I'd had boys flirt with me before but they weren't like this. This was not a boy. This was a man.

"Aspen," I told him.

He reached out and took a strand of my hair letting it twirl around his finger before it fell back to my shoulder. "Please tell me this is natural," he said huskily.

I swallowed hard. "Uh, my hair?" I asked confused.

He smirked. "Yes."

I laughed nervously then. "Since birth."

"Tell me how a sweet thing like you ended up at Kitty's."

"She's my sister," I told him. I left out that Kitty wouldn't let me live alone any longer. I had tried it after Gran had passed away two months ago. When I ended up in the hospital Irish had moved me in to her house.

He leaned closer to me and I hoped that my racing heart was because of my reaction to him and not something else wrong with it. "You planning on working at Devils? Because if you are I need your schedule."

Devil's Lair was the strip club my sister worked at.

I was probably the color of my Auburn hair. My fair skin hid nothing. I shook my head. "No, I'm uh, not a dancer."

"I think that breaks my heart." He reached out and ran the pad of his thumb along my jaw. "This might be the prettiest fucking face I've ever seen."

It felt like fate was making up for all the things I'd missed in life with this one singular encounter. "Thank you," I whispered.

"LEVI!" a male voice called out. "We staying or not?"

He looked back over his shoulder. "Give me a minute," he shouted.

Levi. I liked that name. It fit him.

"Two questions," he said turning back to me. "How old are you, Aspen?"

"Twenty."

A wicked grin touched his lips. "Legal. That just made my night. I need your number, sweetheart."

My stomach felt as if a flight of butterflies had been let loose. "My phone number?" I asked thinking I was misunderstanding him.

He ran his knuckles down my bare arm. "Please."

Okay. Think. This man was here to see my sister. Did I give him my number? What if she liked him? God, who was I kidding? She had to like him. Any woman alive would like him.

I bit my lip hard then let it go. "You came here to see Iri-Kitty," I said. "I can't, I mean, I don't think it would be right for me to give you my number."

He winced. "Fuck, baby. That's painful." His knuckles ran back up my arm. "I can talk to Kitty. She'd understand. We just had some fun. No attachments."

I knew all about my sister's fun. Irish didn't do relationships. She was a free spirit. I envied her as much as I loved her. "Have you… uh… I mean you have slept with her before."

His knuckles went back down my arm. "No, sweetheart, we never slept." The gleam in his eyes made me shiver. I was aware they hadn't slept and he knew that wasn't what I meant. Just like I knew I'd never feel right about giving him my number.

"I can't do that to her. I'm sorry," I said softly.

He winced. He took my hand and brought it to his lips as his eyes stayed locked with mine. "You broke my heart," he said.

"LEVI!" the other man called out.

He sighed and let my hand go then dropped his other arm from the door and stepped back. "Lock up tight. And Aspen don't open it for a stranger again. Promise me that."

I nodded my head and he winked at me before turning to walk away. Unable to help myself I watched him as he made his way back to his motorcycle. Closing the door before he turned and caught me I let out a loud sigh. That man was going to star in my fantasies for a very long time.

I locked up and glanced out the window as the motorcycles drove off. Irish had the best life. I had begged her to let me go back to Gran's house when I'd gotten out of the hospital. She had refused and informed me all my things had been moved here. I knew she blamed herself for letting me live there alone after Gran passed away but truthfully it had been my fault. The moment I had started feeling bad I should have gone to the doctor. I knew better. The result had been pneumonia and with my heart condition that meant hospitalization.

Irish's life was one I could never experience but being on the sidelines and watching it would be more fun than I'd ever had. Especially if men like that one showed up at the door. Smiling, I went upstairs to brush my teeth and get into bed.

COMING AUGUST 27, 2023

ACKNOWLEDGMENTS

Those who are making my insane publishing schedule this year happen:

Britt is always the first I mention because he makes it possible for me to close myself away and write for endless hours a day. Without him, I wouldn't get any sleep, and I doubt I could finish a book.

Emerson, for dealing with the fact that I must write some days and she can't have my full attention. I'll admit, there were several times she did not understand, and I might have told my six-year-old, "You're not making it in my acknowledgments this time!" to which she did not care. Although she does believe she is famous after attending some signings with me. But that is not my fault. I blame the readers ;)

My older children, who live in other states, were great about me not being able to answer their calls most of the time and waiting until I could get back to them. They still love me and understand this part of Mom's world.

My editor, Jovana Shirley at Unforeseen Editing, for always working with my crazy schedules and making my stories the best they can be. This summer she has gone above and beyond with this crazy schedule of mine and the fall it doesn't slow down.

My formatter, Melissa Stevens at The Illustrated Author. She makes my books beautiful inside. Her work is hands down the best formatting I've ever had in my books. I am always excited to see what she does with each one.

Beta readers, who come through every time: Annabelle Glines, Jerilyn Martinez, and Vicci Kaighan. I love y'all!

Damonza, for my book cover. The book covers just seem to be getting better! Especially this one. I think may be my fav one and I've seen the next few covers already.

Abbi's Army, for being my support and cheering me on. I love y'all!

My readers, for allowing me to write books. Without you, this wouldn't be possible.

Made in the USA
Middletown, DE
21 February 2024

49521718R00168